I0769265

HIDDEN
Vows
ERIN
GRAVES

Cover by Dana Isaly (@instalovegraphicdesign)

Editing by Caroline Palmier (@love.andedits)

To those who need a reminder to chase after their dreams.
Go after them.
They're just as important as everything else.

AUTHOR'S
note

Hidden Vows is an open-door romance intended for mature readers, containing sexually explicit and adult content. While this story is filled with friends, family, and love, and a happily ever after is guaranteed, it does touch on some sensitive subjects. You can find a complete list in the back of the book or on my website. Please note, some of the content warnings will be major spoilers for Abbey and Jude's story.

www.eringravesauthor.com

"Could Have Been Me" - The Struts
"something to remember" - Matt Hanson
"Not Now" - blink-182
"All is Well" - Avi Kaplan, Joy Williams
"Slow Dancing" - Aly & AJ
"MIRACLE" - BOYS LIKE GIRLS
"Remember That Night?" - Sarah Kays
"Wave" - Dean Lewis
"i am not who i was" - Chance Peña
"Power Over Me" - Dermot Kennedy
"iris" - mgk, Julia Wolf
"Remember the Time" - Michael Jackson

Prologue

ABBEY

"YOU ASSHOLE!" I shout, shoving at his chest.

"I told you we were too young! That we rushed this! You're only eighteen!" Jude shouts, just as loudly.

There's something in his eyes, but I'm not clear-headed enough to analyze what it is. He's broken something inside of me, and I don't know if I'll ever be able to get it back.

"That doesn't make it better! That doesn't excuse it." I turn away, pacing toward the front door of our apartment—our home. "How could you do this?" My voice is so quiet now; all the fight drained from my body. Slowly, I turn back to him, tears welling in my eyes. "I never thought you could do something like this to me—to us."

"Abbey—" His voice cracks on the single word. He steps forward, reaching for me, but I don't let him touch me.

"No. You don't get to touch me right now." Jude flinches, and I wipe frantically at my face. "I don't know how we fix this." My voice is so quiet and I desperately fight to hold back the sobs building in my chest.

I can't look at him, not with the pain etched across his face. *What right does he have to be in pain?*

My eyes fall to the floor. If I keep looking at Jude I'll break, and I don't feel safe doing that here, not after what I've just discovered.

Squaring my shoulders and with a conviction I don't fully feel, I meet his eyes. "You want out of this marriage, you got it. I'll come back tomorrow to get my things. Please don't be here."

Somehow, I walk out the door without looking back at him. It's the hardest thing I've ever done, but I can't stay—not after this.

Jude may have been telling me for weeks we made a mistake getting married, but I never thought he was capable of hurting me. I never thought he'd go to these lengths to prove me wrong, but maybe I don't know Jude like I thought I did.

Stumbling out the back door of the building, I look around, trying to figure out where I should go. The person I want to talk to most is my mother, but going to my parents' house means seeing my father, and I know he'll gloat about my failed marriage.

The need for my mother's comfort far outweighs the dread of seeing my father. She'll let me cry and scream and feel whatever I need to feel without judgment or comment, and that's what I need more than anything else.

Still refusing to look back at the building that's been nothing but comfort since I first walked through the doors, I steel my spine and walk toward the street.

Maybe the long walk will help me figure out how this happened.

CHAPTER
One

ABBEY

HOW ANYONE CONVINCED me this was a good idea is beyond me. I want—more than anything—to be happy for my friends, but weddings have always been something I avoid like the plague.

But then again...

My eyes drift to the man who's felt like more of a father to me than my own—a man who didn't judge me and accepted me back into his life sixteen years after we last spoke without question.

I couldn't say no to Walt if my life depended on it.

Out of everyone in this town, Walt is the only person who really knows me—even if we've only been back in each other's lives for the last seven months.

The spark in his eyes as he laughs with the women who are now my best friends *almost* makes me smile. But then Declan pulls Quinn into his arms, and the look of love that passes between them has the green-eyed monster rearing its ugly head.

I hate how seeing them happy makes me feel. If anyone deserves this happiness, it's the two of them. I'm amazed they followed through with this wedding, especially considering Quinn's father, Scott, passed away only three weeks ago. But even with my limited time with Scott, I know this is exactly what he would've wanted.

The happiness of those he loved is all Scott *ever* wanted, and it's clear Quinn and Declan are happy together.

"Is it really so bad being here?" A deep voice pulls me from my thoughts, and I can't help the small smile that breaks through at how well this man still knows me after all these years.

I study him for a moment, noticing the deepening circles under his eyes. They've gotten darker over the last seven months, making me nervous. He's too young to look as weathered as he does now.

He's always taken such good care of himself, something anyone can tell from his strong, athletic build. At fifty-eight, he's almost the definition of a silver fox. There's still a decent amount of darkness peppering his hair, but the gray is starting to appear more. With the dimples that often show up and his tattoos on full display, he's got the classic Hollywood look with a rugged, masculine edge.

I used to question why he never got remarried, especially with all the attention he receives, but I understand it now. Even though it's been thirty-six years since he lost his wife, he'll never move on from her.

Looking at him now, though, I'm questioning if he's doing as well as I want to believe.

Shaking myself from my thoughts, I turn to the dance floor. "I'm glad they're happy, especially after everything they've been through," I say, lifting the glass of whiskey to my lips and soaking in the burn as it slides down my throat.

"Oh, mo stór." The weight of Walt's arm falls across my

shoulder as he pulls me into his side. The comforting scent of leather and tobacco invades my nose, making me relax further into his side.

Proving he knows me better than anyone else, Walt continues as if he can read my mind." I wish one of you would just tell me what happened. It kills me to see you both this way." He pauses, his arm around me tightening. "I know neither of you are happy with the lives you're living." I feel his lips press a kiss to the top of my head, exactly like a father would while trying to comfort his child. "I sometimes question if either of you are truly living at all."

The last is said so quietly I know I wasn't meant to hear it, but I ignore the words. Instead, I focus on the solace of being in his comforting embrace.

This is the one topic we've both silently agreed never to talk about, but it shouldn't surprise me it didn't last forever. Asking a man like Walt not to talk about his son is like asking a journalist not to dig into the story of a lifetime.

"My life is nothing like I thought it'd be, but I'm not unhappy," I tell him honestly, smoothing my hand over an imaginary wrinkle in my dress. "I wish I could go back and have you in my life for the last seventeen years, though." I elbow him gently, trying to lighten the mood.

Walt's arm falls from my shoulders as he steps in front of me, catching my eyes so he's looking right at me.

"But are you happy?"

Am I happy? If I'm being honest, no, I don't think I am. I've been going through the motions for the last seventeen years, barely living. I let my failed relationship with Jude dictate every action. I stopped trusting people, and as a result I stopped letting anyone into my life. The less chances there were for someone to hurt me, the better.

It wasn't until Ava started working at the bookstore seven months ago that I really started to open up to people again.

There were a few people who came into the bookstore that I considered quasi-friends, but none I would've called in an emergency.

Thanks to Ava, a woman who dropped everything to come to town to help Scott Marks—one of the best men this town has ever known—with a custody case, I now have more people in my life than I know what to do with. Most importantly, Walt's back in my life, and that's something I'll cherish forever.

Instead of telling Walt any of that or even being the slightest bit honest with him, I shrug. He doesn't have to say anything for me to know he doesn't believe me.

"I'm working on it," I whisper when he doesn't look away.

Walt pulls me into a hug, holding on tight. "I guess that's all I can ask for."

WHY ARE *the lights on at Murphy's?*

There's no real reason to glance at the watch on my wrist; I'm well aware it's past midnight. And realistically, the time doesn't even matter. Murphy's was closed today because of the wedding, and I can't think of a single reason Walt would stop by on his way home.

Quickening my steps, I rush to the door. I'm shocked when the door swings open as I tug on the handle. Walt's usually pretty good about keeping this door locked outside business hours.

"Walt? You here?" I shout, standing at the threshold.

There's music playing softly, but the place is silent. Not a person in sight.

Letting the door fall shut behind me, I step further into the bar, looking around for any sign of life.

I've never been to Ireland, but I imagine if I had, this place would be a replica of a country pub. The second I step inside a rush of warmth overwhelms me. The dark woods and amber lighting create a soft, cozy feeling of a warm living room, inviting you to pull up a chair and chat with friends.

Sometimes, this place feels more like home than anywhere else, and I've missed it terribly. I'll forever be grateful to the women who pushed their way into my life.

If it hadn't been for Quinn and Emily walking into the bookstore all those months ago and forcing me to join them and Ava for a ladies' night, I wouldn't be walking in this door right now.

I wouldn't have been at the wedding either—something I'm not entirely sure I'm grateful for.

"Walt," I shout, moving toward the back of the bar.

Maybe he's in the kitchen? But why is he even here?

My steps falter as I hear a muffled groan from somewhere behind the bar. Without thinking about it, I rush to the bar, lifting myself enough to see over it.

The breath leaves my lungs when I see Walt collapsed there.

Not giving myself any time to think about it, I grab my phone from my purse, dialing 911 as I move to his side.

"911, what's your emergency?" a calm voice says through the speaker on my phone.

"I need an ambulance to 397 Main Street, Ashford Falls, Maryland, at a bar called Murphy's," I say as I crumble to the floor beside Walt, leaving the phone beside me. My hands hover over him, not sure if I should move him or not.

"Is the patient conscious or breathing?"

"I don't—I don't know. Is it okay for me to move him?" I hear the hysteria in my voice and I give myself a second to close my eyes and take a deep breath.

Ignore who this is in front of you and focus. You can break down later.

"Is he talking to you?" the dispatcher asks, bringing me back to the moment.

"No." My voice is stronger this time. "I came into the bar and found him on the ground. He's not moving, but he's groaning."

"Okay. An ambulance is on the way. Will they be able to enter the premises without issue?"

"Yes, the door's unlocked."

"Can you tell me the patient's age? Does he have any medical history the paramedics should know about?"

"He's fifty-eight. I don't know about his medical history."

"And what's your relation to the patient?"

I don't even think before I respond. "I'm his daughter." It may be a lie, but at one point in time I was his daughter-in-law, and I know he'd claim me as his in a heartbeat.

"The ambulance should be there soon."

"Thank you," I whisper.

It's quiet, except for the sounds of sirens growing closer. I'm not sure if the dispatcher is still on the line, but all I can focus on is the fact I can see Walt breathing, and seeing that gives me the smallest ounce of comfort.

It's not paramedics rushing through the door next, but Gage and Ava.

"What happened?" Gage's deep voice demands as he rounds the end of the bar.

It's an odd thing to pay attention to in a moment like this, but I notice he's still in his suit from the wedding. His tie hangs loose around his neck and the top buttons of his shirt are undone, but he still wears his suit jacket. His hair is a little more disheveled than when I saw him as I left the wedding, but then again, glancing at Ava, she seems a little disheveled too.

"What are you doing here?" I ask, a little bewildered at their appearance. There's no reason for them to pass the bar at this time of night, even if they were on their way home from the wedding.

Before he can answer the paramedics push through the door, and Gage helps me stand, moving us out of their way to work.

"Abbey, what happened?" Gage steps in front of me, bending so his face is right in front of mine.

It's strange to notice now, but his eyes seem far more aqua-blue than I've ever realized. I've never paid attention to Gage as more than I friend. I know he's attractive, but I've never thought anything past that, and now's the worst time to focus on it, but I can't stop my mind from drifting. I get it now—why Ava fell head over heels for him with his high cheekbones and chiseled jaw, covered with the lightest amount of stubble. It's not just his looks that draw you in, but everything about him, especially the way he cares for those he considers friends.

"Abbey." Gage's voice, softer now, pulls me back to the moment.

"I don't know. I was coming home from the wedding and saw the lights on. I thought it was strange, so I came to see what Walt was doing here. I found him like that behind the bar when I came in." My eyes shift to the floor where the paramedics are still working on Walt, but Gage moves us, turning my back to the sight.

"What are you doing here?" My eyebrows pinch in as I bring my focus back to Gage.

"We were just leaving the wedding when Lyle called. He heard the call come through dispatch and knows I'm close with Walt."

"Oh."

It's a silly thought, but I wonder if that's some kind of privacy violation, the sheriff calling a friend about an emergency. Then again, Gage isn't just a friend; he's also a deputy. I'm sure there should be some kind of report about the call, especially when we don't know the cause. Though, I think it's safe to say there's no foul play. Nothing is out of place in the bar, and Walt doesn't look physically harmed.

"Abbey?" It's Ava's voice I hear this time, and when I focus back on my surroundings she's the one in front of me.

I don't know when that happened, but as I look around, I realize the paramedics are wheeling Walt out the door, Gage right behind them.

Without acknowledging Ava, I push around her and rush after them. I make it to the ambulance as they're settling Walt inside.

"I'm going with you."

"Abbey—" Gage tries to speak.

"No, I'm not leaving him alone." I toss him my keys. "Lock up the bar and you can meet me at the hospital if you want, but I'm going with them."

"Are you family?" one of the paramedics asks.

"Yes." I don't wait for them to say I can ride in the ambulance; I climb in and take the open seat in the corner.

"We're taking him to Silverleaf Medical Center," the paramedic tells Gage before climbing into the ambulance and pulling one of the doors closed behind her.

Gage gives a sharp nod, glancing at me briefly before closing the other door and tapping it twice. His eyes return to mine through the window as the ambulance pulls away, and I watch as Ava exits the door of Murphy's, practically collapsing into Gage's side when she reaches him.

CHAPTER
Two

JUDE

IT'S FUNNY; no matter what city I'm in, I always search for the bar that reminds me most of my father's. Always searching for that feeling of home I've only ever found at Murphy's, my childhood home, or with Abbey. That feeling I've only ever had back in Ashford Falls, Maryland. The place I want to be more than anywhere—and the place I'll never return to.

The Old Whitaker Tavern doesn't have the hallmarks of an Irish pub like Murphy's, but it has the hallmarks of a small-town bar—just like the rest of Harborview, Massachusetts.

The conversations going on around me show how well the people of this town know each other.

The group of men and women in the corner laughing with each other and talking about an upcoming wedding of one of the couples. The old man at the end of the bar scowling at the empty glass in front of him. The performer for the night packing up his guitar while talking to the woman who stood up front during his whole performance. The bartender collecting empties the waiters gather and place on the bar while talking to customers closing out their tabs.

It all reminds me of evenings spent with my dad while we

worked to close down Murphy's. The camaraderie that can only be found with people you've known most of your life and feel comfortable with.

"Can I get you another one? Last call's in five." The bartender wipes at the now vacant spot next to me, offering a smile I imagine typically has men falling to their feet for her attention.

"I'm good." I lift the pint to my lips, taking the last gulp before placing the empty glass on the bar. "Have a good night." I tilt my head as a final parting, placing a twenty on the bar before heading out the door.

The sea air from the bay has me breathing deeply, and instead of heading straight for The Driftwood Inn, I find myself walking out to the empty dock.

During the day, this dock bustles with people, but at almost one in the morning it's like a ghost town. The boats docked and slumbering for the night, waiting for the next day's work to begin.

Staring out at the calm water, my mind wanders to the place it always does when I allow myself to sit in the stillness of a moment—to Abbey.

What's she doing right now? Is she happy? Does she think of me as often as I think of her?

I can imagine her standing here with me, taking in the quiet calmness of the moment. The weight of her hand in mine feels so real, I stumble at the sudden breeze that rips through the air, bringing me back to the present.

I give myself a few more seconds to enjoy the evening air and the thought of Abbey by my side again before I turn and head back up the dock.

It's late, but I'm not tired—unsurprisingly. Sleep and I haven't been friends for a very long time. My options for where to go are limited...I have one option: the inn. Though, I do have a choice between my room and the library.

Hoping the front desk will be empty at this time of night, I open the door to the inn as quietly as I can. While not technically a bed and breakfast, The Driftwood Inn gives off those vibes. Not really what I'm looking for when I land in a new place and need to work on a project, but it's not the end of the world either.

Luck is on my side tonight—the front desk is empty and the inn is silent.

Closing the door just as quietly as I opened it, I make the decision to stay up in my room once I get there. It's not that the people here aren't friendly, because they most certainly are. It's just that I've never been a talkative person, and trying to feign interest at this time of night is the last thing I want to do.

I'm almost to the stairs when I hear the telltale sounds of footsteps on the wood floor behind me. I contemplate making a run for it, but know my luck isn't normally that strong.

"Oh, hey. Did you need something?" A feminine voice sounds from behind me.

"No, I'm good. Checked in this morning," I toss over my shoulder, hoping that's enough for her to let me keep going.

"I'm sorry." I hear the hesitation in her voice and it has me turning to face her. "I just—I'm filling in for a friend and I'm honestly not sure what she'd do in a situation like this." Her nose scrunches in embarrassment, something most men would probably find endearing, though I don't get the impression she's trying to be.

I reach into my pocket, pulling out the key to my room. "Is this enough?" I show her the Driftwood Inn key chain attached to the room key.

Her eyes shift to a display rack next to the reception counter. A rack that displays key chains exactly like the one I'm showing her.

"It's the tattoos, isn't it?" I ask as I step toward the counter, reaching into my back pocket for my wallet.

I want to say I'm used to being judged on my appearance, and realistically, I am, but it doesn't make it any easier.

"Uh, no." She shakes her head, stepping behind the counter. "I actually didn't notice the tattoos until you held up the key." The woman gestures to my knuckles, seeing the letters and symbols across them—my constant reminder of everything I hold most dear. "I try not to judge people on their appearance. I'm well aware most people often have it wrong."

She's not looking at me as she taps away at the computer in front of her, allowing me a moment to really see her. She's beautiful—a natural elegance that pulls you in. But it's the guarded look in her eyes that has me captivated. It's a look I know well, one that stares back at me in the mirror every day.

"Sorry, I guess I'm used to being judged." I slide my license across the counter, offering her a tight smile as an apology.

"It's all right. I understand." She lifts my license, glancing at it briefly before checking the computer.

I don't know why I do it. I'm normally more than content to sit in the silence, but something has me opening my mouth. "How is it you know your way around the registration system, but you don't know how to handle a guest coming through at odd hours of the night?"

She glances at me, passing my license back across the desk before answering. "I guess that's a valid question. My best friend's family owns the inn. I've sat with her quite a few times while she's worked check-in, and I guess it stuck with me."

"Seems odd to ask you to fill in for her instead of another staff member." It's not any of my business, but for some reason, I can't walk away.

There's this feeling churning in my gut. Like, if I walk away and go up to my room, something bad's going to happen. But I have absolutely no idea what it could be.

"Ah." Her gaze drops to the desk in front of her as she

tucks a piece of hair behind her ear. "Well, that goes back to people judging others. There was a wedding in town earlier this evening, and most people were invited." She shrugs, the implications of what she's left unsaid clear; *she* wasn't invited.

Before I can say anything else, my phone starts to ring.

"Sorry. I have no idea who'd be calling me right now." I reach into my pocket, silencing my phone.

"You better get it. It must be important if someone's trying to reach you at this time of night." She offers me a small smile, but it doesn't quite reach her eyes, that guarded look held firmly in place.

This woman has me quite curious and I want to know her story.

It's not interest in *her* that draws me in, but interest in the mysteries that surround her. It's not uncommon—it's the nature of my job, filling in the blanks to the histories around me.

My phone starts ringing again, pulling me from my wandering thoughts. I glance down at it, seeing my father's face on the screen, and silence the call once more. He can wait one more minute.

"Uh, thanks for the chat..." I let my words trail off, not sure where to go with them.

"Melissa," she says, extending her hand to mine. "Thanks for letting me verify you're actually staying here, Jude."

"Nice to meet you, Melissa. Hopefully you don't have any other guests lurking around this evening."

She laughs but before she can say anything else, my phone rings for a third time. "You better get that. Have a good evening."

"Thanks."

I silence my phone one more time, but turn and rush up the stairs to my room as quickly as possible while still being mindful of the sleeping guests in the inn.

It's not until I'm behind the locked door of my room that I finally answer my phone.

"All right. I know it's been a few days, and I'm sorry, but calling four times in a row is even a little much for you. Someone's gotta be dying if it's that urgent we talk," I chuckle as I fall onto the bed.

It's not silent on the other end of the phone; there's noise in the background, but nothing distinct enough for me to know where he is. It's his silence that has me sitting up at the foot of the bed.

"Dad? You know I was joking, right?"

It's silent for a beat longer before a voice comes clear across the line, but it's not my father's voice I hear.

"Sorry, Jude. I—Jeez, you think I'd know how to handle making a call like this." It's a man's voice, and the way he mutters that last part, I know it wasn't meant for me.

There's a shuffling sound and a muffled noise before everything stops, and the voice comes back, clear as day. "Jude, it's Gage Flynn. The manager of the bookstore next to Murphy's found your dad unconscious at the bar this evening. He's been rushed to the hospital, and they believe he's had a heart attack."

I know Gage continues talking because I hear his voice in my ear, but I have no idea what words are coming out of his mouth. It's like I'm in a *Charlie Brown* movie and his teacher is talking to me—I hear the sound, but nothing makes sense.

My dad can't be going to the hospital. He has to be all right. It's been too long since I last saw him.

My attention is focused on the painting above the desk in front of me. It's a painting of a lighthouse at sunset. It's so realistic it almost doesn't look like a painting, except the colors are so bright that everything practically pops off the canvas. It's truly a stunning piece of art, but what keeps drawing my focus is the inclusion of a man and a child walking hand in hand toward the lighthouse. And even though I hear Gage still talking in my ear, *all* I can focus on is that image.

"Jude, are you still there?" The sharpness in how Gage says my name finally draws my gaze from the painting.

On shaky legs, I stand from the bed and move to the window overlooking the dock I was just standing on. "Sorry. Yeah, I'm here, but I-I missed most of what you said."

"No. Don't apologize." Gage releases a deep breath, and I can almost imagine his entire body slumping at the realization he's the one who has to share this news with me.

It's been seventeen years since I've spoken to anyone in Ashford Falls—outside of my dad—but at one point in time, I thought of Gage as my brother, as one of my closest friends. He may be two years younger than me, but thanks to our dads being best friends, we grew up with each other, and for a period of my life Gage knew me better than anyone—like I knew him.

Gage is one of the few people my dad openly talks to me about during our chats, so I know their relationship is just as close as it's always been. Even knowing Gage has had to make these kinds of calls before due to his job, I know this one is difficult for him.

"They don't know much at the moment, but he's alive."

I want to respond, but I don't know the words to express the thoughts coursing through my brain. Ironic for a person in my line of work.

"I-I don't know if you're close. Your dad doesn't really share much about what's going on with you. I know you don't like returning to town, but I thought this might be the exception..." Gage trails off, and I don't know how to pick up the train of thought.

Gage isn't wrong; I haven't stepped foot in Ashford Falls in almost fifteen years. Though, there isn't a soul on this earth who knows I was there fifteen years ago.

No, to everyone in that town, it's been seventeen years since I've touched the soil of Ashford Falls, and I know there's at least one person there who wants to make sure I never return. But I'm going to have to disappoint them.

There are a lot of choices in my life I already regret, and if I'm not there for my father in his time of need—if I'm not there to say goodbye if he's leaving this world and I was given a chance—well, that's not something I'll ever be able to live with —no matter the consequences.

"I'm in a small town in Massachusetts. Harborview, I think." I turn for my laptop set up on the desk and shut it down.

What sounds like a disbelieving puff of air releases from Gage through the phone, making me pause for a second before he speaks. "I know exactly where that is. You're a lot closer than I thought you'd be."

I'm tempted to ask how he knows where this little town is, but now isn't the time for that. No matter what happens with my dad, I'll be in Ashford Falls for a while. There'll be plenty of time for me to satisfy my curiosity when I get there.

"I'm packing up now and then I'll hit the road. You can get my number from my dad's phone. Text me, and I'll let you know when I'm close to town."

"They've brought him to the Silverleaf Medical Center. I'll keep you updated on any changes, but they won't release much to me since I'm not a blood relative."

"Thanks, man. I'm glad you're there with him."

"Of course, that's what family does."

I stumble over my feet and collapse to the foot of the bed at those words. It shouldn't surprise me that Gage still views us as brothers. That's precisely the kind of person he is. No matter how long it's been, he'll always care for the people he holds dear.

"I gotta finish packing so I can hit the road. Thanks again."

Without waiting for his response, I hang up and do exactly what I told him I would. I've checked out of the inn and am on my bike within ten minutes of hanging up.

I wish I could say my thoughts are entirely focused on my father, but that would be a lie.

My thoughts easily drift to Abbey and the high possibility that I'll see her again.

———

June 21st, 2009

Do you remember the day we met? It was a long time ago—fourteen years, almost to the day. I remember it like it was yesterday.

It's interesting to see what moments stick in your mind as clearly as the moment they happened. I mean, I was six years old. Why does that moment stand out so clearly for me?

You and your mom were the only ones at the park when Dad and I got there, and you were having so much fun running and playing by yourself. It amazed me, even then, how bright your spirit was. Or maybe it didn't, and I'm just older and can recognize you for how amazing you really were. How amazing I hope you still are.

The second you saw me, you came running, the brightest smile on your face. You bravely told me you weren't allowed to talk to strangers but thought your mom would understand that sometimes you have to talk to strangers to become friends. You said you thought she meant it applied more to adults than other kids.

All the same, you introduced yourself and told me we'd be the best of friends. I should've learned to trust you'd always be right—because you were right.

You were my best friend, Abbey. You've always been my best friend, and I wish more than anything that I could take it all back.

I'm sure there's a greater lesson here somewhere—about everything happening for a reason and never regretting something because then you wouldn't be the person you are today. And maybe they're right. But I wonder every day if I'd be a better person if I'd just stayed.

I hate that I don't know who you are anymore. I know it's only been a year since I left, but there's no doubt you've changed. If only simply because time always changes people.

But how else have you changed? Are you still the brightest person in the room? Do you still find enjoyment in the smallest things?

Can you still find the tiniest light in the darkest of times?

Or did I ruin all of that?

Fourteen years after meeting you, and you're still the person I want to talk to most. You're still the person I think about most. You're still the love of my life.

CHAPTER
Three

JUDE

I DON'T KNOW what I was expecting when I arrived at the hospital, but it's not Gage dressed in a suit with a petite woman, in what can only be described as a bridesmaid dress, tucked into his side.

Even disheveled, they make a beautiful couple.

A little pinch in my chest at that thought makes me miss a step. I've spent a lot of my life regretting the decisions I made seventeen years ago, but over the last year I've been thinking more about how I've grown over that period.

Is it possible I would've grown in the same way if I stayed in Ashford Falls? Yeah, it's definitely possible. But there's no way to know for sure, and for that reason alone, I can't live in the past anymore.

It's a new mindset, but it brings me a little peace—probably a peace I don't deserve.

It's the woman who notices me first. I see the way she straightens and elbows Gage lightly in the side. I'm pretty confident it's unease I see filling her eyes.

"Jude, it's good to see you," Gage says, releasing the

woman at his side and pulling me into a hug. "I wish it were under better circumstances, but it's still good."

It takes me a second to return the hug, and I know it's awkward. I honestly can't remember the last time I was hugged. Probably the last time I saw my dad, which I hate to realize was almost six years ago. I should've made more of an effort to see him.

Gage doesn't even acknowledge the uncomfortable air. He simply steps back from the hug, pulling the woman back into his side. "This is Ava Day, my girlfriend. Funnily enough, she's from Harborview."

"Gage, I don't think now is the time to point out the small world we live in." The uneasiness I saw is completely gone when she looks at me. Now all I see is sympathy. "It's nice to meet you, Jude. Your dad always speaks so highly of you." She reaches a hand out into the space between us. This time, I don't hesitate and return the handshake immediately.

"Ava Day, the lawyer?"

"Oh, um, yeah."

I nod my head, a small smile forming on my lips. "My dad talks about you a lot as well." I'm sure I should expand on that more, but I've never been one to fill the silence. It's where I find the most comfort.

Over the last few months, Dad has spoken more and more about Ava Day. He told me about her when he first met her, how she seemed haunted by something and how he hoped she'd find some peace in Ashford Falls. Lately, those conversations have drifted toward how happy he's been for Ava and Gage.

Through him, I know he watched their entire story unfold. Looking at the two of them now, I wouldn't have needed all those conversations to know just how much they love each other.

"Well, uh, can we take you up to his room?" Gage asks after a few moments of awkward silence.

"No. You both have clearly been here all night. You don't need to stick around. I'll keep you in the loop on any changes."

"You sure?"

"Yeah. You can come back in a few hours. After you've had some rest." I squeeze Gage's shoulder, trying to convey my appreciation for all he's done.

"Okay. He's in the cardiac unit, room 211."

It's moments like these that make me wish I was a little more effusive, but it's not who I am—who I've ever been. Instead of saying anything else, I simply give Gage and Ava a quick nod before moving around them and entering the hospital.

The clerk at the front desk smiles kindly as I move toward him. "Can I help you, sir?"

"I'm here to see my dad, Walter Murphy. He's in the cardiac unit, room 211."

"Of course. Just take those elevators there to the second floor and follow the signs for the cardiac unit. Someone there will buzz you in." His smile turns more sympathetic when he looks back at me, and I wonder if it's just his go-to expression when dealing with people coming to the hospital to visit loved ones or if he knows who my father is.

I don't wait around. I follow the clerk's instructions and take the elevator to the second floor. As I step off, the sign right in front of the elevator directs me to the left and I have to think —yet again—that luck is on my side. As I walk down the hall, I end up behind two doctors who are apparently headed to the same place I am, because when I get to the unit doors I'm able to sneak in right behind them.

The unit is shaped like a horseshoe—a nurse's station in the center, with rooms lining the walls around it. The doors to each room are glass, allowing clear lines of sight to all the patients. As I circle the unit, looking for my father's room, I notice most rooms have curtains pulled across, granting a little bit of privacy.

My steps falter as I pass room 205. Across the unit, I see her. She's in profile, her head turned so I only catch a glimpse, but I'd know Abbey Selbey anywhere. I'd be able to find her in a crowded room no matter what.

I knew I'd run into her at some point. Ashford Falls is a small town, and the chances of avoiding her—not that I wanted to—were never strong, but I thought I'd have more time.

I'm not entirely sure why, but I guess I assumed, since Dad never talked about her, that she wasn't part of his life. But then again, why would Dad talk about her? He may not have known all the details about what led to me leaving town or the end of our marriage, but he knew how much pain I was in when I left.

Seeing her now, dressed like Ava was downstairs, the breath is stolen from my lungs.

I can't move.

I can't function.

She looks so different and yet exactly the same.

I thought I was ready to see her. I thought I'd be able to handle it, but even across the unit, through the open door to my father's hospital room, I realize I'm never going to be ready.

Taking a deep breath, I slowly make my way closer to her, only stopping when the two doctors who entered the unit before come into view and step into room 211.

"How's he doing?" the female doctor asks, placing her hand on Abbey's shoulder.

"I don't know. The doctor hasn't been in yet. The nurse said he should be here any minute."

Seeing her stopped me dead in my tracks, but hearing her voice does something to my soul. It's like this wave of comfort washes over me at the smooth sound, and I want so desperately to close my eyes and bathe in it.

"Dr. Croft is one of the best. Walt couldn't be in better hands," the male doctor says as he lifts a tablet, tapping away and searching for something. He looks familiar, but my focus is entirely on the woman sitting next to my father. I don't have the brain power to figure out who the man is.

"I know." Abbey chuckles, but it's a hollow sound. "You mentioned that multiple times while we were in the waiting room." Abbey sighs, her shoulders sagging as her head falls forward. "Sorry, Caleb, that was harsher than I meant." She lifts her head, looking to the male doctor, while reaching to take the female doctor's hand. "Quinn and Declan still don't know, right?"

"As far as I know, no one's told them, but this is Ashford Falls we're talking about," the female doctor offers.

"What about Max and Fiona? Who's with them?" Abbey asks.

Who the hell are Max and Fiona?

"My mom picked them up from the reception hours ago. We already planned for them to stay the night with her since we didn't know how late we'd be."

"I can't find his chart," Caleb mumbles as he messes with the tablet. It's said so quietly I almost miss it from where I stand in the doorway.

"They probably blocked you from it. You know you shouldn't be looking at it anyway. He's not your patient." It's a gentle reprimand, but it's enough for him to lift his eyes to look at the female doctor, and when he does his eyes stop on mine.

"Sorry, can we help you?"

I swallow, taking the final step into the room, shoving my hands in my pockets as my eyes finally travel to the man lying in the bed.

I've always thought of my father as a pillar of strength. While being the biggest teddy bear at heart, my father can appear menacing with his large frame and tattoos. But seeing him now, lying in the hospital bed with tubes and wires all over the place, he looks so small and unassuming. Nothing like the man I've always seen him as.

I bring my eyes back to the man standing at the foot of my father's bed and finally answer him. "I'm Jude, Walt's son."

At the sound of my voice, Abbey's entire posture goes taut. She doesn't turn to look at me, but I can feel the tension pouring off her, and I hate it. Almost more than seeing my father in that bed.

"Oh. Sorry, I didn't recognize you. Caleb Marks," he says, sticking his hand out for mine in a request for a handshake.

I remember Caleb from before I left town. He's a few years younger than me, but growing up in a small town, you know who most people are.

Trying to appear like I have my shit together, I remove my hand from my pocket and accept the request for a handshake. Unfortunately, I'm unable to form any words.

But, like it has a few times this morning, something—or someone—is looking out for me.

"Sorry! I forgot to bring Abbey her things." Ava breezes through the door, Gage right on her heels. Ava only stops once she hands Abbey her bag and registers the tension in the room. "What happened? Is everything okay with Walt?" Ava's eyes bounce around the room, never staying on one person for long.

It's Abbey who finally answers her. "The doctor hasn't been in yet; we don't know anything."

And as if right on cue, another doctor enters the room, pausing just inside the door when he registers how many people there are.

"Well, I know the two of you know better," he says, gesturing to Caleb and the female doctor. "Besides, only immediate family should be in here." The doctor's eyes bounce to Ava and me before stepping to the side and signaling us to leave.

"I'm his son. I don't mind if they stay." I don't know much about these people, but I can see they've been here for Abbey, and if they bring her comfort I don't want them to leave.

"Sorry, I didn't realize. I'm Dr. Croft, your father's surgeon." He glances around the room and sighs before looking back at me. "I had a chance to speak to your sister before the surgery. Did she fill you in?"

At the quick intake of air, my eyes shoot to Abbey briefly. Now I understand why the doctor never indicated that Abbey should leave.

"Yeah, they've kept me updated." It may not have been Abbey keeping me updated, but now I know why Gage had as much information as he did.

I knew in his position, he could get some information about my dad's status, but he shouldn't have been able to get all the details.

"Good." Dr. Croft turns to face Abbey, addressing her when he speaks next. "Your father's surgery went well. We were able to clear the blockage in his heart and place the stent without any problems. The bigger issue is that he hit his head when he fell due to the heart attack. His CT scan does show some bleeding of the brain. We're monitoring it, but doesn't look like it will require surgery. Neurology has recommended he be under sedation to keep him comfortable after the trauma. We're not sure how long he'll stay under, but we'll be monitoring closely." Dr. Croft pauses, glancing over his shoulder at me briefly before turning back to Abbey. "Do you have any questions for me right now?"

"Oh, um, no. I don't think so." Her gaze shifts to mine for only a second before she turns to look at my father.

"Dr. Winters, the neurologist, should be in shortly to answer any questions that might come up. And, of course, if you need anything just let one of the nurses know. They can page me if needed." Dr. Croft turns to me and shakes my hand before leaving the room.

It's silent, minus the beeping from the machines attached to my dad. The tension in the room rises like the tide, making me wonder how many people in this room truly know the history between Abbey and me?

Without thinking about it, my eyes fall back to Abbey. I want to shout at her to just look at me, even if only for a minute. Long enough for me to clearly see the woman she's become.

I thought I knew how much I missed her before but seeing her now—for the first time in fifteen years—I realize I was wrong. Seeing her now, seeing her refuse to look at me, I realize I never knew the meaning of the word.

How can I miss someone who's sitting right in front of me? Someone I have no right to miss?

"Have you been introduced to everyone, Jude?" Ava asks cautiously from her spot next to Abbey.

"I think I'm the only one he needs to meet. You probably grew up with everyone else." The female doctor steps forward, a tentative smile forming on her lips. "I'm Emily Marks, Caleb's wife."

It's more of a struggle than I think it should be, but I turn from Abbey and meet Emily's eyes, offering her a small nod in acknowledgment.

"I'm gonna go." Abbey stands so suddenly from her seat, the chair scratches across the floor.

"You don't have to." I wish the first words out of my mouth to Abbey were so much better than those, but I don't want her to leave.

Selfishly, I want her to stay and tell me everything I've missed since I left, but I know even if she stays, I'd have no right to hear anything about her life.

More importantly, I know how much she means to Dad.

He'd want her here, and I hate that my presence is running her off.

Abbey's gaze finally meets mine, and that comfort I felt hearing her voice is back. There's a shield that was never there before, but her eyes are on mine, and that warmth washes over me again. She's changed over the last fifteen years; she's older, more mature, her features more developed than the last time I saw her, but she's still Abbey.

"Abs." I don't even realize the word leaves my lips until I see something spark in her piercing blue eyes.

"You should have some time alone with your dad. It's been a long time since you've seen him." Abbey doesn't wait for a response before she grabs her things and marches out the door.

I want to go after her, but I know it's not my place anymore.

Stuffing my hands back into my pockets yet again, I let my eyes fall to the floor for a second before lifting them to look at Gage. "Can you make sure she gets home okay?"

"Yeah, no problem." There's a question in Gage's eyes, but being the man he is, he doesn't ask it. He simply reaches a hand out to Ava, waiting for her to take it before they both leave.

CHAPTER
Four

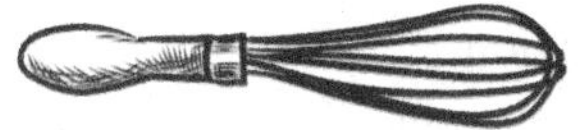

ABBEY

"OKAY, look, I know we're supposed to be at work in thirty minutes, but I can't wait until the morning rush dies down," Ava says as she squeezes past me into my apartment the following morning.

"Ava—"

"No, Abbey, you alluded to something *months* ago, and I let you keep your secrets, but I saw the look on your face at the hospital yesterday. I think you need to let it out." Her voice softens as she continues. "If there's one thing I learned from everything I went through, it's that you can't hold it all in." She pauses, reaching for my hand. "I know I haven't known you long, and you tend to keep people at arm's length, but I'm not going to let you do it anymore."

My lips tip up in a stilted smile. I know Ava's concern comes from a place of friendship, but it doesn't make it easier for me to hear. We've grown close over the last several months, along with Quinn and Emily, but opening up to others doesn't come easy for me—not anymore.

Ava went through a lot over the holidays and at the start of this year. I know it was a call from her brother that brought her to Ashford Falls, but it was running from her problems back home that kept her here—at least at first.

Ava's close with her brother, and he'll always support her in everything she does, but Ava still struggled to share the problems she'd been having when she first got here. It was Gage who ended up being the person she first leaned on, and it was him who convinced her to be honest with Declan.

She eventually shared the whole story with everyone she's grown close to, me included, but it took her until she was put in a really bad situation.

Now she's happier than I've ever seen her, even with the recent loss of Scott, a man who was more like a father to her than her own ever was.

"Abbey," Ava whispers when I don't respond. "You're not alone. I don't think you ever have been, but I won't let you think you are anymore. You told me I'd be a perfect fit, and I know you meant at the bookstore, but I'm a perfect fit as your friend too. You're stuck with me now, so you'll just have to learn to live with it." Her tone is light in the end, but I see the truth in her eyes. She won't let me out of this apartment until I tell her something. Even if that means we're late in opening the bookstore.

"There's not much to tell."

That's such a lie. There's a lot of history between Jude and me, thirty years' worth, but I don't think I'm ready to share that story quite yet.

"Great, we'll be right on time for work." Ava waltzes over to my couch and takes a seat before turning to look at me expectantly.

I take my time joining Ava on the couch, trying to figure out where to start. The truth is, I don't even know the full story, but I know it starts with our parents.

My mother and Walt were born and raised in Ashford Falls. They grew up next door to each other and were best friends. From the stories I heard, they were practically insepa-rable. But Mom went away to college, where she met my dad and fell madly in love, while Walt stayed close to home and met Kimberly. They both lived their own lives while still making their friendship a priority.

But when Mom graduated, Dad asked her to move with him to DC, where he was trying to open his own investment firm. She agreed, especially since she'd just found out she was pregnant with me.

The year I turned five was the year Dad made it big with his investment firm, and it was also the year Mom finally convinced him to buy a house in Ashford Falls.

Which, I guess, is where Jude and my story officially starts.

"Jude and I met when I was five, shortly after my parents bought a house here in town," I tell Ava. "They hadn't intended to live here full-time, but Mom loved Ashford Falls, and DC isn't that far away, so we stayed while Dad commuted back and forth."

"You say there isn't much to tell, yet you're starting the story thirty years ago. How is there not a lot to tell?"

I chuckle lightly. "I'm just giving you a bit of backstory."

"All right. Sorry. I'll be quiet." Ava smiles, lifting her hands slightly in apology.

"Jude and I became the best of friends. We did everything together, and shortly after I turned fourteen, we started dating. I know it's ridiculous to say, but I knew I was going to marry him."

I remember the day Jude and I met like it was yesterday.

We'd only moved to town a few days earlier, but Dad had been called back to the city before we could finish unpacking. Mom had gotten a little frustrated with me and needed a break, so she took me to the park, hoping other kids would be there to play with.

Unfortunately, the park was empty when we got there, but

I was used to playing by myself. Mom was always around and tried her best, but she couldn't entertain me twenty-four seven.

Shortly after we got to the park, Walt showed up with Jude, and without even giving him a chance to do anything, I ran right up to him and introduced myself. From that moment on, he was my best friend—and I was his.

"There's something about falling in love with your best friend. They understand you in a way most people never will, and that's what I felt with Jude. He truly was my other half." We were each other's first everything. There was a comfort in knowing Jude knew all of my secrets—or at least most of them. When it came to him, I never felt self-conscious or afraid. He was my safe place, and I thought I was his. "I thought I knew him better than I knew myself."

"You didn't?" Ava probes when I don't continue.

"I honestly don't know anymore." I stand from the couch, unable to sit still. I move back to the kitchen, where I was packing up the s'mores bars and lemon cookies I made last night before Ava knocked on my door. "We got married, but we kept it secret."

"What?" Ava shouts, standing from her seat and marching into the kitchen. "Married in secret?"

"Yeah, my dad *really* didn't like the idea of Jude and me being together, but we didn't care. We loved each other, and that was all that mattered."

The love I felt for Jude on our wedding day was like nothing I'd ever felt before—like nothing I've ever experienced since. And I thought Jude felt the same. The way his voice wavered as he said his vows, the love that showed in his eyes, the gentle caress of his hands against mine, all of it spoke of the love we shared.

It may not have been the wedding I'd always imagined growing up, but it was perfectly us, and that was all I wanted in the end—a wedding solely about us.

"That's all that should matter," Ava whispers in the silence. "Why didn't your dad like you with Jude?"

"I honestly don't know." And that's the truth. I have some suspicions, but I was never able to get an answer from my mother, and my father refused to talk about it at all. "There was always this perception that the Murphys came from the wrong side of the tracks."

"What?" Ava asks in disbelief. "Why the hell would people go to Murphy's if they thought that?"

"It wasn't everybody in town who thought it, but it was enough." I snap the lids closed on the containers before I continue. "Of course, Murphy's is the only bar in town, so people didn't let their opinions of the owner stop them from spending their money there."

"Right," Ava scoffs. "So, your dad just went along with parts of the town and assumed the Murphys were bad news? Without actually knowing them?"

"My mom was from Ashford Falls. She and Walt grew up together. They were best friends."

"Was it more than that?"

"I don't know." I spin away from her and move to the sink to wash my hands.

Ava doesn't need me to say the word to understand I truly have no idea why my father feels the way he does about Walt and Jude, but that doesn't stop her from returning us back to the original conversation.

"What happened with you and Jude? After you got married?"

I keep my back turned to her, not wanting to see her face when she hears my next words. "We were married in June, shortly after I graduated high school, and three months later I filed for divorce."

"I'm sorry. Did I hear you correctly?"

"You did." I turn back to face Ava, leaning back against the sink.

There's so much more to that statement, but I've walked down memory lane enough for today. And the truth is, I'm already raw from simply seeing him yesterday. Anymore, and I'm not sure how I'll be able to function.

"That's it? That's all you're going to tell me?" Ava asks incredulously.

"Yes, because I may not know Jude like I used to, but I know how much he loves his father. And until Walt is back on his feet, Jude won't be going anywhere." It's not the complete truth, but it's not a total lie either. No matter how much I still hurt from what happened between us, I know what it's like to see a parent lying in a hospital bed, and I wouldn't wish that on anyone.

"So?"

"I don't want to influence what you think of Jude. The town will try to do that enough and no matter what, he deserves to have a little peace while he deals with everything."

"You're too nice sometimes," Ava mumbles.

"No, I'm not." I push off the side of the sink, moving to collect the containers of sweets. "It's been seventeen years since I've spoken to Jude. I have no idea what kind of man he is now, and it's not fair to judge someone based on the mistakes they made as a child. Because no matter how grown-up we thought we were, that's what we were—children."

"Abbey," Ava calls as I walk to the door, making me stop to look at her over my shoulder. "You looked devastated when you saw him yesterday."

Turning to face her head on, I give her another truth. "Because the boy I remember had such a light about him, and the man I saw yesterday was shrouded in darkness. No matter what happened between us, I don't want him to be unhappy."

I'm not entirely sure that's the truth, but it's how I want to feel about him. I want to wish him well in all of his endeavors. If I can do that, it will mean I've moved on from all of it.

And it's time to move on—it's more than time.

"I don't even know the details, but I can imagine based on your face right now, and I don't think I could forgive Gage if he hurt me like that," Ava offers as she moves to open the door for me, grabbing my bag from beside the door and twisting the lock on her way out.

"I've had seventeen years to come to terms with all of it. If you asked me how I felt right after it happened, I would've had a much different response."

"Still, you're a better person than I am."

No, I'm really not.

I don't know how to respond, so I don't.

In the silence, we make our way downstairs and enter Falls Book Haven from the back door. My eyes wander to the right just before I step inside, to the back door of Murphy's, and I wonder how long it'll be before I'll have to start avoiding the bar again.

CHAPTER
Five

JUDE

"ANY UPDATES?" At the sound of the deep voice, I lift my head to see who's come to visit my dad now.

I'd forgotten truly how small Ashford Falls was until yesterday afternoon. I got maybe twenty minutes alone with Dad after Abbey and everyone left before others started showing up. And somehow, even though the doctor said it was immediate family only, they still appeared at the door.

It was nice seeing some of the faces, especially Nick and Laura, Gage's parents. I was a little surprised to see them *so* together, considering the last time I saw them, Laura was married to her second husband, and Nick had only just divorced his third wife. But then again, a lot can change when you avoid your hometown like the plague and refuse to be filled in on what's happening from the one person you keep in contact with.

It was strange seeing some other faces, though. When I left, there were people who stayed far away from anyone with the last name Murphy, only stepping into the bar because they wanted a drink and couldn't get it anywhere else.

I never got the full story, but I know it had something to do with my grandparents and the founding family of Ashford Falls. My dad always said it was a big misunderstanding that people refused to acknowledge. Even when the Ashfords moved away—long before I was born—people still avoided us outside the walls of Murphy's.

But I guess this was another thing that changed over the last seventeen years, because people I swore would be glad to see my father laying in a hospital bed showed up with genuine sympathy on their faces.

This time, it's Gage at the door, dressed casually. He's by himself today, and I wonder if he's technically on duty since his badge is clipped to his belt.

"Nothing new since my last text. They're keeping him sedated and monitoring the swelling in his brain." I stand, stretching slightly before moving to the window overlooking the parking lot.

"Did you get any rest last night?" Gage asks, taking a spot at my side.

"They brought a cot in for me, but I didn't really sleep."

We're both quiet for a few minutes. I have a feeling Gage wants to ask me about yesterday with Abbey, but I honestly don't know what to say. I always knew I loved Abbey, and I knew that love would never go away.

I guess I assumed I could handle it like everything else in my life—leave it in its designated box, buried deep, with no plans to resurrect it. But seeing her yesterday changed everything.

Abbey was never to blame for what happened seventeen years ago. It was entirely my fault, and if I'd been a big enough person to admit I didn't know what to do...if I'd just *talked* to Abbey and my dad, things would be different. But then again, there's no way to know what that "different" would look like. No matter how much I want to hope otherwise, Abbey and I still might not have made it.

People change—or at least they should.

What's to say, our being together wouldn't have stunted that change? Of course, what's to say we wouldn't have pushed each other to be the best version of ourselves?

But that's the point. We'll never know what the future could have been if we made different choices. We can only live in the present. And I might not know how Abbey has changed since I last spoke to her, but I know I want to find out.

"Do you know if Dad has any tenants in the apartment above the bar right now?"

"Oh. Uh. No. I don't think so." He swallows audibly before turning to face me. "But are you sure that's where you want to stay? I'm pretty sure it's completely empty."

"Yeah. I don't know how long I'll be staying in town." And I'm not ready to stay in my father's house without him. That might make it a little too real that there's a possibility he won't wake up from this.

"All right." Gage's eyes shift to look at my father in his bed for a moment, clearly thinking about something before he looks back to me. "I realize we haven't spoken in a really long time, but you've always been one who likes it told to them straight, so I'm just going to say it like it is."

"Okay." I shift, turning to face him head-on, banding my arms across my chest as if preparing to take a hit. It might not be a physical blow, but based on the look in Gage's eye, it's going to be an emotional one.

"Abbey lives in the apartment above the bookstore, the bookstore right next to the bar. The same apartment right across the hall from the one you're asking about."

Well, I didn't see that one coming.

Gage releases a heavy sigh, his eyes bouncing between mine. I don't move, preparing for the next hit.

"Look, I don't know what happened between you and Abbey. I honestly don't think there's a single person in this world who knows other than you two. But I saw the aftermath, and it wasn't pretty." His head shifts, turning to look out the window. "Abbey lost a lot more than you when you left, and it took her a long time to find any kind of peace again." When he turns back to look at me, there's nothing but concern in his eyes. "I obviously didn't see you after it happened, but I know how much you loved her. And if that look on your face yesterday told me anything, you still do."

"Gage—"

"All I'm saying," Gage interrupts, "is that I don't want to see either of you hurt."

I don't know what to say, so instead of saying anything, I give him a terse nod and turn back to the window.

I'm not naive enough to think Abbey was okay after I left, but hearing the words out loud...makes it real. It makes it hurt just a little bit more, knowing the pain I caused her.

Everything I did was with the hope she'd still have her friends and family to lean on when I left. That she'd have the support of this town to help her bear the weight of everything. But I should've known Abbey better. She was never going to tell anyone what happened between us. She never would've wanted to keep me from returning home if that's what I wanted.

She never would've wanted my father to look at me any differently.

On that thought, I can't help but look back at my dad, still so small in his hospital bed.

My dad will always love me, no matter what I do. He's loved me all these years, through all the missed holidays and canceled trips, through all the letdowns and unanswered questions. But if he knew what happened seventeen years ago, he wouldn't look at me the same way. That pride Ava spoke about yesterday would have chinks in it. His faith in me would've wavered, and I never would've been able to live with that.

The fact that Abbey had every right to destroy that faith and devotion but chose not to...it proves how strong she is—how good she is. Her goodness was always the thing I loved most about her. Her brightness and ability to find the best in people and any situation—if she lost that because of what I did, I'll never forgive myself.

"Is she happy?" The words are so soft I wonder if Gage heard me, but when he answers I swear my heart stops beating.

IT'S LATER than I planned when I finally make it up the stairs to the apartment above the bar, my duffle and laptop bag thrown over one shoulder and an air mattress tucked under my other arm.

Gage warned me that the place was probably a mess, but I wasn't expecting it to be as bad as it is. It may be completely empty of furniture, but since no one's been up here in who knows how long, there's a thick layer of dust coating every inch of the place.

Dropping my things in the hall, I step inside. Nothing's changed about this place. It's a predominantly open living space. The only areas behind closed doors being the bedroom and bathroom. The kitchen is directly to the left, the counters running in an L-shape along the walls with a small island in the middle. In the back left corner is the space typically meant for a dining table. In front of me, the area for a living room, and to the right the doors that lead to the bedroom and bathroom.

A wave of nostalgia washes over me, the memories of playing in here as a kid while my dad worked down in the bar, of Abbey and I moving in after we were married, of the happy moments we had in the brief months we lived here, of the night I ruined everything.

I want so badly to only hold on to the good memories of

this place, but it's the painful ones that take center stage. And the reality is, I wouldn't be who I am today without all of those memories flooding my system.

I close my eyes and take a second to center myself. Letting my mind run wild won't do me any good.

Resigned to the fact that I'll need to get rid of at least some of this dust before I can sleep, I head back down the stairs to grab some cleaning supplies from the bar.

Stepping into the bar has its own wave of nostalgia washing over me. Only this time, nothing negative shows its ugly face. All my memories of this place revolve around my father and grandfather, two of the best men I've ever known.

My grandfather immigrated to the United States from Ireland in 1960, shortly after marrying my grandmother. They didn't have a plan when they arrived, but since neither of them had families of their own at that point, they thought it'd be an adventure.

They landed in New York and quickly decided city life wasn't for them, but they thought it'd be fun to hit the road to see the country as a whole before deciding where they wanted to settle. Driving through Ashford Falls was a complete accident after getting lost on their way to Washington, DC. But once they saw this little town, they knew it was meant to be their home.

Owning this bar had always been their dream, and my grandparents worked hard to make it a reality. Opening its doors in 1965 became the proudest moment of my grandfather's life until he welcomed his son into the world a year later.

Even through significant moments of loss and grief throughout all our lives, this bar stood tall, forever their safe space. The joy and pride they both took in running Murphy's will always be the first thing I think of when I step through these doors.

There's a warmth that rushes over a person when they step

through these doors, and that's because of the environment my family built with this place. Keeping the doors open was always one of the most important things to both of them, right behind their family.

No matter how long it's been, it still feels like coming home, and I can't help the small smile that grows. Nothing about this place has changed, and yet it still looks new.

I only give myself a second to look around before searching for the cleaning supplies—something I find quickly enough in the supply closet back in the kitchen. Grabbing a bucket, I toss a sponge, paper towels, and some cleaning solution in before grabbing the mop and trudging back up the stairs to the apartment.

I'm almost to my apartment when I hear the door from outside open. I freeze, knowing there's likely only one person about to come up those stairs behind me.

The bookstore and the bar are technically in the same building, along with a couple other storefronts on this side of Main Street, but the second floor is split in half, with two apartments in each half.

Unless Gage decided to help me get this apartment set up, it's most likely Abbey coming up those steps, and no matter how much I want to see her, I'm pretty confident she doesn't want to see me.

Just as I finally get my feet to start working again, I hear her steps falter behind me.

"What are you doing here?" Her tone isn't harsh. It's cautious, something she's never been with me, not even when we first met, and it tears a little piece of my heart knowing I'm the one that did this to us.

I turn to face her, giving her the truth because Abbey deserves nothing but the truth from me. "I wasn't ready to go to my dad's place without him. It makes the situation a little too real, like I'm preparing to say goodbye to him, and I can't do that right now."

Abbey's eyes move to her door, and I see her visibly swallow before she looks at me again. "Any changes since yesterday?"

"No, they're still monitoring the swelling and keeping him under. Dr. Winters thought it would be better if I left the hospital for a bit, got some rest in a real bed instead of a cot in Dad's room." I watch Abbey's eyes track to the air mattress on the floor by my feet and offer a rueful smile when they come back to mine. "Yeah, so, that's not a real bed either."

Abbey doesn't say anything. I'm not surprised, but I'm also desperate to hear her voice more. I've gone so long without it; now that I've heard it again, I can't get enough.

She shifts uncomfortably where she stands, and I desperately search for something to say that will keep her here a little bit longer. It's not fair of me, especially seeing her discomfort, but I can't stop myself. And that's when my eyes land on the book she's holding, *The Silent Promise* by AJ Doherty.

"I didn't think that book was out yet." I gesture to the book in question, my eyes moving back to hers.

"Oh, yeah. Perks of being a bookstore manager. We can request early copies of books we plan on stocking to blurb them in the store." She shrugs, but I see a spark of excitement in her eye.

"You're a fan of AJ Doherty?"

"Oh god, yes. This man knows how to suck you in and keep you guessing until the very last moment. His twists always blow me away, and his characters are so complex. Even the characters I'm supposed to hate tend to tug at my heart-strings a bit. Of course, I never realize I'm supposed to hate them until the end, so maybe that has a bit to do with it too."

I force the smile tugging at the corners of my lips away, but

I love that Abbey went on a little tangent with me. "A fan of thrillers, I don't think I would've guessed that one."

And just like that, the moment is broken.

Abbey's spine straightens. "Well, a lot can change after almost two decades." She doesn't look over her shoulder as she opens her door, but that doesn't stop her next words from hitting their target. "I'm sure I don't know the first thing about you anymore either."

CHAPTER

Six

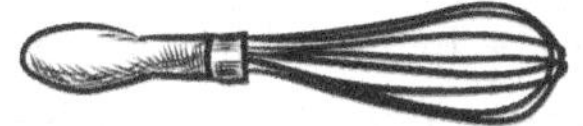

ABBEY

I'M CLOSING out the cash register a few days later when Marybelle Burns, the owner of Falls Book Haven, walks through the door. It's not necessarily late since it's only six in the evening, but if Marybelle makes an appearance in the store, it's normally in the middle of the day.

"Abbey, my dear! I'm glad I caught you." The woman may be in her sixties and shorter than most people, but the way she waltzes into a room with such confidence has always been something I've envied about her.

"Where else would I be, Ms. Marybelle?" *And what an unfortunate truth that is.*

Managing this place has practically become my entire purpose in life. Even with Ava reintroducing me to our little world of Ashford Falls, I still don't go out and do anything unless it's with her, Quinn, and Emily. I might go to Murphy's once or twice a week for dinner, but that's it.

If I'm not with one of them, I'm in this store or my apartment, baking or reading. I used to have such a drive to do more. I strived to learn new recipes, I endeavored to create my own, I volunteered my time. I had friends—a life. I was more than just my job—I wanted more for myself.

I always dreamed of opening my own bakery and coffee shop, but then I had my heart broken, and I mistook losing one dream for losing them all.

"I know, I meant I'm glad I made it here before closing." Marybelle smiles, coming up to the opposite side of the counter.

"Is everything all right?" Concern etches my voice. Marybelle might seem to be in a good mood, but the fact she's here at closing searching me out has my stomach rolling.

"Of course. It's just, well…" She sighs, a half-smile gracing her lips, almost as if in pity. "I've decided to retire early."

"Oh. That's great." I don't know why she needed to rush to tell me, especially since she's been semi-retired for years, but I'm happy for her. Though, the pity in her eyes has me questioning how happy I should be about this announcement.

"It means I'm selling the bookstore," she says gently as if she's afraid of hurting me.

"Oh." My eyes fall to the open drawer in front of me, not entirely sure what to say. I honestly don't even know how I feel. *I should feel sad, right?* "That makes sense." I push the drawer closed and lock it before tucking the key into my pocket. "Do you already have an interested buyer?" That's the logical question to ask.

If she has an interested buyer and they don't plan on keeping this as a bookstore…a*m I going to have to fire the rest of the staff too?*

"No. I just officially decided to retire today. I honestly thought you might be interested in buying the place." Marybelle reaches across the counter, placing her hand on my forearm, waiting for my eyes to meet hers before she continues. "You've put so much of yourself into this place, and I thought you might even be able to turn it into that café you always dreamed about." Her smile is so genuine. I can't bring myself to tell her I have nowhere near the amount of money it would take to buy this place from her.

People like to whisper that the only town secret is about what happened between Jude and me, but the truth is, there are so many secrets this town knows absolutely nothing about. Like the fact that I don't have money stashed away somewhere. They like to assume that since my father has made a lot of money from his investment firm, that I now have money too. But that's not who my father is.

My father worked hard to build his mini-empire, and while he's a very wealthy man with a lot of power, he's always believed that I have to work for everything I want in life. Handouts from him have never been a thing and asking him for money has never crossed my mind—he'd never give it to me.

But he's a businessman at heart. Maybe if I went to him with a business plan, asking for a loan or an investment instead of simply asking for the money with nothing in return...

"Can I let you know in a week?" I ask Marybelle, a plan forming in my mind.

"Of course! I sprung this on you with no warning."

"Thank you, Ms. Marybelle. I really appreciate you thinking of me." And I mean that. The more I think about it, the more excited I get. I might actually make my long-lost dream a reality.

"Always, my dear. And no matter what"—Marybelle reaches across the counter, taking my hand in hers—"I'll make sure you have plenty of time to make arrangements for a new job. I would never leave you out in the rain."

I squeeze her hand and offer her a tight smile. "The thought never crossed my mind."

THE SOUND of knocking on the door to the bookstore jolts me from my laptop in front of me.

I know I should have gone up to my apartment to work on my business plan, but something about being in the space has my creative juices flowing. I couldn't stop jotting down ideas for what I could do with the store.

I'd need to renovate the entire place to make this happen, but I know I can do it if I have the money. Incorporating the café would mean losing a little shelf space, but as Ava pointed out when she first started, a good portion of the traffic coming through the doors of Falls Book Haven is coming for the baked goods, not the books.

Owning this bookstore means I could change up the inventory, and maybe I'd be able to get people interested in the books we sell here instead of just the sweets.

I love Marybelle, but she's been stocking the same types of books for years, and more often than not, it only caters to the older generation of Ashford Falls. The fact that I convinced her to stock some newer thrillers—and, God forbid, romances—was so monumental, I almost fainted.

I have no idea how she's stayed in business as long as she has, but the idea of revamping this space is bringing me back to life in a way I stopped believing was possible.

Glancing over my shoulder, I find Ava and Gage standing at the door, concern etched across their faces.

"Is everything all right?" Ava doesn't even let me open the door before she's pushing through, pulling me into a hug so tight I'm immediately worried.

"What are you talking about?" I may be talking to Ava, but my eyes are on Gage since she hasn't let me go.

"We ran into Rose at The Diner, and she told us Marybelle is selling the bookstore." Gage reaches for Ava, gently pulling her arms from around me.

"That didn't take long," I mutter under my breath,

returning to the chair I was sitting in before they arrived. "Marybelle was here earlier. You heard right. She's retiring and selling the bookstore, but she offered to let me buy it first. She's giving me a week to decide."

"What's there to decide?" Ava practically shouts as she takes the armchair next to me. "You love this place."

"Rebel, tone it down a bit." Gage chuckles softly, perching on the armrest of his girlfriend's seat.

"I will not! This is the perfect opportunity!" Ava's eyes brighten with so much excitement; I can't help but smile at her. "You could gut the whole place and build a kitchen where the storage room and offices are." Ava stands, turning to the space in question. "And you could shift the counter to face the front of the store, putting a few tables in front of that window. You'd probably lose a few bookshelves, but you could become a specialized bookstore and only sell a certain genre or something, so losing the space wouldn't be a big deal."

When Ava spins back to me, her eyes catch on my open computer, the business plan I was working on still on the screen.

"Oh my god! You've already thought of this!" she shouts as she lifts the computer from the table.

"Of course, I'm thinking about it. I just have to figure out how I'm going to pay for it."

Gage's eyes shift to mine, and his brows pinch in, curiosity written across his face. "Your dad won't help you?"

I shift in my seat, discomfort coursing through me. It's been a long time since I've opened up to anyone about the complicated relationship with my father, and the idea of doing so now makes me nervous. But I'm also sick and tired of keeping it all in and doing everything by myself. I want to be a good friend, and Gage and Ava deserve nothing but the truth from me.

"My dad is a firm believer in working for everything you

have. He worked his way up to the powerful man he is from nothing and thinks I need to do the same." I fiddle with the frayed edge of my jean shorts, avoiding eye contact.

It's hard admitting this, especially to a man whose parents would do everything in their power to help their children, no matter the cost to them. "He's a businessman at heart, though. So I'm sure if I went to him with a clear business plan, I could probably get him to invest in the idea."

"How could he pass it up?" Ava bounces where she stands, done holding in the excitement coursing through her. "All he has to do is come in one morning to see the crowd you bring in with your treats. Forget the books. You could only do a bakery and make enough to thrive."

"I love the books, though." My eyes move around the shop. There might be a lot of things I would change about this place when it comes to its inventory, but the atmosphere is something I absolutely love.

"I know you do." Ava moves back to reclaim her seat in the armchair, leaning against Gage as she smiles at me. "What are you going to call it?"

"Oh, I'm not going to change it. Well, not really, anyway. This place has always been Falls Book Haven, and it feels like a haven. I don't want to change that."

"If you're incorporating a bakery, though..." Gage's words trail off, his meaning clear. The name should match the purpose.

"I was thinking Falls Book Haven and Café."

"I love it." Ava beams.

"Don't get too excited. I still have to figure out the money side of things." My eyes shift to the business plan on my computer. I hope I can get this right. The more I think about it, the more I want this to happen. "What about you?" I turn back to Ava. "If I don't get the money, what will you do? There's no guarantee whoever Marybelle sells to will keep this as a bookstore."

Ava's gaze shifts to Gage briefly, her body leaning a little more heavily into his side. "Well, I've actually been spending a couple of afternoons a week helping Benny Meriwether out at his office."

"You have?" I'm surprised but ecstatic about this news. While I've loved having Ava working part-time in the bookstore, I always thought it was unfortunate that she gave up practicing law.

She and I didn't know each other when she first got to Ashford Falls, but I heard how integral she was to Scott keeping custody of his youngest son. There wasn't a person in this town who thought it was right what Caleb and Quinn's mother did to Scott, especially after she abandoned them all when Max was only two.

But even with the win on the case, she was still adamant about moving on from being a lawyer. Hearing that she's spending time at the local law office with Benny Meriwether is great news. I can imagine how happy Benny is with that development. He's been talking about retiring for years but keeps putting it off since the closest lawyer is three towns over.

"Yes, but don't get your hopes up. I'm still not sure it's what I want to do with the rest of my life. There are still a lot of mixed emotions around practicing law. But I'm happy to help you review anything you need to make this café a reality."

"No, I couldn't ask you to do that."

"You didn't ask, I offered." Ava's smile makes it hard to think she's speaking anything but the truth.

The idea that Ava wants to help me shouldn't surprise me, and yet it does. I can't understand why someone would want to help a person that barely lets them in. But then again, Ava understands that better than most would.

I reach across the open space between our seats and grasp

her hand, trying to convey how grateful I am. "I would really appreciate your insight."

"Of course." She squeezes my hand, silently communicating how much she gets it.

"But you both can start on that tomorrow," Gage says, standing from his seat and pulling Ava up. "Now it's time for all of us to go home and get some rest."

"Yes, sir!" Ava laughs as she salutes him, ruining the gesture entirely, but the fond look that crosses Gage's face has a little flare sparking in my chest—wishing I had that kind of connection with someone else.

CHAPTER
Seven

ABBEY

MY HEART RATE SPIKES, and I can't help but be thankful that I'm not the one hooked up to the heart monitor. This book has been such a roller coaster ride and so incredibly different from every other AJ Doherty book I've ever read. The characters are still just as intricate and intriguing, but the storyline follows a path I'm not used to in his books.

It's almost like he's following the formula for a romantic suspense more than a thriller, and I just don't know how I feel about it. I love a good romance novel, but AJ Doherty is the furthest author from my mind when I think of romance. I don't think I've ever seen a hint of romance in any of his previous books, and I've been following him since he published his first book almost ten years ago.

My heart might be pounding, but my brows pinch with the cliffhanger at the end of the chapter. There's no reason for me to close the book right now, but that's exactly what I find myself doing.

Placing my bookmark, I close the book and tilt it to see how much further I have—about halfway there. I could finish it easily, but I still place the book in the empty seat next to me, done reading for now.

My eyes move to the hospital bed in front of me, and I can't stop myself from moving to the edge of my seat, taking Walt's hand in mine. While the doctors have started to wean Walt off the medication keeping him sedated, he hasn't shown any signs of waking up.

"You have to be okay, Walt. I just got you back. I'm not ready to say goodbye yet." My voice is hoarse and I have to swallow to stop the tears building in the back of my throat. "I don't know what to do, Walt," I whisper, dropping my head to the edge of his bed, his hand still held in mine. "How am I supposed to live across the hall from him?"

It's been almost a week since he moved into our old apartment—the apartment I refused to even look at the first few months after I moved into mine.

I almost didn't accept Marybelle's offer to move into the space above the bookstore when I first started working there nearly a decade ago. The thought of all the reminders simply seeing that door would conjure terrified me. To this day, the first memories that run through my brain are some of the happiest moments of my life.

Jude was adamant about carrying me over the threshold the day we moved into the apartment, no matter how ridiculous I told him it was. But there was so much joy and laughter that day. We didn't have much when we moved, but we had each other, and that felt like more than enough.

I lift my head, looking at Walt. I know he won't respond, but that doesn't stop me from talking to him as if he will.

"It might not be fair, but no matter how much time has passed, I'm still hurt. I know I have every right to be hurt, but I hate that I can't let it go. I hate that I'm not stronger." Releasing Walt's hand, I sit back in my seat, my eyes never leaving his face.

Almost a week of living across the hall from Jude, and I've run into him every day. No matter what time I leave—and believe me, I've changed up the time every day—he's still stepping out of his space at the same time. He doesn't say anything, but he watches me carefully as if I might disappear if he looks away.

"I've seen him every day, Walt, and even though he doesn't say a word, it's like I know what he's thinking." My eyes fall to my hands in my lap, afraid of some judgment I know doesn't exist. "Maybe it's because I'm thinking the same thing—how different would our lives be if we made different choices in that one moment?" Standing from my seat, I move to the window overlooking the parking lot.

I'm not sure if I really thought I'd ever see Jude again. I think part of me always knew I would, but then again, I worked next door to Walt for ten years and still managed to avoid laying eyes on him. Not for any reason other than seeing him would always remind me of Jude, and I couldn't handle that pain.

Seeing Walt definitely made me think of Jude, but I was wrong about the pain. It wasn't the thought of Jude that hurt me when I finally spoke to Walt again; it was the realization that I missed out on sixteen years with a man who had been like a father to me. I was in pain because I knew how much I hurt Walt, a man who never deserved that kind of treatment.

"I know I'm not the same person I was seventeen years ago, so how can I treat him like he's the same? How can I feel for him as strongly today as I did back then?"

A noise behind me causes my entire body to jolt. Spinning to see the source of the sound, my heart rate spikes again.

I shouldn't be shocked by the person standing in the doorway—he has every right to be here—but I hoped I'd have a little more time to myself.

"Sorry, I can come back." Jude stuffs his hands into his

pockets but doesn't move to leave, his eyes staying trained on me.

"No. He's your father. You should stay." It takes a moment, but I unstick my feet and move back to the chair I was sitting in.

"He'd want you to be here," he whispers, taking a few steps into the room.

"I've been here for an hour, and it's not like he knows who's here." I reach for my bag on the floor, dropping it into my empty seat as I put my things away.

"Do you really believe that? That he can't hear you?"

"I honestly don't know, but either way, he'd want you here more than anyone else." My voice is harsher than I mean, but I can't control it. It's not something I'm proud of, but I can't find the energy to care right now.

The only sound in the room is the beeping from Walt's monitor, and I take Jude's silence as acceptance, returning to packing my things.

"Are you enjoying it?" he asks, and I look at him, wondering what he's referring to, but find his eyes resting on the book in the seat beside me.

I contemplate ignoring him for only a second before I answer, unable to keep my thoughts to myself. "I don't know, which might say exactly how I feel about it," I mutter as I slide the book into my bag.

"What do you mean?" I hear his feet shuffle slightly, and when I look up, he's standing on the other side of the chair.

"Just that I'm normally already in love with the story and characters at this point in the story." I shrug, shouldering my bag.

"What's different about this one?" His eyes bounce between mine, an emotion swelling in them that I can't quite place.

"Jude." I sigh, my shoulders deflating. I might not be able

to read the emotion in his eyes, but I know this can't be about a book. "Why are we talking about a book?"

"Honestly? I don't want you to go. I know it's selfish and I have no right, but that's the truth." He shifts, removing his hands from his pockets, placing them on the back of the chair, his knuckles turning white from how tightly he grips it. "I've... you're..." His words trail off, and his head falls forward, clearly at a loss for what to say.

I can't blame him. I don't know what to say either.

I've seen Jude every day for the last week, but I haven't allowed myself to study him, and in this moment, I finally allow myself the time to see him.

When I knew Jude before, he constantly fought the stereotype of the boy from the wrong side of the tracks—even if there weren't any tracks running through this town. He was clean-shaven, kept his hair short, and always wore clean-cut clothes. He never looked comfortable in his own skin. But he's changed in the almost two decades since I've seen him.

His golden-brown eyes still show exactly what he's feeling—if you bother to take the time to know him—but his features have matured. His hair is longer, and instead of having a clean-shaven look, he's grown a full beard, though it's well-maintained. He's given up the almost stuffy attire he used to wear and swapped them out for a more laid-back appearance. His jeans hug his hips and thighs, tapering into a pair of biker boots, and at the collar of his plain black T-shirt, tattoos poke out. On his fingers, more tattoos are printed along his skin, though I can't make out what the different symbols are. I can't know for sure since he's wearing a leather jacket, but I have a feeling there are even more tattoos traveling up his arms.

He looks nothing like I remember and yet the same.

He finally looks comfortable in his body, and part of me hates that I wasn't there to see that transformation.

"I'm sorry, Abs." He lifts his head, eyes meeting mine. "I know that's not nearly enough, but I—"

"You don't get to call me that anymore," I say, cutting him off and bending to pick up the book. "You're right, though." Standing straight, I meet his eyes, and the pain I see in them makes me pause.

It's not only pain. The pinch in his brow and the slump of his shoulders show a devastation I only remember seeing in him once before. Everything about his stance makes me wonder how he can still be in so much pain over everything.

"Sorry isn't enough, and you don't get to ask me to stay."

"Abbey. I-I'm not the same person anymore." His voice is so soft I almost miss it.

"I know," I whisper. "Neither am I."

It hurts realizing we don't know each other anymore. I thought I'd see every version of Jude Murphy, but because of one stupid moment, I'll never know the versions of him I missed.

He studies me for a second, and I see the moment something clicks in his brain—his eyes clear and his posture straightens. "I'm going to prove that to you."

I step around the chair, moving toward the door. "Jude—"

This time, he's the one to cut me off. "I know you're not ready." I hear his steps behind me and feel his heat at my back. "But soon, we're going to sit down and talk about it. All of it," he whispers.

My eyes fall closed, and his voice is so close to my ear the warmth sends a shiver up my spine. I pray that he doesn't notice how my body responds. Without saying anything or looking back at him, I step from the room and try not to run out of the hospital.

How can he still have that kind of power over my body— and my heart?

—

February 28, 2012

Do you remember our first kiss? Nothing was the same after that, but it's a moment I wouldn't change for anything.

You felt left out because all your other friends already had their first kiss, and you thought they were leaving you behind. We were still just friends, but we were best friends, and you trusted me not to judge you. You thought it was an experience we could share, just like everything else in life up to that point.

We were at your fourteenth birthday party, and we'd just blown out your candles. It was your party, but you knew my dad couldn't throw me one for my birthday a few days later.

You'd always been so adamant about sharing your birthday with me, no matter how much it upset your dad.

You came up to me in the hallway and pushed me into the bathroom, demanding I kiss you. I remember being so nervous. I had the biggest crush on you—I don't know if you ever knew that.

It may have been your birthday wish to have your first kiss, but it was my wish to have my first kiss with you. I tried to talk you out of it, telling you that you should experience it with someone special, but you told me there was no one more special than me.

Even then, I knew I wasn't good enough for you but I couldn't say no. You were—and still are—my greatest wish, Abbey.

I cupped your cheeks in my hands and pulled you in close. You closed your eyes immediately, but I watched you until the moment our lips touched. It wasn't anything more than a press of our lips, but I still felt it in my soul. I knew in that moment you were the only one for me.

I saw it in your eyes when we pulled

away—the shock you felt. I was relieved I wasn't the only one who felt the shift. We didn't talk about it right away, but it wasn't long after that we officially started dating. Your dad was pissed, but we ignored him.

Maybe we should have paid more attention to it. Maybe there was something more we should have done. Maybe...

CHAPTER
Eight

JUDE

I KNOW I SHOULDN'T, but I can't help myself when I step into the bookstore Wednesday morning—it's as if it's entirely out of my control.

Seeing Abbey through the front window—one elbow propped up on the counter, her chin resting in the palm of her hand—reading a book. She's too tempting to ignore.

Since I watched her walk out of my dad's hospital room, I've made it a point to stay in the apartment above the bar until I hear Abbey leave. Not because I don't want to see her, but because I wanted to give her time to accept what I told her Sunday afternoon—I will prove to her that I'm not the same person I was when I left town.

Three days probably isn't enough, considering what happened between us, but I've gone so long without her, and now that I've seen her again I don't want to waste any more time.

I never thought I'd be back in Ashford Falls, let alone see Abbey again, but I don't know how to ignore this opportunity. There's no other way to say it: I was an idiot when I was nineteen. I made the wrong decision and I've had to live with it.

But now I'm thirty-six, and I'm doing pretty well; I don't have to rely on anyone else to be successful anymore, and that means I can take care of myself and anyone else I might choose.

And I'll always choose Abbey.

No matter how much time passes or where we are, she's always been and always will be the person I want to be with most.

I never wanted our story to play out the way it has, and I can't help but view this as a chance to make things right with her.

Abbey is the love of my life.

Ever since I told her we'd talk about everything, I can't stop the possibilities from running through my head. I never stopped wanting her; I wasn't strong enough to fight for that, but I am now.

Walking into the bookstore may not be what Abbey wants, but it's what I need. And unfortunately for her, I can't wait any longer to address things between us. Maybe that was my issue back then, not being brave enough to prioritize my wants above others, but I'm more than capable now.

The bell above the door rings, giving my entrance away before I'm ready for it, but I don't let it stop me.

It takes Abbey a second to register it's me walking through the door, but she straightens from her position as soon as she does, her body going taut.

"Jude—" she tries to speak, but I don't let her finish.

I have eyes only for her. "Here's the thing," I start, stepping up to the other side of the counter. "I know you're not ready to talk, and I want to respect that, but I also know you won't be ready to talk any time soon, not if I don't push a little."

Her eyes bounce between mine, but she doesn't open her mouth to say anything.

"I don't want us to act like the past didn't happen, but I

know we're not in a place to talk about that yet, so let's try to focus on something outside of you and me. I don't care what it is. It can be as small as the weather, but we have to start somewhere."

Abbey's eyes stay trained on mine, but I see her fingers start to fidget with the corners of the book in front of her—it's as good a place as any to start. "That's a new book. Did you finish the other one?"

She bites her lip, her eyes falling to the pages in front of her for a moment before her spine straightens and her eyes meet mine, determination burning bright. It's a struggle smothering the smile that pulls at the corner of my lips. Abbey's fight was always something I loved about her, and I'm glad she hasn't lost it.

"I did. Definitely his worst work yet." Her brows pinch as she studies me. "You're really interested in my thoughts on that book. Are you a fan of AJ Doherty?"

"You could say that." I feign indifference, but it's harder than I imagine.

Am I a fan of AJ Doherty? That's one way to put it. A better way, a more honest way would be to tell her the truth—*I am AJ Doherty*. But if I tell her that now, there's no way she'll be honest about her opinions on my work, and Abbey's opinion is the one I care about most.

I've had negative reviews before—been torn apart by editors and publishers alike—but something about Abbey not liking my work hurts in a way none of the others have.

"When you say worst, what do you mean?" Trying to appear nonchalant, I lean against the counter, bringing myself close enough to get a brief whiff of lemon and lavender— *Abbey*.

"Well, I mean, I absolutely hated it. It's nothing like any of his other work. It felt far more like a romance than a thriller, and he clearly doesn't have the knowledge to write a romance."

She turns, grabbing a pile of books from the shelf behind her and marching toward the shelves in the back of the store.

"What does that mean?" I follow behind her but finally let my eyes travel the store.

This place is a reader's dream.

The shelves span almost three walls, standing floor to ceiling without an inch of open space. Their deep mahogany color with large armchairs in front of them help create a cozy atmosphere. It feels more like a cozy home library than a bookstore.

"I know this was a fictional story, and I shouldn't apply real-world logic to it, but characters that in love with each other should have better communication." She shrugs, returning books to their proper place on the shelves. "What made it worse was that the first half was phenomenal. It was everything I expect from an AJ Doherty novel, and then he threw it all away in the second half. And that spicy scene?" She scoffs. "What the hell was that? Has the man ever had sex?"

"Wow, don't hold back," I mumble.

I want to disagree with her but struggle to find a leg to stand on. My editor and agent had very similar comments when they read the manuscript. They both seemed surprised the publisher picked it up. But I'd built a name for myself and had proven time and time again I could sell books, so they ran with it.

It helped that I'm a faceless author writing thrillers. The mystery behind who I am seems to drive fans mad, sending them out to buy my books, looking for clues in my writing to figure out who I am. My publisher ate it up and uses the mystery to their advantage.

I ignored all of it and focused entirely on the writing. I would've laughed in your face if you asked me when I was younger if I ever thought I'd be a *New York Times* bestselling author. The idea that I—a kid with no future beyond running the family bar—could make such a big name for myself was so far out of this world it never crossed my mind.

When I left Ashford Falls, I took whatever job was available in the town I stopped in for a short time. It's a miracle so many people were willing to take a chance on someone like me. A kid with no plan, simply passing through on their way to who knows what.

"Sorry." I think I detect a small wince, but it's gone before I can be sure. "I know you're a fan, but I'm not willing to lie about my feelings on a book. There are too many in the world for people to waste their time reading something that's not good."

"It's so bad you'd tell people *not* to read?"

Her lips purse for a second as she looks at me, but then she's spinning back to the shelves. "I can't think of a single person I'd recommend it to, which says a lot about my feelings. I can always find at least one reason to recommend a book, but this one?" She shakes her head like she can't even bring herself to say the words.

My gaze shifts to the section of thrillers to our left, my eyes landing on the shelf filled with my books, specifically the little notes under my previous releases. I can't read them from here but I imagine it's praise for the books.

I wish I could say I don't remember what led me to write in the first place, but I remember it like yesterday.

It started with a journal.

Almost a year after leaving everything I loved, I officially ran out of money and needed to stay in one place long enough to save up again before moving on. Somehow, I ended up in a little town in Minnesota where the local mechanic took pity on me. He gave me a job cleaning up after the guys and organizing the office at his shop. It wasn't fancy, but it paid.

He also let me stay in the shop's backroom—at least until

his wife found out. Once she learned I was sleeping on a cot in what essentially was the supply closet, she gave me the spare room in their home.

I thought it'd be easy enough to go unnoticed in their house, but she wouldn't have it. Barely there two days, and she made sure I joined them for every meal, making sure I shared things about myself. It was hard, but she saw me for who I was: a kid suffering from so much guilt I thought I didn't deserve their kindness.

To this day, I still don't think I do, but I'll be forever grateful they gave it to me.

Willie and Mae were barely old enough to be my parents, but they felt something like parents all the same. Even though I stayed in constant contact with my dad, his support from miles away never felt like the support I got from the Larsons. I still make it a point to talk to them regularly and visit them whenever I'm in their area.

Staying with them for those few months set me on the path of healing—even if I haven't achieved the final goal yet, I'm much closer to it because of them.

Mae was the one who gave me my first journal and told me I was only making it worse by keeping it all locked inside. She said if I couldn't talk to her or someone else, writing it all down was the next best thing.

She was right, of course.

I started writing in that journal, and I couldn't stop. It became a part of my daily routine, to the point I couldn't sleep if I didn't write in it—even if it was only a few words.

One journal turned into two, two turned into ten, and ten turned into twenty. Even being the nomad I am, I still own every one of those journals. They may not go on the road with me, but I know exactly where they are if I need them.

And one of those journals, started in another small town in the middle of nowhere, inspired my first novel.

I never thought it would turn into what it did, but that little town was hit with a terrible kidnapping case that had my mind spinning with all the possibilities, and I couldn't stop writing them down. That fascination with the case turned into a need to get the words out, and the first draft of my first manuscript was the result.

I'd gotten better about saving money over the years after staying with Mae and Willie, and while I questioned my decision to spend a large chunk of that money on a laptop, it turned out to be one of the smartest decisions I've ever made.

That manuscript sat on my computer for another few years, and more and more manuscripts were added. Just sitting there with no plans to do anything with them. But in one of the most unoriginal moments of my life, everything changed.

Sitting in a coffee shop in New York City, a man at the table next to me saw what I was working on and struck up a conversation. Turned out he was an up-and-coming literary agent; adamant he could turn my books into something. With nothing to lose, I figured, *why not?*

That "why not" moment changed my life. Ten years later, I'm about to publish my thirtieth novel, and I want for nothing —well, nothing material anyway.

My eyes move back to Abbey, tracking her movements as she continues putting books away.

She's right—in a way. This book is different from all my others. I started writing it a little over a year ago after yet another conversation with Mae. I never told her the complete story of Abbey and me—I never told a soul—but Mae knew enough to know Abbey was my reason for everything: my guilt, my pain, my sorrow. Everything that held me back from living a full life.

She said something during that call that got me thinking. It wasn't anything new, but the way she said it finally had it clicking. No matter what you believe, there's a path we all follow in life—it's different for everyone, but a path nonetheless—and we have to keep moving forward. If we focus on the things we wish we could change, we get stuck, and what good does that do anyone?

I wished for so long I could redo that moment with Abbey, but time travel doesn't exist, and wishing for something that would never happen was a waste of time.

The Silent Promise became my therapy. It wasn't Abbey and my story, but I definitely took inspiration from our past, and a lot of healing was done while writing that first draft. That's why I fought my editor and agent as hard as I did. I *needed* this story to be out in the world, the same way I needed to fix things with Abbey now.

The bell above the door rings, bringing me back to the present.

"Dad, you're here early." Abbey smiles, striding past me without a second glance.

My entire body goes rigid. Edward Selbey has never been my biggest fan, and I have no doubt seeing me with his daughter will make him very unhappy.

"I hope that's not an issue." You'd think his voice would be softer when talking to his daughter, but all I hear is a businessman.

"Well, Ava's not here yet to watch the store." Abbey fiddles with the skirt of her dress, rubbing the material between her thumb and forefinger.

Before Edward can say anything else, I march toward the door, offering Abbey the smallest glance as I pass her. "Thanks for the recommendation, Abbey."

I don't see it, but I imagine a flicker of confusion crosses her face. She didn't recommend a single book to me.

CHAPTER
nine

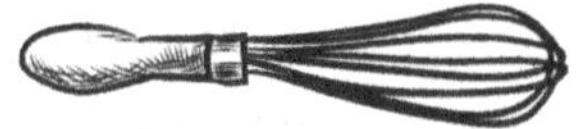

ABBEY

"JUDE'S BACK IN TOWN." No question, just a statement. One I'm sure is supposed to come off as indifferent, but I see the anger burning in his eyes.

"Dad." I sigh in exasperation. "Of course, Jude's back in town; his father just had a heart attack." I turn away from him, returning to the books I was restocking before he walked in.

Dad never liked Jude—something I've never understood—but I would've thought he'd be past all of it. Especially since we're divorced and haven't been a part of each other's lives in such a long time.

"Is this the first you've seen him?"

I let my eyes fall closed for a second, my shoulders slumping as I spin to look at him. "No. Not that it should concern you, but I was at the hospital with Walt when Jude got into town. Jude's also staying in the apartment above the bar, so we run into each other." My voice is stronger than I thought it'd be, but maybe that shouldn't surprise me.

I'm done letting what happened with Jude dictate my life.

Jude's right. We aren't the same people we used to be and it's time to move on. I don't know if we need to rehash everything that happened between us, and I don't think we can ever be friends again, but co-existing peacefully in this town? That's something we can do.

"Your happiness will always be my concern." Dad takes a few steps toward me, his hands reaching for me, but I shake my head.

"Jude has nothing to do with my happiness, not anymore. And whether or not he's part of my life is my choice, not yours." I release a breath I didn't realize I was holding, and my voice gentles with my next words. "I need you to respect that."

His eyes study mine, searching for what I don't know, but it doesn't surprise me when he ignores my words and changes the subject. "You went through my assistant for a meeting. That's unusual for you."

For once, I'd like to have an open and honest conversation about all of it with my father—his hatred for Jude, his refusal to move on from it, his need to control who's in my life. But now isn't the time. I asked him here in a professional capacity, and if I allow myself to be distracted by this conversation, I'll never get the investment I'm looking for.

Shaking away the disappointment from his brush off, I stride to the front counter, grabbing my laptop and the folder with the business plan. "Yes. I have a business proposition for you, and I wanted you to view it as such. Going through your assistant made it more official, which felt right."

His brows lift in surprise. "Color me intrigued. What business?"

And as if on cue, Ava rushes through the door. "Sorry, I'm late! Benny called this morning to see if I could stop by the office and I lost track of time."

"It's all right. Dad and I were just getting ready to sit down." I step next to my dad, introducing the two of them. "Dad, this is my friend, Ava Day. Ava, this is my dad, Edward Selbey."

Maybe I should be more concerned that this is the first time my dad is meeting a person I've become close to for almost seven months, but it doesn't surprise me. Dad doesn't spend much time in Ashford Falls, and when he is here he doesn't leave his house often. I think it has something to do with being surrounded by Mom. Even though she's been gone fifteen years, that house still feels like her.

"Nice to meet you, Mr. Selbey." Ava extends her arm for a handshake, a friendly smile stretching across her lips.

"Ava Day? Aren't you a lawyer? Didn't I hear that name in connection with a case between Scott Marks and his ex-wife?" Dad returns the handshake, but there's judgment in his tone.

"Oh, um, yes," Ava offers hesitantly. "I guess I'm technically still a lawyer, though practicing law isn't my primary focus anymore."

"Interesting that you'd give up such a lucrative career to work at a bookstore."

"Dad!"

"No, it's fine, Abbey." Ava straightens, waving me off. "He's not wrong. But luckily, I recently learned that I really don't care what other people think." A saccharine smile twists her lips. "I'll work on organizing the back room." She turns away from my father, a genuine smile meeting her lips. "I'll listen for the bell, but since you're out of treats, I'm sure it'll be a slow afternoon."

"Thanks, Ava." I squeeze her hand as she walks past, my eyes narrowing on my dad as I do.

It doesn't faze him as he strides over to the armchairs in the back corner of the store. "Well, she may have made a stupid choice giving up her job, but I can appreciate that she doesn't let anyone bring her down about it."

"Of course you do," I mumble, sitting in the chair beside his. He may judge her for giving up a job he thinks is far more valuable to society, but he'll respect her for standing up for herself.

"So, what business did you want to discuss?" He unbuttons his suit jacket before sitting in his chair, crossing one leg over the other.

I sit straight in my seat and hand him the folder. "I wanted to discuss an investment opportunity."

"SO, HOW'D IT GO?" Ava rushes to my side as my father walks out of the store.

"He said he wanted to review the numbers on his own before making a decision." I can't stop myself from staring in the direction he walked, even long after he's gone. "I honestly don't know what he'll do," I mumble more to myself than Ava.

"I'm not one to talk; you know about my parents, but your dad seems like he actually cares about you. My parents never would've sat down to hear a business proposal, and they definitely don't call to check in on me the way your dad has." Her arm snakes around my waist as her head lands on my shoulder, offering comfort in a way I didn't know I needed.

I drop my head to hers and wrap my arm around her shoulder in return. "I know he does, but that doesn't mean he'll just give me whatever I want."

"That business plan is genius." She straightens, removing her arm from around me. "The only corrections I made were grammatical ones. There's no way he doesn't invest." She spins away, marching over to the books I never finished putting away. "I'm manifesting that shit!"

I don't even try to stop the laugh that bursts out of me, and it feels good to let it out. For too long, I've let the heaviness of my past hang over me. I've let it weigh me down and dictate not just my actions but my emotions too.

Somewhere along the way, I started to think I didn't deserve to laugh and have fun. Like, by admitting defeat and getting divorced, it meant I wasn't allowed to try again so why put myself out there?

Maybe it's time to change all that, to really open myself up to the possibility of more—not just with people I'm starting to consider my true friends, but with others too.

I'd been so closed off to everyone around me, refusing to let anyone know me, even in a small way. Before Ava walked through the door of this store all those months ago, I can't even remember the last time I laughed or the last time I'd gone out on a date.

I haven't exactly been celibate over the last seventeen years, but I wouldn't call what I've been doing dating either. There were no outings around town or shared anecdotes, just a couple of men I'd let close enough to feel comfortable allowing them into my home for a few hours. It was safer that way—no chance of getting close or getting hurt again.

And if I'm honest, that first time felt too much like cheating on Jude—even if it had been years after our divorce was finalized.

From the moment we had our first kiss, I thought I'd marry Jude, and when we did marry it was like all my dreams came true. I couldn't imagine being with anyone else. And no matter what happened between us, I didn't *want* anyone else.

The guilt I felt after the first time with someone else was like nothing I'd ever experienced before, and I know it was made worse by the fact it was someone I knew nothing about. I may not remember his name, but I remember everything else about that night.

I'd finally convinced myself to take a little trip—not far, just a few towns over—but I never made it further than the bar. It was nothing like Murphy's, and I hated it the second I walked through the door, but it didn't stop me from claiming a seat and ordering a drink.

I wouldn't say I was drunk, but I was definitely tipsy—so was the guy. He was cute and the complete opposite of Jude, exactly what I thought I needed. He was kind and attentive, making sure I was okay with everything happening between us, and he honestly wasn't bad. The issue wasn't anything he did or said; it was that he wasn't my husband, the man I'd always be in love with.

The guilt that overcame me the second he pulled out and rolled off me was unimaginable, yet somehow I kept it together until I made it to my car. I broke down the second I was behind the wheel, my heart shattering into a million pieces all over again.

As soon as I could see clearly, I drove home and never looked back. It was another few years after that before I ever tried again.

"Hey." Ava's voice breaks through my thoughts. "Where'd you go?"

"Sorry." I shake my head, clearing my mind of those feelings. "I got lost in the past."

"Do you want to talk about it?"

"No." I give her a small smile. "I think it's time to move on." I turn, heading for the register. "Besides, we've got more exciting things to think about. Like what kinds of sweets should I make for our grand re-opening."

"Yes!" Ava shouts, running over to me and bouncing on her toes when she hits the opposite side of the counter. "You have to make the lemon bars, that's for sure. Those things sell out so fast."

And that's how we spend the rest of the afternoon, imagining a future where I get the money from my dad and build the business I've always wanted.

———

August 10, 2015

Do you remember the night we first made love?

Looking back on it, I realize we were too young to be making adult decisions. But when you came running to my house that night, all I saw were the tears on your face and the heartbreak in your eyes.

It was the first time you lied to me. Eleven years without a lie between us, and that night changed it all—again.

I trusted that you knew what you were doing. I trusted that you knew your mind better than I possibly could.

I sometimes wonder if that was the right decision. I know you never regretted it, and I know you felt the love I had for you, but everything about that night now has a cloud over it.

I wish you'd been able to tell me what happened. I know the truth now, and I understand why you felt like you couldn't share it with me, but I still wish things had been different.

Looking back, I can see that night for what it really was—the start of the end for us.

We should've realized your father would never accept me in your life. The history between our parents was too much for him to overcome.

I've always hated the story of Romeo and Juliet, but I get it now: how you can love someone more than life itself and still have to let them go.

I loved you then, and I love you more every day. Even though I'm not with you, I fall in love with you all over again every time I think of you.

You're in my soul, never far from me, even if you're thousands of miles away.

CHAPTER
Ten

JUDE

"I THOUGHT I made it clear you were never to step foot in this town again."

I turn slowly to see Edward Selbey standing at the threshold to Murphy's, his face clear of all emotion. To any onlooker—if there were any—he'd look like any other businessman stepping into a bar.

"Not even going to play at pleasantries?" I smirk, knowing it will irritate him.

I'm not surprised he stopped by after finishing his conversation with Abbey—I expected it. That's why I'm sitting in an empty bar and not my apartment. But I can't say the same for the animosity; maybe that was wishful thinking. The man has proven he knows how to hold a grudge.

"You know me better than that, Mr. Murphy." His voice is laced with disdain, his anger starting to bleed through.

There was a time when I found the man standing before me intimidating, but now I see him for what he truly is—insecure. And that is something I pity.

Closing my laptop, I turn in my seat, giving him my full attention.

"Sometimes, I think I'm the only person who knows the real man behind the mask"—I stand, shrugging as I shove my hands in my pockets—"but I don't really care. I'm not a kid anymore, Eddie."

He tries hard, but I see the muscles in his jaw tick, anger flashing in his eyes at the nickname. "I still have the power to destroy this bar, boy," he hisses.

It used to bother me when he called me "boy," but now it rolls right off my shoulders. I hoped I'd be able to at least *appear* unbothered in front of Edward Selbey, but I'm not faking it. I truly don't care what this man thinks of me—not anymore.

"I know you do, but you really expect me to stay away when there's a chance my father might die? Even you aren't that cruel." This man may hate me—for reasons I can't quite understand—but I think even he can understand the importance of family.

"I may be able to look past you being in town to see your father in his time of need, but the second you wormed your way back into my daughter's life again is the moment you lost my understanding," he seethes, moving closer.

"It's a small town." I don't move, unwilling to give even an inch to the man before me.

"And yet." He strides closer, coming almost toe-to-toe with me. It's a move I'm sure he wants to be intimidating, but I'm taller than him, and I've put on muscle since the last time he saw me. "I'm sure if you really tried, you could stay out of my daughter's way. You're no good for her. You never have been."

"There might have been a time I believed that, but I don't anymore. You can do whatever you want to me or this bar." I smirk at him, proving my next words true. "I know my worth, and I'm far more confident than I used to be."

His nostrils flare as his eyes bounce between mine, his

words more of a snarl than anything else. "I guess we'll have to see about that, won't we?"

Before either of us can say another word, the door to the bar opens, and Caleb Marks steps through. It doesn't take long for his eyes to find mine, silently asking if everything is okay. But I don't even have a chance to shake my head before Edward straightens his jacket and turns to leave the bar, only offering a slight nod in Caleb's direction as he passes.

"What was that about?" Caleb asks as he makes his way behind the bar, grabbing a glass and pouring himself a pint of beer.

"Nothing new." I retake my seat in front of my computer, gently smoothing my hand over the top. A silent reminder that my words to Edward were true. I'm not the same kid anymore, and I have way more life experience and grit than I did back then.

"And what exactly does that mean? Because I still don't know what happened before you left. I don't think anyone does." Caleb moves back to my side of the bar, taking a seat a few stools down from mine, his body angled toward me.

"Well, you won't be the first person I tell, considering Abbey doesn't even know."

His brows lift, shock painted across his features. "Are you saying you're finally going to tell the truth about what happened back then?"

Now it's my turn to be surprised. I turn to him slowly, trying to mask my own shock. "What do you mean? What truth?"

"Oh, come on, Jude. I may not know whatever you wanted Abbey to believe, but there's no way you did anything to hurt that woman—not really."

"Caleb—"

"Abbey was your whole heart," Caleb interrupts me, not giving me a chance to stop him. "You loved her more than anything and anyone else—even your dad. You may have some people fooled, but you could never fool me, you could never fool Gage, and you could never fool your father." He pauses, taking a sip of his beer. "And I think deep down, you could never fool Abbey. She's been too blinded by whatever lie you told her to think clearly."

"I don't even know what to say to that." I stand from my seat, moving behind the bar to get my own pint of beer.

He laughs, taking another sip before staring at me across the bar. "Just tell me you're finally going to come clean about it. It's time you came home and lived your life again."

I scoff, unwilling to admit how right he is. "I have been living my life."

"No, you haven't," he scoffs. "You've been going through the motions, but you haven't been living." He studies me for a second before pointing his finger at me. "You don't think your dad talks to people here?" He pauses, but before I can say anything he starts again. "You might have made him promise not to talk to you about Ashford Falls and the people in it, but he made no such promise to the rest of us. I may not know everything you've told him, but I know you haven't dated anyone since Abbey, and I know you never stay in one place long enough to make lasting connections with people."

I open my mouth to argue—Willy and Mae being a prime example that's not true—but Caleb plows on before I can say anything—again.

"You're a nomad through and through, searching for something. The only problem? You found that something when you were six years old, and you let it go when you were nineteen."

"You seem to have it all figured out," I mumble, taking a large gulp from my glass.

"That's the thing. I have no idea what's going on with you. But I can't believe you'd pass up an opportunity to take it all back if you could."

"It's not about taking it back. Abbey is the love of my life, and she always will be," I admit, my eyes falling to my closed laptop on the bar, thinking about the words I was writing before Edward walked through the door.

I wish, more than anything, I believed that Abbey and I would've made it through the last seventeen years if I'd made a different choice back then, but I don't think we'd have been strong enough. I was too focused on how other people viewed me, and trying to fit the mold I thought they wanted me in, to fight for Abbey.

Now, though, after everything we've been through? I know I'm strong enough to fight for Abbey. And if Abbey is even half the woman I knew her to be back then, she's strong enough to learn the truth.

"But?" Caleb asks when I don't continue.

Bringing my eyes back to him, I give him the truth. "I wouldn't take any of it back. I don't know who Abbey is anymore, but I know who I've become, and while I wish I could have become this person without causing anyone pain, I know I wouldn't be who I am today if I stayed in this town."

"Jude—"

"No." I put my hand up, stopping Caleb from continuing. "This isn't me putting myself down or fishing for validation. I am who I am today because of everything I went through." My hand falls, holding the edge of the bar in a tight grip. "And while I don't know everything about Abbey right now, in my gut, I know she's exactly who she's supposed to be because of everything she's endured."

"So, that's it? You're just going to let the love of your life go? You're going to leave town and never look back?"

Without hesitation or taking my eyes off his, I give him another truth. "No. I'm going to fight like hell to get Abbey back, and I'm never leaving this town without her by my side again."

"Hell yeah!" He fist pumps the air, a goofy smile taking over his face. "What's the plan?"

The corners of my lips tip up in a small smile. "Nope. I don't want anyone's input."

"Oh, come on! I wanna help!"

I laugh, grabbing his empty glass and refilling it. "You sound like a five-year-old."

"So what? Let me help." And now he bounces in his seat like a five-year-old.

I shake my head, placing his fresh pint in front of him. "If I need help I promise I'll ask, but I want to try this my way first."

"Fine," he grumbles, taking a deep pull from his beer.

"Enough about me." My smile falls. I don't want to bring down the mood, but this is the first time I've seen Caleb since that night in the hospital, and unfortunately for all of us, I'm not the only one going through something. "I heard about your dad. I'm so sorry for your loss. I know that's not enough, but—"

"No." He shakes his head, his eyes falling to the bar before him for a second. "It's enough."

We're both quiet for a minute, sitting in our own thoughts, but I've got a lot to catch up on, not just with Abbey but with the other people I've hurt as well.

"Tell me what else I've missed."

CHAPTER
Eleven

JUDE

"WHAT MADE you decide to open the bar?" Gage asks from his seat across from me a few days after my conversation with Caleb.

"Honestly, I needed something else to do besides sitting by my dad's hospital bed. I love the man, but it's a little boring watching him sleep nonstop." I attempt a smile, trying to bring a little levity to a heavy topic.

The honest truth is that the doctors can't tell us why he hasn't woken up yet, and it's starting to scare me. The swelling in his brain has gone down, and they've weened him off the meds that were keeping him sedated and removed the breathing tube, so there's no easy explanation for why he's still isn't awake. The only thing keeping me from going completely out of my mind is that all their scans and tests show that he has normal brain function, meaning he's not brain-dead, just... stuck in limbo.

"What do you normally do? When you're not here, I mean. Like, what have you been doing for the last seventeen years?" There's no judgment in his tone, only curiosity, and that makes me smile because that's the same Gage I've always known.

"I've done a little bit of everything since I left town." I wipe down the bar top next to Gage, not because it needs to be cleaned, but to have something else to focus on. I'm not sure if I'm ready for everyone to know about my secret author career. That *is* one thing I swore my father to secrecy on.

"Okay..." He lets the word hang before setting his beer down and leaning forward. "But what have you been doing recently?"

Gage probably thinks his patient look as he stares at me silently will make me uncomfortable enough to tell him the truth. Bad news for him...I don't break that easily.

"I'd just gotten to Harborview the day you called. I wasn't doing anything quite yet."

"Speaking of Harborview. How crazy is it that you were in the town Ava and Declan grew up in?"

It's nice to know not everything changes. Gage may want to know what I've been up to since I left town, but he won't push me when I've avoided the same question twice. The man before me still knows me just as well as I know him.

"I've met Ava, obviously, but tell me more about Declan."

Caleb told me a bit about his sister and new brother-in-law, but he focused more on his wife and new daughter than anything else. The look of pure love and devotion as he showed me picture after picture made me both happy for him and incredibly jealous.

It made me even more motivated to do everything in my power to get Abbey back.

Out of the corner of my eye, I see someone step up to the bar. Tilting my head at Gage in apology and lifting my finger to motion *one second*, I turn to help the unfamiliar face. It doesn't take long to pour them a couple of pints before I'm back in front of Gage. "Sorry about that."

"I'm used to it." He chuckles. "This happens all the time with Walt."

It doesn't surprise me that Gage has stayed so close to my dad. Just like Gage's mom and dad became surrogate parents to me when we were growing up, my dad became a surrogate parent to Gage—especially after Gage's parents divorced.

I love that Gage still comes around and spends time with my father at least once a week. It's comforting to know my dad still had someone to take care of in a way.

But it's also a reminder of how much my father loves this place. His devotion is clear in the way he's always here, behind this bar, serving everyone who walks through the doors. I love his dedication to keeping these doors open, but when he makes it through this—because I refuse to believe he won't—things are going to have to change around here, and I can get some of those changes started.

Step one? Hiring some staff to help out around the place.

"Declan is Ava's older brother, and now husband to Quinn Marks." Gage lifts his beer, taking the last sip before continuing. "He moved to town about six years ago and is the art teacher at the high school."

"I heard about the wedding from Caleb earlier this week."

"Well, there's not much else to it. He and Ava grew up in Harborview with parents who probably shouldn't have had children. He got married, got divorced, and realized just how shitty his parents were, so he left and ended up here." Gage shrugs. "He met Caleb, who dragged him to a family dinner, and you knew Scott..."

"The second he knew about Declan's family life, Scott pulled him into the Marks family fold," I finish for him.

"Exactly. The rest, as they say, is history."

"Do you want another?" I ask as Gage fiddles with the empty glass in front of him.

"Not right now. I'm waiting for Ava." His eyes track to the

door before falling to his watch. "She should be here soon. She was catching up with Abbey next door."

My spine tingles at the sound of her name. I haven't seen her since I walked out of the store Wednesday afternoon. It was intentional, trying to give her space to think about everything we talked about, but it's been torture for me. Knowing she's so close and yet still so far away.

The moment I decided to fight for Abbey, I knew it'd be hard. She's always been stubborn—and I hoped she still was. Arguing with Abbey—though our only real fight was that last one—was one of my favorite things to do. She's never been afraid to speak her mind or fight for what she thought was right, and I can't wait to see that fire in her again.

"Well, tell me more about Ava." The smile that takes over his face has the green-eyed monster rearing its ugly head yet again. What I wouldn't give to have that kind of light in my life. To be happy simply at the thought of the person I love.

"She's amazing, man." He aims his goofy grin at the bar, shaking his head slightly before lifting his eyes back to mine. "I don't know why she picked me, but I thank my lucky stars every day that she did."

"You're a good man, Gage. It doesn't surprise me that she'd pick you."

And he spends the next ten minutes telling me all about what brought Ava to town—a custody case between Scott and his ex-wife—and how they met—one day at the courthouse—and how they fell in love—sitting here at this very bar with both of our fathers and their meddling nature—and how he has no doubt that she's the love of his life.

"I'm truly happy for you."

"Thanks." His smile falls as he studies me. "I know you have your reasons for being so secretive and refusing to answer my questions earlier, but what about you?"

I sigh and fall forward, leaning against the back of the bar across from Gage. "It doesn't feel right filling you in on everything before talking to Abbey about it." I shrug as I speak, standing straight behind the bar again. "I know that doesn't make sense, but—"

"No," Gage cuts me off. "I completely understand that. I may not have a few months ago, but I do now."

I can't help but feel guilty at the idea of giving Gage absolutely nothing about my life since I left. He was my best friend, the person I talked to about everything happening in my life. There was only one time I didn't talk with him, and I imagine if I had my life would be very different right now.

"I've truly done a little bit of everything. The first town I stopped in, I got a job as a dishwasher at the local inn. After that, I worked as a custodian in a local law office. There was a period I worked the front desk at a mechanic's shop. Once I turned twenty-one, I started bartending a lot. I even toyed with the idea of being a tattoo artist for a spell."

"Now that one doesn't surprise me." Gage chuckles, gesturing to my arms, covered in tattoos.

"If I'd been more open to the idea of staying in one place long enough, I would've done it. But I never stayed in one place longer than six months."

"Why not?" There's that genuine curiosity again, and I find myself giving him the truth.

I let my eyes wander to the floor for a second, swallowing the lump that forms in the back of my throat. "I never wanted to leave Ashford Falls." I'm so quiet I wouldn't be surprised if Gage misses the words entirely, but he doesn't say anything when my eyes meet his. "The idea of staying anywhere long enough for it to start feeling like home terrified me."

"Jude..." He trails off, a stretch of time passing between us before he speaks again. "Did you let yourself have anything since you left?"

I open my mouth to answer, but I'm cut short by the door

practically flying open, Ava marching in with a bright smile on her face.

"We need shots!" she says as she slams her hand on the bar next to Gage.

"Are we celebrating?" Gage asks her, his eyes bouncing from Ava to the door as it opens less dramatically as Abbey steps through.

My breath catches at the sight of her. It's not just her beauty or radiant smile that has me at a loss for words. It's the fact that she's voluntarily walking through the front door. I thought it would be so much longer before I saw her here.

Ava turns to Abbey. "Well? Are we celebrating?"

"Yeah, we definitely are." She slides into the empty seat next to Ava, offering me a small smile as she does. "Whiskey for me."

"Make it two!" Ava shouts, her excitement getting the better of her.

I chuckle as I grab the shot glasses, catching Gage's eye and silently asking if he's having one as well. At the shake of his head, I grab the bottle of Redbreast from behind me and pour the ladies their shots. Abbey's fingers brush mine as she takes the shot from me, and the simple touch does more than it should. The spark that travels up my arm and straight to my heart has my breath catching.

"What are we celebrating?" I ask as the two of them slam their shots back, shaking myself slightly but unable to take my eyes off her.

"Abbey's stick-in-the-mud father is giving her the money!" Ava's hands shoot in the air, and she bounces on her feet. Her excitement is almost contagious enough for me to forget the words she said.

I have no idea why Abbey needs the money, but based on the energy flying off Ava and the smile stretched across Abbey's face, she's happy about it. I want to be happy for her, but I can't help the worry that courses through me. Knowing her father, there must be strings attached, and I don't believe for a second he's told her the truth about those strings.

"Another round!" Ava demands.

I want to ask Abbey more about why she needs the money and exactly what the deal is with her father, but I don't get the chance. Ava pulls Abbey out of her seat and toward the middle of the bar, where there's a little more space, and starts dancing.

Gage can't stop the laugh that bursts out of him at the scene, and I can't blame him. Murphy's has never been a bar for dancing, but that doesn't stop Ava.

It takes Abbey a moment to feel the beat of the music, a large smile forming on her lips as her head falls back, and her eyes close as Ava spins her around. Her hips sway to the music and my eyes are transfixed by the sight. She's carefree in a way I haven't seen in far too long, and I want to make sure she stays that way.

"Turn the music up! And get us another round!"

Gage glances at me, the crinkles at the corner of his eyes more prominent than I've ever seen them. "You heard her. Turn up the music."

I follow orders, turning up the music before pouring another round of shots for them, and then I watch. I know I shouldn't be as enthralled by the sight as I am, but I can't tear my eyes away. It's been so long since I've seen Abbey this happy, and I don't want to miss a moment.

I'm nervous about the deal Abbey's made with her dad, but as I watch her dance and have fun with Ava, I realize I'll do anything to make sure that smile never leaves her face again.

CHAPTER
Twelve

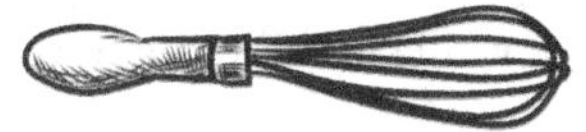

ABBEY

"I'M DRUNK," I slur as I collapse onto the empty bar stool.

"So what?" Ava shouts as she falls onto the seat next to me, leaning back against Gage, who can't stop smiling at her antics.

I smooth a hand over my chest, trying to brush away the tight pinch. It's stupid how envious I get at the little moments of affection between the two of them. After everything Ava went through with her parents and Brian, and after the threat of Gage almost losing his job because of it...if two people deserve their current happiness, it's them.

And honestly, I'm so incredibly happy for them. It just hurts knowing I don't have that—and realizing that maybe I never did.

"The question is, how drunk are you?" Gage asks, standing from his seat and practically holding Ava up in hers.

"Hmm..." I take inventory of how my body feels, trying to figure out just how drunk I am. My head feels a little loopy, and I don't think I walked in a straight line to the bar, but I'm pretty sure I'm seeing clearly. "Too drunk to drive anywhere, but not drunk enough to forget where I am or what happened this afternoon." I can't help the smile that takes over my face.

I still can't believe my dad agreed to invest in the bookstore —for a fraction of the profit I originally proposed. It's not that I thought the business proposal wasn't a good one—it's an amazing business plan—it's just not where he normally spends his money. Maybe I should be questioning why he's taking the chance on me, but I can't bring myself to think of anything other than my excitement.

This is my dream, and the idea that I'm only a few steps away from achieving it makes me so happy I can't focus on anything else—except maybe the man walking up behind the bar.

"How are we doing down here?" There's a small smile on his lips, but it doesn't quite reach his eyes. Part of me wants to know what he's thinking and why he's not truly happy. Maybe it's the alcohol part of me, or maybe it's a bigger part—one I'm not sure I'm ready to acknowledge.

"I think we're going to get out of here." Gage looks down at Ava, smoothing the hair that's fallen out of her ponytail from her face. "Trying to figure out if Abbey's coming home with us or if she's okay to stay on her own."

"I'm definitely okay to stay on my own." I lift a finger as if trying to make a point but quickly forget and drop my hand back to the bar.

"You sure? We've got the space if you want to stay with us." The furrow of Gage's brow deepens as he studies me, and my smile grows as I look at him.

"You are a good man, Gage Flynn, but I promise I'm okay on my own. I'm not that drunk, I swear." I hold up three fingers. "Scout's honor."

"Abbey." He chuckles. "You weren't a scout."

I shrug, not worried in the slightest.

Jude shuffles his feet, his mouth opening and closing a couple of times before he finally speaks. "I'll make sure she gets up to her apartment."

"I don't need help walking up a set of stairs. I'm fine." I stand from my seat—admittedly, it may be a little too abrupt.

Without meaning to, I stumble.

Gage and Jude both reach for me, but it's Gage who catches me before I fall.

"Alrighty. Either I'm walking you up to your apartment before Ava and I leave, or you're letting Jude help you."

My eyes narrow. I know I'm not sober, but I wouldn't call myself drunk. I'm perfectly capable of getting myself home on my own—it's a set of stairs and I'm there. But then I see Jude out of the corner of my eye, and I have to wonder if my resistance has more to do with the idea of relying on Jude than the idea of Gage thinking I'm too drunk to take care of myself.

Before I can open my mouth to protest, Ava jumps in, a mischievous glint in her eye. "I think I might be sick." She stands from her seat far more gracefully than I did but still leans heavily against Gage. The twinkle in her eye when she looks at me makes me think she might not be as drunk as she leads the rest of us to believe.

Gage's eyes bounce between mine and Ava's, looking as if he can't quite decide what his course of action should be.

Sometimes I hate my people-pleasing tendencies.

"Go on. Get Ava home." I fall back onto my seat, elbow on the bar and my chin resting in the palm of my hand. *I'm definitely pouting.*

"Love you, Abbey! I'll see you tomorrow." Ava surges forward, pressing a sloppy kiss to my cheek before standing straight and gliding out the door, Gage right behind her.

"There's no way she's that drunk," Jude mumbles as he watches the two of them leave.

"Nope, she's attempting to play matchmaker." I spring up in my seat, my eyes widening when I realize the words I just said. "I didn't mean that the way it sounded. She *is* drunk and not thinking clearly."

Jude's eyes soften as he looks at me and I shift in my seat, avoiding his gaze.

"How about a glass of water while I finish closing up?" He turns for a clean glass and fills it with water before placing it before me. My eyes catch on the tattoos dotted across his knuckles, but he pulls his hand back before I can identify any of the letters or symbols.

It's not until I'm lifting the glass to my lips that I realize he didn't put any ice in it—exactly how I prefer it.

He doesn't stand around waiting for me to say anything but moves out from behind the bar, passing the door and flipping the lock before he starts wiping down the now-empty tables.

I can't help but track his movements around the bar. There's a grace to him I've never seen before, a confidence in how he holds himself. When we were younger, he used to walk around with his shoulders hunched forward as if trying to make himself invisible. Now, he stands straight as if proud of who he is.

I always thought Jude was good-looking, but seeing this new, more confident version of him is far more attractive than I'd like to admit. *Why couldn't he have gotten worse with age?*

It's hard not to notice how much muscle he's gained since he was a teenager. I can't know for sure, but I imagine they were made from hard work and not some egotistical power trip. Jude and I may not know each other the way we used to, but he's never been one to let ego drive his motivations.

"I know you were celebrating that your dad is giving you some money, but what do you need the money for?" Jude's voice breaks through my thoughts, forcing me to focus on something other than his firm ass as he bends to pick up a dropped napkin.

"Oh." I spin away, toying with the rim of my glass so I'll stop looking at him. "Marybelle's retiring and decided to sell the store. She knows I've always dreamed of owning a café and thought I could buy the store from her."

"And you don't have the money." It's not a question. Jude knows how my father feels about working for what you have. Sometimes, I think that might be why he judges Walt and Jude so harshly. While Walt's parents worked like hell to get this bar off the ground, Walt inherited it. Of course, you only need to step into this bar once on a Friday or Saturday night to know how hard Walt still works to keep this place running.

"No, I don't." I peek at him over my shoulder, but he's focused on the task in front of him. "I wrote up a business plan and presented it to him earlier this week. The day you stopped by, actually."

Jude sidles up behind the bar, slowly making his way closer to me as he wipes it down. "Did you ask him for a loan?"

"I thought about it, but since he runs an investment firm, I stuck with what he does." I lift my glass and drain the last bit of water as Jude stops in front of me. "He's agreed to a probationary period as a silent partner with a small portion of the profits. The plan is to reevaluate within three months of our grand opening."

He studies me for a second before his eyes fall to the rag in his hands. "You're happy with the arrangement?" he asks quietly as if he's afraid to voice the question.

"Yeah." I smile. "I'm really happy about it."

Jude's head bobs up and down absentmindedly. "Good," he murmurs so softly I wonder if he even meant for the word to pass his lips. "I'm glad you're getting what you want." His eyes meet mine, and I see the sincerity staring back at me, but something else is mixed in—something I can't label before he's turning away from me.

It's not fair, the words that come out of my mouth next, but it's honest. "It's probably time I start going after the things I want instead of holding myself back for fear of being hurt."

He freezes, his entire body going taut for a second before he slowly turns back to me. He doesn't say anything, simply continues staring, his eyes moving over every inch of me as if memorizing the moment.

"I'm sorry, that—"

"No. Don't apologize," he interrupts. "I don't want you to hold anything back from me, no matter how much it might hurt to hear." He shuffles his feet, moving both toward me and away from me all at once. "Abbey." His spine straightens as he seems to make a decision and moves around the bar, coming to take the seat beside me. "I know you've been drinking, and it's not the right time, but I want to talk about what happened. I—"

"No."

I can't talk about it—not yet. I don't know if I'll ever be able to talk about that night with him, but I know I can't do it right now. Not when I'm just starting to put myself back out there. Not when I'm just starting to chase my dreams again.

"Abbey..." It's the sound of my name on a broken whisper that has me turning.

"I don't know what the future holds, but I don't want to live in the past. Not anymore."

"What does that mean?" He visibly swallows, his eyes bouncing between mine.

"You're right. I don't want to live like the past never happened, but I don't want to talk about it. So, when it comes to the two of us..." My words trail off. I don't know how to say the next part, not when I see the hurt etched across his face already.

"Abs." If it were anyone else, I'd call the sound that comes out of his mouth a choked sob. But it's not anyone else, and Jude has never been a person to be run by his emotions.

"I don't know what that means for us, but I don't think we can ever be more than acquaintances." I mess with the frayed edges of my shorts, trying my hardest not to break eye contact with the man across from me.

I'm not sure if I mean the words coming out of my mouth, but I don't think my heart can afford to be more than acquaintances with Jude.

Looking at him now, seeing the man he's become, I want to know more about how he got here. And part of me hates that I'm still desperate to know more—after everything he did—but he was my everything for the longest time, and even with the pain of all that happened, he's still important to me. I'm just not sure if I'm strong enough to handle another heartbreak at the hands of Jude, no matter how unintentional it might be.

It's Jude who breaks eye contact, his head turning away from me. A few moments pass, the two of us standing motionless, and I can't help but let my eyes track over his tattooed arms. I've seen flashes of them for weeks now, but I haven't been able to study them long enough to figure out what they are.

There's both a randomness and cohesiveness to them. It's almost like he got tattoos as the mood struck, but went back at some point to blend them all, creating such intricate pictures. He's still too far away for me to identify all of them, but one peeks out from the bottom of his sleeve that has me gasping.

My eyes shoot to his when he turns back to look at me. Whatever emotion he was fighting is gone, and a mask of clear indifference is in its place.

"I understand where you're coming from, and I'm going to respect it. At least for now." He stalks forward, coming within inches of me. "But I think you should know I plan on fighting with everything I am to get you to forgive me."

"Jude—"

"No, Abbey." He steps closer, still not touching me. "I made the biggest mistake of my life that night, and I won't make it again." His eyes move over my face, and it feels like he might as well be touching me with the way the shiver runs up my spine. "I know you're not ready to hear everything I want to say, but I'm not going anywhere—not this time."

"Jude," I release on a breath. I want to say more, but I can't even form the words in my brain, let alone out loud.

"Do you want me to walk you up to your apartment, or are you okay on your own?" He's close enough that his breath ghosts over my cheek as he says the words, and I can't stop my eyes from falling shut. It's like a gentle caress—one I haven't felt in almost two decades. "Abbey?" he whispers when I don't respond.

My eyes spring open, and I step back, trying to put space between us—physically and emotionally. "I-I'm fine. I can make it on my own."

"Okay. I'll see you soon."

I stand there for a few more seconds, watching him stuff his hands in his pockets, his eyes never leaving mine, before turning and marching away.

What the hell was that?

———

June 18, 2018

Do you remember the day we got married? Of course you do. Maybe the better question is, do you wish you could forget it?

I don't.

Even with everything we went through after, I wouldn't change marrying you for anything. I hate that we're not celebrating our tenth wedding anniversary today. I hate that instead of spending the day with you, I spent it wallowing in self-pity.

We're living in a world I forced upon us, and ten years later, I still don't know if it was the right call.

When you walked into the courthouse, you took my breath away.

We were both so young.

We may have been adults in the eyes of the law, but we were still children—we were teenagers getting married.

I know our wedding was nothing like you ever imagined, but it was ours, and my love for you was unyielding.

I know you don't believe that, but it's the truth. My love for you has never wavered, and it never will.

The look in your eyes when we exchanged our vows—I'll never forget it. If I ever doubted your love for me, all of it was wiped from my memory when you looked at me standing before that judge.

I know how badly you wanted your mom and my dad there, but it was the right call leaving them in the dark the way we did. It kept them safe.

You gave me my wish for traditional Irish vows, and in return I broke your heart. I wish I'd done better. I wish I'd been better.

Ten years later, these vows are still true, no matter what you might think.

I vow you the first cut of my meat, the first sip of my wine, from this day it shall only be your name I cry out in the night and into your eyes that I smile each morning; I shall be a shield for your back as you are for mine, never shall a grievous word be spoken about us, for our marriage is sacred between us and no stranger shall hear my grievance. Above and beyond this, I will cherish and honor you through this life and into the next.

CHAPTER
Thirteen

JUDE

"COME ON, DAD." My eyes never leave his face as I lean forward, taking his hand in mine. "I need you to wake up. I need your wisdom." My grip tightens, hoping he'll respond in kind. It's only when he doesn't that I let my eyes fall on our clasped hands.

Laying his hand flat on the bed, I let my fingers trace over the tattoos across his knuckles. He's had these tattoos my entire life, but I've never paid much attention to them. I remember asking him about them when I was young, but the true meaning of the symbols never resonated with me—not until I started getting tattoos of my own.

On his thumb, he got the Irish harp to represent joy, music, and celebration. Dad always said the Irish harp was meant to bring prosperity and health.

On his index finger, to bring protection, he got the Triskelion to represent the physical world, the spiritual world, and the afterlife—the idea that life will always carry on.

On his middle finger, he placed a shamrock—one of the most common symbols of his heritage—to represent good fortune and bring good luck.

On his ring finger, instead of wearing his wedding band, he got the Dara Knot to symbolize the union of two people—to bring happiness.

And finally, on his pinky, he placed the Celtic cross. He could never tell me exactly what it meant, but he liked to say it represented knowledge, strength, and the compassion to manage life's ups and downs—for life would always have many ups and downs.

"I guess we're going through a pretty big down right now, aren't we?" I whisper as I trace the final tattoo. "I don't know what to do. I know what I want to do, but I don't know if it's right." I let my hands fall back to my lap, clasping them tight. "I shouldn't have listened, but I heard her talking to you. I know there are still feelings there." I fall back into my seat, my eyes moving to my dad's face. "Who am I kidding? I didn't need to hear her talking to know that. I see it every time she looks at me."

Abbey may have said we can only ever be acquaintances, but how her body melted at my proximity tells a different story. I know she wants her words to be true, and I should respect that, but I've never stopped loving her, and the idea that I might have a chance to have her in my life again is something I can't pass up.

My need for Abbey is as strong as my need to breathe.

"I need you to wake up so I can tell you everything," I whisper, leaning forward, my elbows on my knees. "I know you'll be disappointed, but I need to tell you the truth. It's time I stopped hiding." I'm silent as I watch him for a moment, hoping and wishing he'll open his eyes. "Come on, Dad."

I hear the steps before the person clears their voice, alerting me to their presence. I know it's her even before she speaks. I could go an entire lifetime without her in my life, and I'd always know when she's near.

"Sorry, I didn't mean to interrupt. I can come back later."

Her voice is like a blanket draped over my shoulders on a cold night, comforting in all the best ways.

Shifting in my seat to look at her, I offer her a small smile. "No, it's fine. I interrupted your time with him; it's only fair you get to do the same."

She wavers slightly, her weight shifting back and forth before she steps further into the room and places her bag in the empty seat beside me. "Any changes?"

"No, but the doctors say that's not necessarily bad."

Abbey moves to the other side of the bed, taking his hand in hers before bending to place a kiss on his forehead. "Hey, Walt. Don't you think it's time you woke up now?" she whispers, still bent over his frame. "I think you've milked this long enough." Her eyes shift to me for only a moment before returning to my father's face, but I can't take my eyes off her. I'm transfixed. "You got him home. Don't sleep through your time with him."

"I'm not—" Her eyes cut to mine so quickly, a clear message of "shut up" pouring through. I stop talking.

It's not until she takes the seat next to me that she speaks again, her voice so quiet I have to lean closer to hear. "He doesn't need to know you don't plan on leaving—not yet anyway."

"You believe I'm staying?" I don't mean for the words to come out, but when she walked away Friday night, I thought I may have ruined the small bit of progress we'd made. But the fact she's sitting next to me, looking at me with such kindness in her eyes, I can't stop the hope from burning inside.

"I know you'll stay until your dad is back on his feet. I knew that the second you walked through those doors." Her eyes stay trained on mine like she's trying to make sure I don't miss the words she's about to say. "And I believe you're going to do everything in your power to make things right between us. I just don't know if we agree on what that looks like."

Shifting in my seat, I angle my body toward hers. "Abbey, I need to talk about what happened back then. I want to tell you everything." I want to reach for her, take her hand in mine, but I hold back, unsure if I could withstand her rejection in this moment.

"And I wanted you to tell me everything back then." There's no malice in her tone, just honesty. "Now, I need to move on." She's the one who reaches for my hand, sandwiching it in hers. "I'm not trying to be hurtful, but I've lived in this weird stasis since you left, and I'm finally starting to go after the things I've always wanted. I *need* that to be my focus, and rehashing the past with you won't help me with that goal."

I let my eyes roam over her face, studying every inch. It's been seventeen years since I've been this close to her, since I've been able to count the faint freckles across her cheeks, and I never want to go that long again. I never want to miss seeing how her face changes over time. I know the only way I'll be able to do that is to show her I mean what I say, and that means giving her what she's asking for.

"Okay." I squeeze her hand still holding mine, a soft smile spreading across my lips. "We'll focus on getting you your dreams."

THIS WAS A BAD IDEA. *Why did I agree to this?*

The mantra for my day continues on a loop as I walk up to the front door. My knuckles barely touch the door when it opens, and Ava's smile greets me.

"I'm glad you could make it."

"Happy birthday," I say as I pass her. "I had no idea what to get you, but I remember Dad saying you like Guinness, so I took a chance and bought you some good Irish Whiskey."

"Oh!" She smiles, taking the bottle. "You didn't have to get me anything, but thank you." She gives me a quick one-armed hug as she studies the bottle. "Redbreast? Is this what you served Abbey and me at the bar last week?"

"It's the same brand, but not the same bottle. My dad would probably disown me if I gave out shots of this stuff without charging." I chuckle, trying to make a joke.

"Twenty-one-year-old whiskey..." Her brow lifts. "That can't be cheap."

I shrug, trying to act like I didn't spend 450 dollars on a bottle of whiskey. "Benefits of running a bar. You can get some pretty nice discounts if you know the right people."

Ava doesn't believe me, if the glint in her eye is any indication. "All right. If that's the story you want to go with..." Her words trail off as if giving me a chance to tell the truth, but when I don't open my mouth, she laughs softly, shaking her head. "Come on. Everyone's out back. Let me introduce you."

"I didn't get anything for your brother. His birthday is next week, right?"

"Tuesday, but I don't think anyone will blame you for not getting a gift for someone you've never met. I didn't expect you to get me a gift when you barely know me." She laughs as she pushes open the screen door to the backyard.

"I was always told to never show up to a party empty-handed."

Ava glances at me over her shoulder, that brow lifting yet again. "I've met your dad, and while he's a very kind man, I wouldn't have guessed he was teaching you about proper party etiquette."

I can't help the chuckle that escapes. "No, it wasn't my dad who taught me that."

Ava doesn't get a chance to respond before Gage walks up and pulls her into his side. "Hey," he says, extending his hand to mine. "Glad you made it. Did Ava introduce you to everyone?"

"What do you think?" She pushes at his stomach, but the smile on her lips shows that she's not actually upset with him. "We just walked out the door."

"You're slacking in your hostess duties, Rebel." The look the two of them share—one of an intimacy I've rarely seen between two people—has me glancing away. I try not to look too closely at the fact that my eyes, without even trying, immediately find Abbey. She's like a magnet, always drawing my gaze to her, no matter where she is.

She's stunning. It's the first thought that crosses my mind. In her cutoff shorts and loose shirt, with her natural waves pulled up in a messy knot on top of her head, and not a stitch of makeup on her face, she takes my breath away.

The fact she's laughing with another man shouldn't cause the pinch of pain in my chest, but it does all the same.

"You got a little something..." My eyes whip to Ava as she flicks a finger to the left corner of her lips, a teasing smile growing.

I grunt. I know it's childish, but I do it anyway, making Ava and Gage laugh.

"Everyone," Ava shouts, gaining the small crowd's attention. "This is Jude. If you don't already know him, introduce yourself; if you do, say hi. We want him to be happy with his decision to return to Ashford Falls and maybe fall a little in love with it again while he's here."

A chuckle goes around the yard, but most people return to the conversations they were having before Ava interrupted them. One couple breaks away from the little group they were talking to and makes their way over to us.

"Jude Murphy, as I live and breathe." It takes a second for me to recognize the woman walking up to me, but I place her as soon as I see her eyes—Quinn Marks, Caleb's younger sister. "It's good to see you." She pulls me into a brief hug, the smile on her lips shining in her eyes. "This is my husband, Declan."

The man in question extends his hand. "Nice to meet you."

"You too," I say as I shake his hand. "And happy birthday."

"Oh, thanks."

My eyes drift back to Quinn's. "I was sorry to hear about your dad. He was a good man."

"Thanks," she whispers. Declan wraps his arm around her waist, pulling her into his side. "I'm glad I was home with him the last few months. I don't know what I would've done if I'd missed out on that time." The silence that takes over becomes awkward the second she remembers why I returned to town. "Oh god!" She slaps a hand to her forehead. "I didn't mean for that to sound like it did."

"It's fine." And I mean it. I know it's been three weeks since Dad's heart attack, but the doctors are adamant he'll wake up soon, and that's what I have to keep believing. I can't let myself think about the possibility of him never waking up.

"No." She reaches for my hand, squeezing tightly. "That was so insensitive of me."

"Quinn, it's all right." I squeeze her hand in return, wanting to make sure she hears my words. "Never feel bad about having time with your dad. What I'm going through doesn't take away from your experience."

She doesn't shy away from me as the tears build in the corner of her eyes. "Thanks, Jude."

I give her a quick nod, and Ava jumps in, changing the subject to something brighter. My eyes drift back to Abbey. She's still talking to the same guy, but this time, her eyes are on me, concern pinching in the corners.

This was a bad idea. Why did I agree to this?

CHAPTER
Fourteen

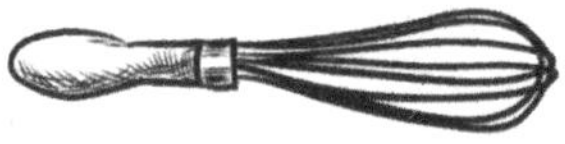

ABBEY

I KNEW he'd be here today. He'd always been close friends with Gage, and after that night at the bar a week ago, Ava really started to like him. I can't say I blame her; even knowing what Jude did all those years ago, *I* struggled to dislike him.

He's worming his way back into my life, and I'm letting him.

He's respecting my wishes and keeping his distance—to an extent. I've seen him every day since that conversation in Walt's hospital room, though never for more than a few minutes. But he never tries to bring up our past; he focuses entirely on my future.

Seeing him today shouldn't be such a shock to my system, but it is. Maybe it's not simply seeing him that's a shock, but seeing him interact with people as if he's only been gone for a short period instead of almost two decades. Even with all that time away, even though he never believed it, he fits in this town. He was always meant to be in Ashford Falls.

"You all right?" Reid's voice pulls my focus back to him.

"Sorry. I'm fine." I offer him an apologetic smile, trying to focus on the conversation.

Reid grew up in Ashford Falls, like most of us at this party, but I didn't really get to know him until Ava and I became friends earlier this year. When she pulled me out of my shell after everything happened with her parents.

He's close friends with Gage and works as a local deputy, so he's been around a decent amount. And I noticed he's attractive and kind—the kind of guy who likes to flirt—but that's as far as my notice has ever gone.

"Reid," I interrupt. "I've gotta ask, why are you standing here talking to me?"

"What do you mean?" he asks, almost offended by the question.

"No." I shake my head. "I mean, you've been standing here talking to me for well over thirty minutes, but there's a woman over there who hasn't stopped looking at you since she walked in." I gesture between the two of us. "We both know nothing will ever happen here, and you're not one to usually pass up the opportunity to..."

"Spend time with a woman where something might happen?" he offers when I struggle to find the words, causing us to laugh.

"Yeah. While I appreciate you didn't want to seem rude walking away in the middle of a conversation, you don't have to keep up the charade."

"Honestly?" He glances over at the woman in question so quickly I wonder if he really sees her. She's pretty and definitely his type—petite, curvy, with fiery red hair. "I've known her for a while. She's my ex-girlfriend's younger sister."

"Oh. That's—"

"Complicated." His eyes fall to the ground for a second before he looks at me again. "I don't know. I've run into her a few times this year, and I thought something might've been growing between us, but..." His words trail off, and I see the hurt in his eyes.

"Well, I'm probably not one to take advice from, but if I had to guess, whatever you're feeling isn't imagined. She feels it too. No woman will spend ten solid minutes staring at a man while he talks to another woman if there aren't serious feelings involved."

His eyes move back to her, and this time, they stay trained on her. "God, this could get messy," he mumbles.

"Sometimes the messy situations are the best ones." Now it's my turn to let my eyes wander. When they land on the man I can't seem to stop thinking about, his eyes are already on me, and I can't look away.

"Are you going to forgive him?"

I'm slow bringing my attention back to Reid.

Am I going to forgive him? I don't know how I can, but I'm also starting to question what really happened that night. The Jude I knew back then never would've done what he said he did. But I can't understand why he would lie about any of it either.

"I don't know what I'm going to do," I tell Reid honestly. "Right now, I'm focusing on my dreams. Everything else is going to have to wait."

Reid's smile is small, but I see the pride shine through in his eyes. "Good for you, Abbey. It's about time you went after the things you want."

"Hmm," I hum. "Maybe you should take your own advice," I offer as I step away, the redhead moving to take my place.

"Reid, I'm sorry..." Her voice fades as I move further from them, and I can't help the smile that slowly grows across my lips. I don't think I've ever seen Reid so at a loss with what to do when he likes a woman—it's kind of nice to know even the playboys can stumble.

I look around the backyard, taking stock of everyone who showed up for Ava and Declan's joint birthday party. It's not a large group, but I feel lucky to be included with the people they want to celebrate with.

My eyes land on Quinn and Declan first. It's been three weeks since their wedding, and while I know they got home from their extended honeymoon last week, this is the first time I've seen them since the wedding. I'm stunned when I realize the sight of them cuddled together doesn't cause the same pinch in my chest as it did a few weeks ago. Standing across from them are Ava and Gage, and the way Gage looks at Ava while she tells an animated story doesn't cause the twist in my gut that I've grown accustomed to ignoring in their presence. It's nice seeing them so happy together.

I let my eyes wander across the yard to find Emily and Caleb talking to Max. There are smiles on their faces, and I'm genuinely happy for them. I haven't seen Max much since he moved in with them, but I know how hard it is losing a parent, and at twelve years old I can't imagine the pain he must be in.

"Hey," Jude says softly, pulling me from my spiraling thoughts.

I spin to look at him, and it surprises me to realize there's a comfort in hearing his voice. "Hey," I reply just as quietly.

This week has been different. Like there's a peace settling between us that I honestly never thought we'd have again.

I've lived the last seventeen years in this weird limbo of trying to move on but not really letting go of the past. Somehow, Jude coming back into my life is the thing that finally pushed me to move forward.

Silence falls between us, and for the first time since he got back, it's comfortable.

It's in that silence and comfort that I take him in. His tattoos are on full display as he stuffs his hands into his pockets, and I finally have the chance to see that I was right about the randomness sprinkled throughout the shading that brings them all together.

The tattoos—all in black on one side and mostly in color on the other—almost seem to create an intricate maze leading your eyes up his arm. The same tattoo I caught a glimpse of under the sleeve of his shirt the other day still captures my attention, but I'm still unable to see it in its entirety.

"How are—"

"What have—"

We both start and stop at the same time, and my head falls forward—a genuine smile forming on my lips. That's something we would've done as kids. "You go," I say.

"I was just wondering what happened when you talked to Marybelle about the store."

"She was ecstatic." I laugh. "She's so happy she said I can get started on the renovations right away."

"Wait. What?" He shakes his head in disbelief.

"Once I told her that Dad was investing in the business, she said we didn't need to wait for all the paperwork. There are still a few details to iron out, but I've already set up a few meetings with some contractors, and Ava and I start packing the inventory next week."

He stares at me, stunned for a minute, before the corner of his lips lifts in a small smile. His arm twitches, almost like he wants to reach out and touch me but holds himself back. "That's great, Abbey. I'm really happy for you."

"Thanks." I beam. "I'm really happy for me too."

He opens his mouth but closes it almost immediately, shaking his head before glancing away for a moment. When he looks back at me, the smile on his lips doesn't reach his eyes. "I definitely don't have the knowledge to do most of what you need, but I worked in construction for a bit, so I'm happy to take a look or help out wherever I can."

My eyes widen in surprise. That's the first bit of information Jude's offered about his time away from Ashford Falls, and if I'm being honest, it makes me that much more curious about what he's been up to.

"Thanks," I whisper. "I might just take you up on that." And I'm shocked to realize I mean it.

CHAPTER
Fifteen

JUDE

THE DOOR to the bar slams open, startling me from my staring contest with the blank word document on my laptop, and my eyes jump to the door to find Edward Selbey glaring at me.

It's my fault. The bar doesn't open for another hour, but my secret hopeless romantic heart leaves the door unlocked when I'm here, wishing the woman always on my mind will walk through those doors.

"How's it going, Eddie?" I close my computer and stand from my seat, shoving my hands in my pockets as I face him. I shouldn't egg him on, but his entrance has me on edge and I just don't care what the man thinks of me. "Anything in particular I can help you with?" My tone is flat, though my heart is racing from the surprise. I was under the impression Edward had gone back to DC for work.

I might not go out around town for fun, but I do need groceries if I want to survive, and one aspect of living in a small town where everyone knows everyone is hearing all the gossip whenever you step outside. Abbey and Edward have been a popular topic of conversation since the news broke of her buying the bookstore, and anyone who knows our history loves to make sure I've heard the news.

Everything I've heard has been incredibly positive. For the most part, people are excited to see what Abbey plans to do with the space. But the one thing they're all getting wrong is how she has the money to make this dream a reality. They're not wrong in where the money came from, just wrong in the way Abbey received it.

I know even if people knew the truth, the way they talk about Edward wouldn't change. Or maybe it would, but only in a positive manner for him. Somehow that man is always depicted in the best light around Ashford Falls, even if he's rarely around for town events, and was absent from most activities Abbey had growing up.

This town can't stop gushing at how much he loves his daughter. How could he not since he's given her the money to open the store?

I still don't know what strings he's attached to the purse, and I'm pretty sure Abbey doesn't either, but I know they exist.

"You're spending time with my daughter..." He lets his words trail off, the threat implied in his tone.

"We've already been over this. I'm not going out of my way to avoid Abbey." He doesn't need to know I plan on going out of my way to spend time with her. I'm sure he already guessed that if he's showing up like this.

"Let me make something very clear, Mr. Murphy." He takes a step closer on each word until he's standing toe-to-toe with me—exactly like he did the last time he was here. "You *will* stay away from my daughter. I don't care what you have to do to convince her not to be around you, but you'll do whatever it takes to make sure that happens."

I keep my eyes on his, but silently count to three before responding. I want so desperately to egg him on more. But while I may not care what he thinks of me, I don't want to be responsible for any issues between Abbey and him. Abbey and I may not be together, but if I get it my way we will be, and I won't be responsible for Abbey losing her only remaining parent.

"Sir, I wish I understood what I did to make you hate me, and I wish I could do what you're asking, but the truth is, when it comes to your daughter, I'm incapable of staying away. She's my true north, and no matter what, I'm always drawn to her."

His eyes sharpen and if this were a cartoon, steam would be pouring out of his ears.

I know my words won't change anything, but I can't stop them from spilling out. "The only way I stay away from Abbey is if she asks me to. I'm done letting anyone else decide what we do with our lives."

"You're just like your father."

I'm not entirely sure I'm meant to hear those words, but that doesn't stop me from responding. When it comes to my dad, I'm nowhere near the kind of man he is, he's far better than me.

"I don't think that's the insult you want it to be. My father's an amazing man, and if I can be half the person he is, I'll be happy with my life."

"Only a blind man would say that about your father."

I want to be cordial, but when it comes to others insulting the people I love, cordial goes flying out the window. "What the hell happened between the two of you? Is there some imagined wrong he committed? Or are you jealous of the relationship he had with Grace?"

"Don't you dare say her name!" he booms, taking another step closer to me. "She was too good for the likes of this town. None of you deserved her."

I know Edward loved his wife, it was hard not to notice in

the way he looked at her, but sometimes it was easy to forget how much he loved her with how often he was out of town and how often Abbey said she heard them fighting.

I don't back down from him, he's angry, but I know he won't do anything to jeopardize his reputation in town. He may hate it here, but he also can't stand the idea of others disliking him. He cares too much about what other people think—like I used to.

"You're right that she was a far better person than most, but this town absolutely deserved her—simply because she wanted to be here."

Edward seethes, his face red with anger, and part of me honestly feels sorry for him. To love someone as much as he loved Grace, only to lose her far too young. It's a horrible reality to live.

I don't understand it entirely; while I lost Abbey, she wasn't gone from this world. I always knew where she was and could've come back to her if I'd been able to get over my own issues. My loneliness was of my own making, and, to an extent, so is Edward's, but losing the love of your life? I wouldn't wish that on anyone.

"Sir, I get that you love your daughter and you want to protect her from what you think might hurt her, but have you ever thought you might be wrong about me?"

Nothing in Edward's countenance changes. The anger still sits under the surface, barely held in check. I wish I knew the full story. I wish I understood what happened to make him hate me and my father, but I know he'll never tell me, and until my father wakes up, there's no other person to ask.

If only I'd been smarter in the past, I could have talked to my dad about it. Instead I held the secrets of how badly Edward treated me from everyone.

"I don't know what you think happened in the past, whether it was something between my dad and Grace, or some history with my grandparents, but I swear to you, Abbey is the most important person in my life." He flinches at the sound of his wife's name, but he doesn't interrupt me. "I'm not disappearing from her life—not again."

The door to Murphy's opens, stopping Edward before he can say anything. We both turn to find a woman with deep brown hair stopped in the doorway. It's not hard to imagine why when the tension in the air around us is palpable.

"Sorry, I saw the help wanted sign in the window and wanted to ask about the position." She stays where she is on the threshold, the door held open as she decides what her next move will be.

I help the decision along, stepping back from Edward and addressing her directly. "I've got a couple positions open, but I'm interested in hiring a bar manager first."

"We aren't done, Mr. Murphy." Edward's words are quiet enough only I can hear them, but the anger is still more than evident.

"I think we are." I keep my words just as hushed as his. "I think it's time you go." I don't back down from his stare, making sure he sees how serious I am. Nothing he can say or do will make me leave, not this time.

Without another word, Edward spins on his heel and marches toward the door. The woman has just enough time to press her back into the door, making space for him to breeze past her. I take only a second to release the tension from my shoulders before finally addressing the stranger.

"I'm sorry about that." I reach forward, presenting my hand for a handshake. "I'm Jude Murphy, the owner's son."

The woman hesitates only a moment before she accepts my handshake. "Jane Smith." When she speaks, her voice is clear and direct. It's clear whatever made her nervous isn't going to stop her from doing what she came for, and I respect that. "I just moved to town, and while I've never managed a bar before, I do have experience managing a store."

My brow lifts at her name—it's a little too generic for me not to question its validity—but I don't comment on it. I know what it's like landing in a new town looking for someone to take a chance on you, and after everything I've been through, I like that I have a chance to pay it forward.

"Come on in. Let's sit and talk about the position."

Dad may not love that I'm hiring staff to help with the place, but he's not going to have a choice when he finally wakes up. If this heart attack should teach us anything, it's that he needs to take better care of himself first and foremost.

Besides, I'm not going anywhere this time and I want to make sure we have plenty of time to catch up with each other. I've missed too much and I refuse to miss more time.

CHAPTER

Sixteen

JUDE

THE BELL above the door sounds as I step into the disheveled bookstore. My eyes immediately roam the cluttered space, searching for a head of sandy blonde hair, one that belongs to the woman I've always loved.

"I come bearing coffee," I announce into the store.

It's comical how quickly two heads pop up from behind piles of boxes and books in the back of the store from those four simple words.

"My hero!" Ava practically sprints around the boxes in front of her, springing to grab one of the cups from the carrier in my hands. "I know I should be holding a grudge against you on Abbey's behalf, but I have to be honest; you're making it very difficult," she whispers so Abbey can't hear.

I chuckle, appreciating Ava's honesty. I like a person who isn't afraid to speak their mind, but knowing she's the person standing by Gage's side makes me like her even more. Even if I've only known her for a little while, I can see how perfect she is for him.

"You think Abbey will forgive me if I keep going down this

path?" I ask just as quietly, appreciating I might have an ally in my fight to win Abbey back.

"Hmm." Ava shifts to stand beside me to better see Abbey, still packing the box she was working on before I entered the store. "Keep supporting her and trying to be her friend, and I think you might be able to accomplish your goal." She pats my shoulder before turning for the door and calling over her shoulder, "I'll be right back! I'm just going to return that call from Benny real quick."

Abbey looks up but doesn't get the words out before the bell above the door rings again, this time with Ava's departure. Her eyes move to mine, and the hesitation I've grown accustomed to seeing in them is gone. Instead, I find a genuine smile gracing her lips and a softness in her eyes I haven't seen since before I left all those years ago.

"Coffee?" I have to force the word through the lump in my throat as I lift the holder in the air. *Maybe that conversation at Ava's birthday party was more significant than I thought.*

"Yeah. That'd be great." I don't even try to fight the smile at her words.

We meet in the middle of the store, our fingers brushing as Abbey takes the cup from my hand. The simple touch has both of us freezing. I know I felt the spark all the way to my toes, and from the stunned look on Abbey's face, so did she. It's not the first time we've touched since I returned home but this touch feels different.

I can't stop myself from stepping further into her space, but that movement shakes something in Abbey—her eyes leave mine as she steps away from me, moving back toward the boxes she was packing moments earlier.

"Thanks for the coffee." She fidgets, tucking a piece of hair behind her ear. "You really don't have to keep bringing it, but I appreciate it."

"Of course." I watch her as she takes a sip before setting

the cup on a closed box. "Marybelle's really ready to retire, huh?"

"Oh, yeah." Abbey laughs. "The sale doesn't officially go through for another week, but she's adamant I get a jump start on packing everything so I can start on renovations immediately."

"When do the renovations start?" I follow Abbey's example and place my cup on a box, moving to the shelf Ava was working on before I came in. I can't help but chuckle when I see she was working in the "thriller" section.

"One of the many benefits of small town living." Abbey glances over her shoulder to watch me for a second before she focuses back on the shelves. "George said he can send a crew over next week to get started, but we have to get all the stock boxed up and put in storage before they arrive Monday morning."

"So you're going with George?" Abbey wasn't joking at the party last week when she mentioned she had meetings set up. She met with three contractors on Monday and had proposals from all three by Wednesday.

"Yeah. He wasn't the cheapest, but he had the best ideas to accomplish my goals and the fastest timeline." She laughs, more to herself than anything else. "Besides, in this small town? How could I go with anyone else? People would've boycotted the shop on principle alone."

"You're not wrong." I chuckle. "Do you have a place to store all these boxes?" I ask, looking around at all they've already packed and the shelves of books that have yet to be touched.

"Yeah, we've got one of those pod things. I wish I'd been a little smarter and culled some of the inventory before we started packing. I think I'll have to do a big sale on books during the grand re-opening..." Abbey continues talking, but my mind drifts when I reach the shelf filled with my books.

When I saw them a few weeks ago, I noticed the little plaques with blurbs, but I didn't realize there was one for each of my books on the shelf. They don't stock all of my books, but for the ones they do, Abbey has written a few words recommending them.

It surprises me how many they have in stock, though. I don't know if it's a good thing or not, but I had the ideas and my publisher loved them, so over the last ten years I'd been able to publish two books a year. Even with my success, it's rare to see a store have all my books on their shelves.

But what surprises me the most is when my eyes catch on my debut novel, *The Echoing Silence*. Don't get me wrong, there are debut novels out there that will stand the test of time, but I don't think mine is one of them. Then again, we are our own harshest critics.

With a slightly trembling hand, I can't stop myself from picking up the note Abbey wrote.

> This book transfixed me in a way no other author ever
> has. The complexity and emotional depth of the charac-
> ters is like no other. I felt seen.

The words are so simple, and yet it's knowing they came from Abbey—it's knowing that my words touched her in a way I never imagined when I wrote them. It's knowing that, even though I was hundreds of miles away from her, we were still connected—even if we didn't know it.

"Jude, you okay?" The feel of Abbey's hand on my shoulder brings me back to the bookstore.

"S-sorry. What did you say?" I ask, swallowing the lump in my throat before looking at her.

"Just asking if you're okay. You've been quiet and unmoving for a few minutes now."

"Oh." The concern in her eyes has me looking away,

unable to hold it after reading just one of her recommendations. "I'm fine, just got distracted reading the little blurbs you wrote for this author." I gesture to the shelf I'm standing in front of. "Isn't this the author we talked about a few weeks ago? The one whose book you hated," I ask, knowing we are one and the same and trying to come up with a valid excuse for my off behavior.

"Yeah. I think that might have been why I was so harsh. I've been a fan of his since the very beginning." She reaches for a copy of *The Echoing Silence*, thumbing through the pages as she speaks. "I read this book when it first came out. It's actually what got me back into reading. It's also what landed me the job here with Marybelle."

"I didn't realize you stopped reading." Slowly, without letting Abbey see, I slip the note into my pocket.

Her eyes meet mine. "Yeah, shortly after you left, Mom's health declined pretty rapidly. I spent a lot of time with her, reading books aloud, and after she passed I couldn't get into it the way I used to."

"It reminded you of her."

"Yeah, and I just wasn't ready for that."

"I was sorry to hear about Grace. I know it wasn't a surprise, but that doesn't make it any easier."

Grace Selbey was more than kind to me. She'd been the only mother figure I had growing up.

My father was my whole world as a kid. He was there for every milestone, scraped knee, school activity—anything you'd wish for your father to be, he was it.

But he couldn't fill every shoe I needed—though he tried his damnedest. Where my dad missed, Grace was there, filling the gaps.

When she got sick and was diagnosed with ALS a few weeks after Abbey and I were married, it nearly broke both of us—not our relationship, but our spirits. Grace was our biggest supporter and was so happy when we told her about our marriage. She'd been sad she wasn't there, but we didn't have to explain why we did it the way we did—she just got it.

Grace knew better than we did how Edward would've reacted had he known about the wedding before it happened, and she understood why it had to happen in secret. But her joy when we told her was unlike anything I'd seen from her before.

"She loved you," Abbey whispers, and the words just about break my heart.

"I know," I say around the lump in my throat. "I hate that I wasn't here for you both in the end," I tell her honestly.

I see the tears well in the corners of her eyes before she can look away. "Well..." She swallows. "It happened a long time ago." She turns to the shelf she was working on and begins packing boxes again.

I know it's a defense mechanism, and I understand it. I want to say more, but that would mean talking about the past, and I can't do that if I want to stick to my plan. I told Abbey I'd help her focus on her future, and that's what I'm going to do. Once she opens this store, I'll focus on getting her to talk to me about that night and the last seventeen years.

My fingers ghost over the note in my pocket once more before I get back to work, ignoring the rest of the notes. I can only imagine what the rest will do if *one* note sent me into a tailspin.

———

August 5, 2019

Do you remember the night about six weeks after we got married?

That's a stupid question. I have no doubt that night will forever be ingrained in your brain. I came home plastered and way later than was acceptable.

There's so much I wish I could change about that night. First and foremost, I wish I told you the truth about what happened.

It's interesting how all the moments we lied to each other—and there weren't many—come back to your father. But, then again, maybe it shouldn't be a surprise.

It's funny. Your mom always wished she'd been strong enough to stand up to your father, and when I was put in a similar situation, I did the same thing she did—I caved to his demands.

I couldn't be the reason my dad lost the bar. He would've told me not to worry about him, but I couldn't do it. It was all he had left from my grandfather.

And I couldn't be the reason you'd never see your mother again, especially when your time with her was already limited.

Your father knew exactly what he was doing when he talked to me that night. He knew exactly what buttons to push.

He knew you and my dad were my greatest weaknesses. You two were the most important people in my life—you still are.

I couldn't stand by and watch you both suffer. Though, I guess...in the end, I did.

I'll never forgive myself for that night, even if it didn't happen the way I let you think it did.

CHAPTER
Seventeen

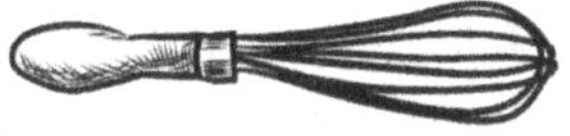

ABBEY

MY EYES DART to the clock above the door at the sound of the soft knock. *Who could be knocking on my door at almost one in the morning?*

It's rare for me to have people visiting my apartment at any time of the day, but this late at night makes me nervous. I tiptoe to the door, trying to make sure I don't make a sound and peek through the peephole. The sight of the person shouldn't surprise me. He's been true to his word, focusing on helping me make my dreams a reality. I don't think there's been a single day he hasn't stopped by the bookstore to bring coffee and help in some way. He never made it in today, and if I'm honest, it hurt a little.

"Hey," I whisper as I open the door to Jude. There's no reason for me to whisper. I can't disturb anyone else when the only apartments in this hall are mine and Jude's.

"Hey." He stuffs his hands into his pockets, his shoulders shrugging slightly. "I know it's late, but I didn't make it into the store earlier, and I just wanted to make sure everything was okay." His voice is so quiet and soft it almost makes me melt. I lean against the door instead.

"You took a chance I was still up?" I smirk, ensuring he knows I'm kidding.

His smile in return is small, but it still does something to my insides. "I heard the TV. I thought I'd take a chance."

"Things were good at the store. They finished with all the demolition today. They need to finish hauling out all the debris, and then they can start rebuilding."

Staring at him now, I can't stop my thoughts from reeling. How is this man still ingrained in my soul? How can I still be so comfortable with him after everything that happened?

He more than broke my heart seventeen years ago—he broke my spirit, and I'm not sure I ever really got it back. And yet...

"Do you want to come in?" I ask softly.

"I don't want to keep you up. I just..." His words trail off, and I can't help but wonder if it's because he doesn't know what he wants to say or because he's trying to respect my wish to only focus on the bookstore.

"I'm not really tired yet. Which honestly amazes me." I chuckle. "I've been getting up and helping the crew downstairs every day this week."

"It's probably the excitement of everything." He shrugs. "You're getting everything you dreamed of. It's exciting."

"Not quite everything," I whisper. How can I still love him? Want him?

"Abbey." His smile falls, and he pulls a hand from his pocket, lifting it to cup my cheek. He moves so slowly, and I know it's because he's giving me time to move away, but I can't. I need his touch more than I thought I would.

My eyes fall closed the second his skin touches mine. This isn't the first time we've touched since he came home, but this is different. This is more than a simple touch; it's comfort in a way I haven't felt since he left.

I lift my hand, holding his in place as I turn my head

slightly, letting my lips rest against his palm. I should flinch at the roughness of his palm, at the callouses I feel, but I don't. All they do is remind me of all the years I felt those callouses—all the years I knew exactly what he did to get those callouses, and all I want now is to know where the ones currently caressing my face came from as I relish the way they feel against my skin.

I don't see him, but I feel him as he steps into me, leaving only inches of space between us. "Abbey," he whispers. "I'll do everything in my power to give you all your dreams. Every last one of them." The conviction in his voice has me opening my eyes.

I don't let go of his hand, still holding it against my cheek as I tilt my face to look at him. What are my dreams now? It's true I always wanted to open a café, but there was a time when my only real dream was spending my life with Jude. I truly didn't care what we did or where we were; I was happy as long as we were together.

But that wasn't fair to Jude, was it? Putting all my hopes and dreams on the two of us being together. That wasn't fair to me either. I should've had dreams outside of the two of us. I should've always been my own person.

I guess I thought I had been, but looking back on it now, I lived for the time I got to spend with Jude, and I can't help but wonder if he gave up some of his dreams and wishes to make mine come true.

"What about your dreams?"

"My dream is you." I swear his voice breaks on the word you, but he says it so softly I convince myself I imagined it.

I pull his hand from my cheek, holding it between us, trying to soften my next words. "We can't be each other's dreams, not anymore."

"Abbey—"

"No," I interrupt. "We can't. We have to have dreams of

our own. Dreams that have nothing to do with the other person. If the past has taught me anything, we can't rely solely on someone else."

His eyes fall to our clasped hands. "It's not wrong to lean on others for help."

"I know," I whisper, finally able to read the word across the knuckles on his right hand. *WISH*, what an appropriate word for this moment. "I'm not saying we can't rely on other people. I'm saying we can't rely *only* on other people. We have to be able to support ourselves. To go after our own wants and needs without leaning on someone else to get us to the finish line."

His eyes soften and I just know the next words out of his mouth. "Abbey, I—"

"Were you with your dad today?" I ask before he can say anything else.

His eyes bounce between mine, and I see the regret pooling in their depths, but I'm not in a place to hear those words. I don't know if I'll ever be able to hear those words from him again.

No, that's not right.

I don't know if I'll ever be able to believe those words from him again.

"Yeah." He gently removes his hand from mine, stuffing it back in his pocket as he steps back. "The doctors wanted to meet to talk about our options."

"Has something changed?" I ask, worry coating my words.

"No. He's been off life support for weeks now, and brain function is still completely normal. They have no idea why he's not waking up."

"So, what options are there?"

"Moving him to a different facility. A nursing home."

"What?" I breathe.

"They don't see a reason for him to stay in the hospital since there's nothing for them to treat. In all honesty, it sounds like they should have moved him weeks ago. I think your friends, Caleb and Emily, have something to do with why they kept him there for so long."

"They're your friends too."

"I don't know if I can rightfully call anyone in this town a friend. Not after abandoning all of you." I open my mouth to respond, but he shakes his head. "I'm not saying that for sympathy. It's just a fact. I haven't been a friend to anyone here, and the fact that they're all letting me back into their lives without question is a testament to the people they are."

It's silent between us, and I don't know how to respond. It doesn't surprise me that Ashford Falls pulled Jude back into the fold as if he never left. People knew we were together, and they knew I was heartbroken when he left, but we were so young.

It felt like this big, all-consuming, adult love back then, but now? I wonder if it was everything we thought it was. Seeing the relationships around me—Quinn and Declan, Ava and Gage, Emily and Caleb—I can't help but wonder if Jude and I would've had what it takes to make it work. Would we have fought to make it through the natural downs all relationships have?

Obviously not, if we couldn't weather our first big conflict.

I shuffle my feet, discomfort at that thought coursing through me. "So you're moving him to a nursing home?" I ask, focusing back on the safer topic of Walt.

"Yeah. I just have to pick one."

"Let me know how I can help. I have tons of time now that demolition is done. There's very little I can help with in the rebuild of the shop." I force a laugh, trying to lighten the somber mood.

"I think I'll take you up on that offer." His smile is tight, and I know he's forcing it too. "They gave me a list of places that aren't too far away. Maybe we could sit down and look at a few, maybe schedule some walkthroughs before deciding?"

"Yeah. We can sit down tomorrow morning. Before you open the bar?"

"That'd be great. Ten sound good?"

I nod, giving him a tight smile. *Where did the comfort between us go?* "I'll be there."

He stares at me a moment longer before striding across the hall and entering his apartment, not looking back at me once. I should close my door and head to bed, but I'm trapped where I stand.

Maybe I can forgive him for what he did all those years ago, not for him but for me. Because I think I'd rather have him in my life than not. I think I'd rather have his friendship than not have him at all.

Forgiving him doesn't mean he needs to become my everything again, and it doesn't mean we go back to who we were before everything happened. It just means that we're moving forward with our lives.

I smile as I close the door to my apartment, a weight lifting from my shoulders.

CHAPTER
Eighteen

JUDE

FIVE WEEKS, and I'm still staring at a blinking cursor on a blank screen. I can't remember a time I've ever gone this long without writing a single word, not since I started publishing.

The advice every author, agent, and editor has ever said plays on repeat in my head. *Forget about the end result and get the words on the page. The first draft isn't meant to be good.*

I know it, and yet I'm still struggling to start. My mind keeps returning to last night, standing at the threshold of Abbey's apartment.

I wasn't planning on knocking on her door last night, but when I heard the soft rumbling of voices I couldn't stop myself. My first thought was that someone was there with her, and I couldn't stand the thought of another man in her apartment. I had no right to care one way or another if she was with someone else, but feelings are rarely logical.

When she opened her door, a soft smile on her lips, I wanted nothing more than to go inside and just be in her space. Reaching out and touching her may not have been the smartest, but I needed to feel her skin against mine. And when she relaxed into the simple touch, I felt like I was soaring.

It sparked the hope I kept pushing down inside me. Maybe all hope isn't lost. Maybe there's room for me in her life. Maybe we can find our way back to each other.

The sound of the door opening pulls me back to the blank screen before me, and I turn to find Abbey standing just inside the door.

"Sorry. I know I'm a little early."

"No, it's fine. I'm not doing anything that can't wait for another day." I close my laptop and switch it with the stack of brochures I laid on the bar next to me. "Can I get you anything to drink?"

"It's a little early for a drink, don't you think?" She laughs as she steps up to the seat next to me.

There's a lightness to her that wasn't there last night when I left, and I can't help but wonder where it came from. There may not have been any harsh words between us last night, but there was a discomfort between us, one that I haven't felt since the birthday party three weeks ago.

"I was thinking more along the lines of coffee or water. Maybe a soda? But they say it's five o'clock somewhere, so I'm happy to pour you a drink if you want one instead." I smile as I stand from my seat and move behind the bar.

"I thought you didn't like coffee."

With my back turned, my smile grows. I like that she still remembers things about me, even the things that don't matter. "I don't, but you do."

"Hmm," she hums. "I've already had a few cups this morning, so I'll go with water for now."

I grab a glass and turn to fill it, my eyes catching on her as she flips through the brochures, pulling her hair over one shoulder. She's in what I've realized is her every day look—cut-off shorts and a loose shirt—but instead of her hair piled on top of her head, she lets the natural waves fall down her back. No matter how long I've known her or how many times I see her, she always takes my breath away.

How have I gone so long without seeing her? How have I survived it?

"Have you looked through any of these yet?" Her voice breaks me from my trance, and I reach for the soda gun, filling the glass with water before placing it on the bar in front of Abbey.

"I glanced through them. There are a few nearby, but they don't seem the best." I want to move back around the bar and sit next to her, but I think staying on this side of the bar might be smarter—for now.

"What do you mean?" she asks, looking up at me, her brows pinched.

I fidget with the rag sitting on the underbar, not entirely comfortable with the words I'm about to speak. "The ratings aren't great and, from the pictures online, they seem pretty run down." I take a breath and let my shoulders fall. I hate that I'm in this situation, but I'm not going to put my dad some place I'm not positive he'll get the care he deserves.

"Oh." Her eyes fall to the brochures, a frown marring her beautiful face. "How far do you have to go for nursing homes that have good ratings?"

"There's a couple of private homes a town or two over that I'd like to look at."

"Can Walt afford the private homes?"

"On his own, no, but I've got some money saved to help make up the difference." I force myself to meet her eyes even though every inch of my skin itches with the half-truth I've just given her. It's not the biggest lie I've told, but I hate that it's a lie at all. I know I should tell her the truth about me being AJ Doherty, but now doesn't feel like the right time.

Her eyes return to the brochures, her fingers toying with

the edges. "I'd like to help too," she says so quietly I almost miss it.

"Abbey, it's not necessary. I've lived a pretty cheap life-style"—not a lie—"when I say I have some money saved up, it's a decent amount," I tell her, placing my hand on her arm.

I love that Abbey wants to help my dad—that he still means so much to her—but I won't let her spend money she doesn't have when the truth is that I have more than enough to cover his stay at any facility.

Her eyes lift to mine, studying me. I don't move, letting her take in whatever she needs. Her mouth opens and closes a few times before her eyes fall back to the brochures. "What have you been doing since you left?" she asks softly, as if she's afraid of the answer.

"A little bit of everything." I shrug. Abbey might be afraid of my answer, but part of me fears telling her. Not because I don't want to share every aspect of what happened over the last seventeen years—and have her share the same with me—but because I don't want to cause her pain.

I know hearing what I missed out on while I was gone will hurt, maybe more than leaving ever did, but I can't learn about the woman she's become without knowing what I missed. And I want so badly to know the woman Abbey's become. From the little bit I've learned so far, she's more amazing than I ever imagined.

"When I first left," I start, watching her closely for any signs of distress, "I went to this little town about thirty miles north of here, in Pennsylvania. I ended up at this little family-owned inn where I got a job as a dishwasher."

Her eyes lift to mine, and the interest I see in them keeps me telling her more.

"It's not the stereotypical tourist town, but they have a higher population in the summer and fall, so they hired me and gave me a place to stay. The couple who owned the inn had three kids; their oldest was a year older than me, and I think they did it because they would've wanted the same for their son if he'd been in my shoes."

"Your shoes?"

It's my turn to look away from her. I don't know if my words will cause her pain, but I know they'll cause her discomfort, and I don't want that. But I also don't want to lie to her—not anymore.

Stonebridge Hollow felt more like Ashford Falls than any other town I ever stayed in. Maybe it's because it realistically wasn't far from home, and it felt easy enough to go back if I wanted to, but out of all the places I've lived—and there have been many—Stonebridge Hollow is the place I would pick if I were looking for a home outside of Ashford Falls—even after staying with Willie and Mae in Minnesota.

"I never told them exactly what happened to make me leave home, but they could see I was hurting, and I think they just wanted to lessen as much stress as they could." I lift my gaze back to hers, offering a small smile. "They were good people. It was a good place to land right after everything that happened."

She's quiet, her eyes moving over my face as she thinks. I have no idea what's going through her head, but the look in her eyes is still inquisitive. "How long did you stay there?"

"About three months. I moved on to a new town in Ohio, one a bit bigger than Stonebridge Hollow but still small. There, I got a job cleaning a few businesses in town. It started as just the local lawyer's office, but he recommended me to a few other people, which helped significantly. I was only there a couple of months before I ended up in Chicago." I shake my head, remembering how much I hated it there.

Not only was it harder to find someone willing to take a shot on a kid, but it was even harder when they saw I hadn't stayed in my two previous jobs long.

"That's where I got my first job in construction. I picked up a couple of skills and quickly moved on. I learned definitively in Chicago that city life wasn't for me." I notice she's finished her water and grab the empty glass to refill it. "I think I was only there a month before I moved on."

She runs her fingers over the rim of the glass, her eyes tracking her movements. "Did you ever stay anywhere long?"

"I stayed in a little town in Minnesota for about six months. I got a job at a local mechanic shop. The owner and his wife let me stay with them and quasi-adopted me," I tell her honestly. "I never lost contact with Dad, but that first year wasn't easy."

"Why?" she blurts.

I fight the smile at the Abbey I used to know peeking through. "He wanted to know what happened, and I wasn't ready to hear the disappointment in his voice."

"Jude—"

"I know he would've supported and loved me no matter what," I interrupt. "But I didn't want him to look at me differently. Though, I think in the end, he still did."

There was a disappointment I felt from him in our conversations that first year, but it was a disappointment I could live with. One based on wishing I trusted him enough to tell him what happened. And I guess, it was always my fear of disappointing a man who did so much for me as a father that kept me from telling him the truth.

To this day, I have no idea what my dad would've done if he knew all the details of what led to my and Abbey's divorce.

I can guess, though, and it would've meant losing something he loved and cherished more than most things in his life.

"So, six months in Minnesota?" Abbey asks in the silence, bringing us back to the moment.

"Yeah. From there, I moved all over the country, picking up whatever job I could to support me for however long I was there. If you can think of it, I probably did it. I generally stayed in town for a season before moving on to the next, and I only stayed in smaller towns after Chicago. Though, I found myself hitting some tourist spots along the way."

"What kind of tourist spots?"

I can't stop the laugh from breaking through. "Any and all of them." And even though we're supposed to be spending this time looking at the brochures for different nursing homes and scheduling time to visit a few, we spend the next forty minutes before opening the bar talking about all the places I'd been.

CHAPTER
nineteen

ABBEY

"JUDE'S BEEN AROUND A LOT LATELY." Ava falls onto the couch beside Quinn, passing her a beer bottle.

"Wait." Quinn spins to look at me, her eyes wide. "I know I saw you two talking at the birthday party a few weeks ago, but I didn't realize you were spending time together. What did I miss while I was on my honeymoon?"

The last I know is more rhetorical, but it still makes us chuckle. No matter what she might have missed here, her honeymoon was exactly what she needed and wanted it to be.

"We're not *spending* time together. He's just..." My words trail off and I have no idea how to finish that sentence.

Technically, we have been spending time together. If we're not working on finding a nursing home for Walt, or he's not at the bookstore helping out with the renovation, or I'm not at the bar helping wherever he needs it, then we're generally in my apartment hanging out.

Not that these women know about that last part...

"I don't know what's going on." I look down at the baby in my arms, avoiding the look I know Ava is throwing my way.

She's seen us together at the bookstore and Murphy's a few times now.

I'm glad we decided to have a ladies' night in at Emily and Caleb's house—something we've started doing more often since Emily had Fiona—but right now, I wish their focus was on someone else. I'm still so confused about what's happening between Jude and me. My heart and brain aren't on the same page, and it's more than frustrating.

How can my heart be open enough for Jude to sneak back in? When he left, it broke me. It's melodramatic, but there were days I didn't know how I'd survive them. Losing Jude wasn't just losing my husband and a man I loved; he was my best friend—my everything.

Maybe that was too much pressure, and maybe that's what led to our downfall.

"You know exactly what's going on," Ava says. "That man is trying to make you fall in love with him again."

"Hold up. Someone has to fill me. I feel like I'm missing something." Emily moves around the kitchen island, joining us in the living room and passing me the bottle she made for Fiona.

"You know what? I don't think I know the full story either, and I lived in this town," Quinn says.

"Well, be prepared. She's not going to give anyone the full story. I already asked." I swear I see Ava pout as she sinks back into the couch.

"There's not much *to* tell." My eyes stay trained on Fiona as she drinks her bottle, her little hand wrapped around my finger.

"Oh, now we all know that's not true. Anyone watching you at the party could see there's serious history between the two of you." Emily scoffs.

"Fine. Jude was the love of my life, and he broke my heart," I say in exasperation.

"Well, that's a start, but it's more than that." Ava's voice is much softer this time. "Abbey, if you don't want to talk about it, we'll respect that, but you don't have to keep anything bottled up if you don't want to. We're family, and family is there for one another—no matter what."

"Ava's right. And believe me, we all understand the drive to keep things to ourselves." Quinn laughs softly, but I know she's speaking from experience. For three years, she held onto a secret that led her to abuse drugs and alcohol and living in fear that she was exactly like the mother who abandoned her.

"I don't think I've ever realized how true that is. What is it that drives us to hide from the people who care about us most?" Emily asks, her eyes falling to Fiona. "I'm sure it has something to do with fear of being judged or letting someone down, but if we really support one another, then there's no judgment or disappointment." Emily leans over, stroking a hand over her daughter's head. "I hope this little girl never feels like she can't come to me about something."

"Jude and I met when I was five and he was six," I blurt, my eyes lifting to meet Emily's. "We grew up together. We fell in love with each other and got married."

"Wait, you got married? How did I not know that?" Quinn interrupts.

"Well, you were, what? Ten years old? I doubt that was something you paid attention to."

"Sure, but this town loves to gossip, and the question of what happened between you and Jude was popular. How did no one ever talk about you two being married?"

"We didn't tell anyone we were doing it, and then we only told Walt and my mom afterward."

We never planned to make a big announcement about our marriage, but we never intended to keep it a secret either. We figured with the gossip mill in Ashford Falls, people would find out in a matter of weeks. I still don't know how no one ever figured it out.

"You didn't tell your dad?" Emily asks.

"No." Fiona's grip on my hand loosens and when I look down I see she's fallen asleep. I put the bottle on the table next to me and settle into my seat to tell the story. "My dad never liked the idea of Jude and I together. It's why we got married in secret."

"I still don't understand," Quinn whispers.

"Honestly, I don't understand either. I don't know what my dad held against Jude. I know there was a history between Walt and my mom, but she always said they were only ever friends. Like Jude and me, the two of them grew up together."

"You think Walt and your mom ever dated?" Ava asks.

"I guess it's possible, but I don't think my mom would've lied to me about it. She loved that Jude and I were so close. She was the one who made sure we stayed in each other's lives after we first met—even if she and my dad fought about it."

My mom and I had so many conversations about why Dad didn't like Jude, and while I know she never told me the whole truth, she was adamant there wasn't more to her and Walt.

I remember asking her once why she wouldn't answer my questions directly, and she said she never wanted to influence my relationship with my dad. She wanted my relationship with him to be about the two of us and nothing else. Like outside influences might make me think differently.

She wouldn't have been wrong. With Dad working in DC most of the time, our relationship was never the strongest, and it was easy for me to become upset with him because of that absence. The more I think about it, the more I can't help but wonder what kind of man that makes my father—if my mother felt she couldn't speak candidly about him.

Two people in love should have kind things to say about the other person. There should be some kind of emotion attached, but I can't recall my mother ever talking about more than facts about my father. It was always where he grew up, what he studied in school, what he did for a living, or who his family was.

She talked openly about when they met and how they fell in love, but she never spoke about anything that happened from the moment they found out she was pregnant with me. The love they had for each other was still evident whenever they were together, not because of the way they couldn't stand to be away from each other or always needed to be touching, but simply from the way they looked at each other.

It's ironic that she didn't want to say anything to influence my relationship with him. I think her lack of sharing anything meaningful about him still ended up impacting my relationship with him.

I still hated disappointing him, no matter how strained everything was between us.

"So you went against your dad's wishes and married Jude, but when he found out, you did what he wanted and kept it secret?" Emily questions.

"Not exactly. My dad demanded we get the marriage annulled, and we refused."

I still remember the look on his face when he came into the living room as Jude and I told my mom. There were tears of joy in her eyes, but when Dad saw them the anger in his terrified me. He immediately started demanding Jude leave and never return, shouting nonstop about how he always said Jude would cause us pain. I tried to jump in, but it was Mom who got him to stop. A simple touch of her hand to his arm and his focus immediately went to her.

She told him in her soft, calm manner about the wedding and how happy she was about it, how it was one of her greatest wishes come true. While Dad had calmed down considerably, it hadn't stopped his demands for an annulment—demands we refused.

"We agreed not to make a big deal, but we told him we wouldn't lie or stop living our lives the way we planned."

"What did you have planned?" Emily asks.

"Honestly? Not much." I laugh softly. "Jude was already working with his dad at the bar and knew that was what he wanted to continue doing. And I was enrolled to take a few classes at the community college starting that fall." My eyes drift down to Fiona for a moment, watching her sleep peacefully. "We moved into the apartment above the bar and went about our lives like nothing was different. And other than living in a new place and with the person I loved most in the world, nothing was different."

"Until it was," Quinn murmurs.

"Yeah, until everything changed," I say, my eyes never leaving Fiona's face.

I hear the shuffling of feet, but it's not until I feel the hand resting on my knee that I lift my eyes to find Ava sitting on the floor before me. "Abbey, what happened?"

"I don't know anymore," I whisper, tears slipping out the corner of my eyes.

"What do you mean?" Quinn moves to the floor beside Ava, her hand resting on my arm.

"He told me he cheated on me." It's silent, the three of them staring at me in shock, and it takes me a minute before I can continue. "He came home drunk one night not long after we were married. He was late and hadn't told me where he was. I'd been worried about him, and then he'd stumbled through the door, ranting about how my father was right and that we shouldn't be together."

"Abbey," Ava whispers, her thumb rubbing back and forth across my knee.

"I remember that night so vividly. Jude was usually such a

happy drunk. He was a little handsy, but only ever with me. It was always so affectionate and loving, never overbearing or creepy. But that night, he rambled about my dad and how he wasn't good enough for me. He went on about how much he loved me but that he'd only cause me pain and heartache."

"When did you find out the truth about that night?" Emily asks quietly.

I shake my head, unable to form any words. According to Jude, it wasn't only that night. That night was the start of many nights. "It was a few weeks later he told me about the affair."

"It was more than once?" Quinn asks in bewilderment. "I never would've thought Jude capable of that," she mumbles.

"He told me it started the night he came home drunk. He made it clear that sleeping with her wasn't a result of the alcohol but that the alcohol was a result of the guilt he felt *after* sleeping with her. He said that while he felt ashamed, he couldn't stop going back."

"Abbey," Ava chokes on a gasp.

It's silent except for the tiny snores coming from the baby in my arms. When a tear lands on her soft cheek, I turn to Emily. "Can you take her? I don't want to disturb her."

Ava and Quinn shift, allowing Emily to step in and take Fiona from my arms. I try to stand from my seat, but Quinn stops me with a hand on my leg. "I don't know what to say. I-I can't believe he would do something like that."

"I can't believe he would show his face around you after doing something like that." Ava scoffs.

"Walt means everything to Jude—"

"That's a little hard to believe since he's never shown his face around town before now," Emily mumbles.

"But he talks to Walt almost daily." My eyes fall to Ava, remembering how I refused to tell her these details when she first asked five weeks ago.

"How can you be in the same room as him?" Her voice is laced with disbelief.

"I don't know. He's nothing like I remember him, not from those last few weeks." My eyes fall closed as I picture him.

I remember the way he couldn't look me in the eye when he told me about the affair and the way his voice was completely void of any emotion.

Now, though, he won't stop looking me in the eye, and all I hear when he speaks is emotion.

"He's tried to talk to me about all that happened back then, but I won't let him," I whisper, opening my eyes again.

"Why not?" Quinn asks.

"I'm afraid."

"Of what?"

"Learning even more was a lie."

"Abbey—"

"No," I interrupt Ava. "Like I told Jude, I don't want to focus on the past anymore. I've let it run my life for too long. I just want to focus on my future." My eyes bounce between the three women, and while I don't see pity in their eyes, I do see sadness. "I don't want you to treat Jude any differently now that you know."

"Abbey—"

"And I know it's not fair of me to ask, but I'd appreciate it if you didn't tell the guys." In the silence between us the three of them share a look. "Besides, none of us are the same people we were when we were nineteen. It's not fair to assume Jude is either." Ava opens her mouth but snaps it shut quickly. "He deserves to visit with his dad in peace, and if you won't do it for Jude, do it for Walt."

"Oh, that's just dirty." Ava stands from her seat by my feet, moving back to the couch. "But for Walt, I'd do almost anything."

"Thank you."

She studies me for a moment, her eyes and face clearing before she speaks again. "If Gage asks, I'll tell him you've asked to keep it between us. I'm sure he'll respect that, but I won't lie to him."

"I can respect that," I tell her.

Quinn and Emily agree to do the same as Ava, and slowly the three of them move on to happier subjects, but I can't focus on them to save my life.

Quinn is right. Even having experienced that night and those weeks after, I can't fathom Jude cheating on me. He'd hurt himself before he hurt me. But then, why would he lie about something like that? And why is it only now that I'm realizing it?

———

August 28, 2020

Do you remember that night it all ended? I still wish I could forget it. I still wish I could take it all back.

Nothing had been the same since that night I came home drunk. Just over two months married, and I forced you to throw it all away.

I wish I found a different way to make you see that our being together would never work, but at the time, the only way I could see you letting us go was to make you hate me.

It was the coward's way out, but it accomplished what I needed it to.

I hope somewhere deep down, you know it

wasn't the way it seemed. Hurting you broke me in a way I never thought a person was capable of hurting. You are the love of my life, and you always will be.

I've lived in countless cities, traveled to a dozen countries, and met people from all walks of life. Not a single person has come close to making me feel the way you do.

If I could do it all over again, I would. Even with everything I've experienced and learned over the last twelve years, I'd give it all up to be with you again.

Nothing and no one has given me the peace I had with you by my side.

I want more time with you, Abbey.

I want it all with you.

CHAPTER
Twenty

JUDE

THE KNOCK at my door surprises me. Not many people know I'm staying here instead of my dad's place, and considering three of the people I've spent the most time with since I got home left the bar thirty minutes ago, I think it's safe to assume it's not them.

Looking around the sparse apartment, I can't help but regret that I haven't taken the time to furnish the space. To anyone looking at this situation, it appears that I have no plans to stay, and that's the furthest thing from the truth. My only plan is to be wherever Abbey is, and after this past week, I'm starting to think that might actually be a possibility—regardless of what Edward wants.

It didn't surprise me when he showed up at the bar yet again this morning, but fortunately for me, he wasn't there long. His plans were thwarted when he barged in and found Jane and me interviewing someone for the open bartender position. He seemed poised to fight, but quickly decided against it and left.

He didn't need to say the words; I knew what they were— *stay the hell away from my daughter.*

I stand from my seat at the kitchen island and move to the door, peeking out the peephole briefly before opening it. I'm happy it's Abbey standing on the other side, but I can't stop the worry from washing over me.

It's late—almost two in the morning—and if I heard correctly from the guys when they were at the bar, it was ladies' night at Caleb's this evening.

"Hey," I whisper as my eyes land on her. Her gaze is firmly on the floor, and the pinch of her brows grows my unease. "Is everything okay?" I ask softly when she doesn't move.

She lifts her eyes to mine, but it takes her a minute to speak. "I don't know."

My shoulders fall at her words. I don't know if it's relief—that she might finally let me tell her about the past—or dejection—that she might be done letting me into her world.

I step back, opening the door a little wider and ask, "Do you want to come in?"

She hesitates, but only for a moment before she's nodding her head and taking a small step over the threshold. Her eyes immediately move around the space, and I wonder if she's taking in the emptiness of it as it is now, or imagining it with all the warmth and comfort she infused into the space when we lived here together.

Has she set foot in this apartment since she walked out of it seventeen years ago?

Gently, I close the door before stuffing my hands in my pockets. I want so desperately to touch her, to hold her, to offer her comfort for whatever is troubling her, but I don't know if that's something she'd accept right now, and I don't want to stop whatever this conversation will be.

It takes her a few minutes, but when she's done looking at the space around us she turns to me, and I hate that I can't read what she's thinking.

"Didn't you have a ladies' night over at Caleb and

Emily's?" I ask when she doesn't say anything. I know the answer, but I can't think of anything else, and this conversation has to start somewhere.

"Yeah. I just got home." Her eyes don't move from mine, but something in her shifts. It's like I can almost see the shield going up around her, like she's preparing to take some kind of hit, but when she doesn't say anything, I think I might be wrong.

"Abbey," I whisper, afraid she might run if I speak too loudly. "What's wrong?"

"I told them what happened," she blurts before her eyes fall to the floor, her fingers toying with the strap of her bag slung across her shoulder. "Back then—why we split." The words are simple and yet they still hit some imaginary wound across my soul.

It's a wound of my own making.

I'm the one who messed up.

I'm the one who broke us.

But it still hurts more than anything else in my life.

"Abbey—"

"No," she interrupts. It takes her a moment to continue, but when she does, her eyes meet mine straight on. "I know it's not smart, and I know it doesn't make sense, but I don't want to talk about it." She draws her shoulders back as she drops her purse to the floor, her posture straightening as she readies herself to say the next words. "I'm pretty sure you lied to me back then, and while I should demand to know the truth, I know you wouldn't have lied to me if you didn't have a really good reason." Her voice wavers, but she takes a step forward, closing the space between us. "If I'm being honest, I'm afraid to know the truth. I'm afraid of knowing the reason you lied to me."

"Abs." My voice breaks and I have to fight with everything

I have not to reach for her. There are more words I need to say, but in the moment I can't find them.

"No. I know it's stupid and goes against everything you are, but I don't want to talk about it. I've lost so much already, and I'm not ready to lose more." Another step and another foot of space gone.

I could so easily wrap my arms around her and finally feel her body pressed against mine, but I hold back. I won't take this moment from her—whatever it is.

"What do you want?" I whisper.

"For you to love me again." Her words are just as soft as mine, but I hear them as if she shouted them in my head.

There's nothing in the world that could stop me from reaching for her—not at those words. Slowly, so she can still back away if she wants, I cup her face in both of my hands, tilting it so her eyes meet mine. "I never stopped loving you."

Her feet shuffle and she closes the last bit of space between us, her hands rising to grab my wrists, holding them in place, as if I have any plans of moving them. But it's the tears building in the corner of her eyes that finally breaks me.

How can she possibly think I don't love her anymore?

My lips crash to hers with a desperation I've never imagined. It's like a drink of cold water on a hot summer day or the first day of spring after a harsh winter.

It's like coming home.

I've known from the moment I walked away from this town that I'd never be the same again. Leaving Abbey was the hardest thing I've ever done, and I've constantly thought about a world where we got another chance, but my imagination never conjured up anything like this.

It's not gentle, not at first. This kiss is fierce and built on seventeen years of want and need. It's built on a lifetime of love, because there hasn't been a single day that's passed that I haven't loved Abbey with everything I am.

Without pulling away from her, the pressure of my lips against hers gentles, becoming tender as my tongue coasts along her bottom lip, begging for entrance. I feel her tears wet my palms where they cup her cheeks as she melts into me, her hands leaving my wrists and trailing down my arms. She opens her mouth and meets me with equal desperation.

The feel of Abbey pressed against me, her hands at my waist, and her lips moving in tandem with mine, all of it feels so familiar and like everything I've always wanted. I can't believe I made it this long without it.

"Abbey." I pull away, only enough to see her face. I need to know she really wants this. I need to know this isn't some itch to scratch or some momentary lapse in judgment.

I need this to mean something real.

We may have spent the last seventeen years apart, but she can still read me as easily as any book on her shelves. "I've missed you." Her grip on my shirt tightens. "I've missed this." Her lips brush over mine lightly as she moves to her toes and whispers in my ear, "I'm done wasting time."

She moves to press her lips against mine, but I don't let her. I want this more than anything. To be back where we were before I left—before I messed everything up—but not talking about the details feels like setting us up for failure in the long run. It feels like a Band-Aid on an injury that requires surgery.

"Abbey. We can't pretend the past didn't happen." My voice is gentle, trying desperately to make sure she doesn't view this as rejection.

"I know, and I'm not asking to. I'm asking to put that conversation on hold." She doesn't fight against my grip. She leans back just a bit more, enough to make sure I can see her face. To make sure I can read how serious she is. To make sure I know she's telling the truth.

And just like she could read me, I can read her.

She knows what she's asking for. She knows what she wants, and I don't know how I'm supposed to say no when it's everything I want too.

Releasing her face, I drag my hands down her body and around her waist, lifting her as my lips crash back to hers.

There's so much for us to talk about, so much she doesn't know. She thinks I lied to her before, and I know how stupid it is for us not to clear the air before this goes any further, but when I drop her onto the one piece of furniture I've purchased for the apartment and she stares up at me with that much lust in her eyes, there's nothing I can do to stop us.

There's nothing I *want* to do to stop us.

Abbey sits up at the foot of the bed, her eyes never leaving mine as she reaches for me where I lean over her, my hands braced against the mattress on the outside of her thighs.

"Are you sure?" I ask, my eyes roaming her face, searching for even an ounce of hesitation.

Her answer is instant. "Positive."

It won't be the last time I check in with her tonight, but it's all I need to let the dam break. My lips are back on hers. Abbey scoots back on the bed, pulling me with her, and not a single morsel of me fights her on it.

Seventeen years later, and we still move together as if it's only been hours since we were last together. Her arms snake around my shoulders as she lays back against the bed, my hips fall into the cradle of her thighs as she arches into me, and I can't stop my hands from roaming up her sides under the hem of her T-shirt.

I don't even try to stop the groan from breaking free when I finally feel the heat of her skin under the calluses on my palms. Nothing has felt better—well, that's not completely accurate.

"Jude," she moans as her hands grip the back of my shirt,

tugging and pulling desperately. Her body melts into the bed when her fingers finally meet bare skin.

Thank God I'm not the only one desperate to feel skin.

I pull away, sitting up on my knees—opening her legs wide around me—as I pull my shirt over my head. My eyes are back on her the moment I toss my shirt to the floor, but instead of falling back on top of her, I let my gaze roam her entire body. I've barely touched her, but her chest is already heaving, and I honestly can't blame her. The pressure of my cock pressed against the zipper of my jeans is truly painful, but I do absolutely nothing to relieve it.

Abbey's back arches, her hips driving into the bed as she seeks some kind of friction, and I feel bad for only a second before I'm letting my hands coast up the outside of her bare legs. Her hips move again as I pause at the waistband of her shorts, but I'm not ready to give her that relief quite yet.

"Patience, love." I lift her shirt, placing a feather light kiss to the skin right above her shorts.

"I don't want to wait." Abbey has never been one to blindly take orders. She's always been an active participant in everything she does. It really shouldn't surprise me that she pushes me away to sit up and tear her shirt over her head along with the lacy bralette she's wearing underneath.

My eyes drink in the sight before me as she falls back onto the bed, a smirk forming across her lips. I'm not the only one who's marked their skin. I want to say the first thing I notice is the elegant script under her left breast, but it's the glint of silver at her nipples that captures my attention first.

I don't even think about it as I reach for her left nipple. My fingers barely brush the pebbled tip when I hear her little moan and my eyes spring to hers. The way she bites her lip as she stares at me has my cock pulsing. *It's entirely possible I'm going to come in my pants without her laying a hand on me.*

"When did you do this?" I ask, pinching her nipple around the barbell piercing.

"A few years after you left." I appreciate that she doesn't shy away from saying it. It's proof that she wasn't lying when she said she didn't want to forget about the past.

"And this?" My fingers trail down her breast to the words tattooed across her ribs. My breath catches when I register the words.

...and until we meet again...

A line from an old Irish blessing my father gave us on the day we told him about our wedding.

"The day our divorce was finalized." Her voice is soft, but I don't hear the pain I thought I would. And when my eyes meet hers, all I see is sincerity. She's not saying it to hurt us, she's simply stating the truth.

I let my gaze fall back to the words, watching as my fingers slowly trace each letter. Goose bumps pop across her skin, but I can't stop.

I bring my lips to the tattoo and finish the blessing against her skin. "May the joys of today, be those of tomorrow."

"Jude," she begs, reaching for me.

This time I don't make her wait, my lips crash to hers.

CHAPTER
Twenty-One

ABBEY

I HAD every intention of going home when I left Emily's house. It was an emotional night. One filled with so many questions—from everyone, including myself. But walking up those stairs and seeing Jude's door was like someone looped a rope around my waist and I couldn't stop myself from being pulled in.

I needed to see him. I needed to talk to him. I needed to feel him.

I needed *him*.

If I'm being honest, while I hadn't planned on kissing him or falling into his bed, the second I laid eyes on him, I can't say the thought didn't cross my mind. It was quickly followed by the thought that it would only be scratching an itch, but the second his lips touched mine I knew it would never be only scratching an itch with Jude Murphy.

His name is written across my soul, and I can't imagine anything changing that.

In the grand scheme of life, it hasn't been long since I slept with someone, but I've never felt the connection I had with

Jude with anyone else. Being with him has always been—and will always be—so much more.

No matter how much time passes, Jude and I fit together in a way I've never experienced with anyone else and in a way I've only seen few other couples display.

Being with Jude is like coming home.

Is it smart to ignore the elephant in the room—the possibility that he lied to me all those years ago?

It's probably the stupidest mistake I've ever made.

I don't have any proof he lied. He's never lied to me before, so why is it so easy to believe he lied about this? But then again, if he did cheat on me—have an affair with someone else—all those weeks were lies.

Talking myself in circles proves how stupid I'm being *not* talking to him. That thought doesn't stop me.

If he did lie to me about the affair, I know it was for a good reason. And giving myself the time to actually think rationally? I have a pretty good idea what that reason might have been. It's a reason I don't want to think about because it means losing the one person I had after he left and my mother died.

I may have more people in my corner now, but for so long I only had one, and no matter what, he's my family.

But I don't want to think about any of that right now. We may have lost seventeen years, and we may have a lot we still need to work through—knowing the truth won't magically fix the fact that he lied and let someone else control our lives—but I still love him.

I never stopped loving him.

"May the joys of today, be those of tomorrow," he whispers against my skin. Against the words I had permanently etched across my ribs. Finishing a blessing I've held onto like a lifeline. Hoping and wishing our ending wasn't truly written yet.

It's the reverent tone that breaks me. "Jude," I beg,

reaching for him, needing his lips on mine. Needing the weight of his body on mine.

With that simple word he knows exactly what I need, the same way he always does. His lips meet mine in a scorching kiss. One filled with so much love and devotion, it's hard for me to fathom.

How can that still exist after all these years? After all this time apart? How can we both still feel so strongly for each other?

Keeping his lips pressed to mine, his hands trail down my sides and smooth back up, his thumbs brushing my peaked nipples. There's a gentleness behind the touch I didn't realize I was missing and I can't stop the whimper that breaks through.

Jude settles his weight on the bed, his hips cradled between my thighs and his hands resting on my ribs just below my breasts. When he releases my lips from his kiss, there's nothing but tenderness in his eyes. "Is this okay?"

"Yes," I breathe out, wrapping my arms around his shoulders and pulling him closer to me. The feel of his bare chest against mine has never felt more right. My entire being relaxes, all thoughts other than Jude and me leaving my mind.

His eyes bounce between mine and I see the wheels turning, but before he can say anything else, I bring my left hand to his cheek. The coarse hair of his beard brushes my palm and his eyes fall closed as he leans into the touch. "I know there's still so much to figure out, but let's worry about it tomorrow," I whisper. "Let's just be together and only focus on this moment right here." His eyes meet mine and all I see is love. "Everything else can wait."

"I don't want to lose whatever it is we've been building since I got back. You mean too much to me to ruin any of it."

I don't just hear the worry in his voice, I see it in his eyes too—and I get it. I don't know the future and I'm pretty sure I don't even know the past either, but I know what I want, and it's to have Jude back in my life.

I'm willing to fight for that now.

I know *how* to fight for that now.

"You won't." I pull his lips back to mine, trying to prove with my actions how much I mean those words. My kiss is determined, but my touch as I move my arms around him is soft. There's a clear purpose and intention behind all of it. I don't want anything that happens tonight to be seen as anything other than love. I don't want him to say it was out of desperation. I need him to feel the truth and depth of emotion.

It's when his body relaxes into mine that I know he's living in the moment too, cherishing everything that's happening between us.

His lips leave mine, and the whimper I release quickly turns into a moan when his lips move across my cheek and down my neck. The trail he leads to my breast is tender, and the moment his tongue touches my left nipple I'm lost to everything but the feel of him. He might be just as lost if the grinding of his hips against mine is any indication, but he's not lost enough to forget about my other breast. He brings his hand to the other side, pinching and soothing in rhythm with his tongue and teeth.

My fingers tangle in his hair, holding his head in place, like I have any kind of say in what's happening between us. Jude might ask me if I'm okay with what's going on, but I know he has almost all the power here—and I love it. I don't want his attention anywhere else other than my chest, but I also can't stop my hips from pressing against his. The pressure building in my core is like nothing I've ever felt before.

"Babe," I breathe out, and everything freezes. It's been seventeen years since that word has slipped past my lips. It's a simple word. A nickname I've heard plenty of people use. And yet...that simple word expresses just how much I meant what I said earlier.

I'm done letting life pass us by. I'm done pushing him away.

Jude pulls away from me, his eyes meeting mine and the tears I feel in the back of my eyes are reflected in his.

"Mo ghrá." It's barely a whisper, but those words have the tears breaking free.

He brings his left hand to my cheek, brushing the tears away and I can't stop myself from holding him in place. My eyes fall closed as I turn my face, pressing my lips to his palm.

"Abbey," he murmurs after a few minutes of stillness.

I don't turn to look at him, but I open my eyes and they catch on a spot on his ring finger. Jude's body instantly goes taut and when my eyes shift to his I see a hint of panic in them.

I push at his chest, forcing him to his knees as I move to sit up in front of him. His mouth opens, but without letting him say anything I take his left hand back in mine, finally giving myself a chance to truly study the tattoos.

Just like his father, he has symbols going across the tops of his fingers, and while I don't know what each one is, I know they stem from his Celtic heritage, something that has always been so important to him. Unlike Walt, he also has a word stamped across his fingers. I don't know for sure, but I'd guess the word is Gaelic. I want to know all the stories associated with each tattoo branded onto his skin, but none of them are what caught my attention.

Turning his hand to the side, I force his first two fingers closed, revealing the inside of his ring finger. There, etched on his skin is the letter A.

"Jude..." My words trail off, unable to decide what I want to say.

My eyes fly to his, but he doesn't open his mouth to say anything and it's then I let my eyes fall to his chest and arms.

All of his tattoos are finally on full display—nothing's in my way. I'm shocked it took me so long to see them for what they are—our story.

On his left pec is a swing, our wedding anniversary twined within the ropes. On his left shoulder, the oak tree that represents Ashford Falls—that represents his home. On his right shoulder, the logo for Murphy's. I can't stop my eyes from studying every piece of art decorating his skin. The contrast of color on his left side to the simple black tattoos on his right has as much meaning as the pieces themselves, I'm sure. Jude is too intentional for that not to have meaning.

My eyes find his and the pain I see makes me lose my breath. I don't know what happened seventeen years ago, and I thought I could do this without knowing, but seeing the dedication Jude's always had for me, even when we were thousands of miles apart—doing this tonight, without talking about it—I think it might ruin us.

"I'm sorry," I whisper before rushing off the bed and grabbing my shirt from the floor.

I don't pause to put it on. The chances of anyone being in the hallway between our apartments is essentially zero. I hold the shirt to my chest, rush to grab my purse, and run out the door. I thank whatever higher power exists that I didn't lock my apartment door as I hear Jude calling after me.

I've already locked myself inside and collapsed to the floor with tears pouring down my cheeks by the time Jude is knocking on my door.

CHAPTER
Twenty-Two

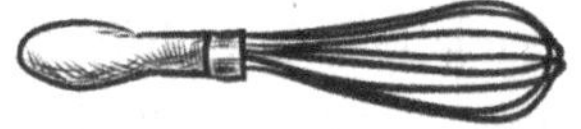

ABBEY

AVOIDING Jude is harder than I thought.

It took him over an hour to finally walk away from my door that night. And I imagine, if he knew I planned on sneaking out, he would've sat there all night.

Friday night was a mess of things I didn't plan—knocking on his door, kissing him, almost sleeping with him, running to my dad's house. None of it was planned and most of it wasn't what I wanted.

I knocked on Jude's door needing to know the truth, needing to know if I was right about the lies, but knowing the truth was going to change everything. There aren't many people in the world who aren't afraid of change. People might be open to change and they might embrace it, but I don't believe there isn't a single part of them that isn't afraid of change.

Seeing his tattoos, seeing our story play out across his skin, it struck something in my soul and I couldn't follow through. Not without knowing the complete truth.

Should I have stayed and talked to him like the adult I am? More than anything, I wish I had. But I think I also needed these days surrounded by the home I was raised in. If there was ever any doubt whether or not my parents loved each other, it's all thrown out the window when I walk through the doors.

The house still has all the touches of my mother. And the pictures lining the wall and mantel are a testament to the good times the three of us had. I don't understand it, especially when my mom so often refused to talk about my dad, but there was something the two of them shared that no one could damage, even Mom's relationship with Walt.

My dad and I may not be close, but he's the only family I have, and family has always meant something to me. It's always been important. I know my father has many faults—he's not perfect and he's made plenty of mistakes—but he's always taken care of me. He may push me in ways I don't agree with and he may be distant, but he loves me.

None of that changes the fact that he likely played an integral role in the dissolution of my marriage. And running to his house—even though I'm surrounded by my mom too—was the last thing I wanted to do. But I also knew it was the last place Jude would look for me.

Growing up, the only time Jude ever came to my childhood home was for our joint birthday party every year—not that it was ever planned as a joint birthday party. My father barely tolerated the presence of Jude and Walt at those parties. It was all Mom's doing that got them through the door.

It wasn't a stretch to think Jude still wouldn't want to show up on this doorstep if he thought he might run into my dad. Of course, seeing the changes in Jude—seeing how the last seventeen years have shaped him—I can't really say what he'd do anymore.

He's been fighting for me in little ways since he came home. Quietly showing up every day to support me in whatever I'm doing and gently pushing me to open myself back up to him.

Ava wasn't wrong. Jude has been around a lot and I've *liked* having him around. I want him to keep being around.

And yet...

I'm hiding out at my dad's so Jude can't corner me at home. I'm keeping the bookstore door locked so he can't come in to help me. And I'm avoiding visiting Walt in case Jude's there spending time with his dad.

I'm such a coward.

The sound of a key in the lock makes me jump and the refrigerator door slams shut as I spin to the back door, my father's brows pinching at the sight of me standing here.

"Abbey. I wasn't expecting you to be here. Is everything okay?" he asks as he wheels his suitcase further into the kitchen, the door closing behind him.

"Oh, yeah. I just wanted to stop by and make sure everything was all right." I step up to the kitchen island, toying with a dish towel lying next to the mess I've yet to clean up from the cookies now baking in the oven.

My dad lifts one brow, not believing me for a second. There's no way I would be making cookies in his kitchen if I was only stopping by.

"I needed a break from all the construction going on at the bookstore. I figured since you were out of town it wouldn't be a big deal." I avoid looking at him as I start gathering the dirty dishes and walking them to the sink.

"You know you're always welcome here." I still don't look at him, but I hear him moving closer to me. "This will always be your home," he says before pressing a kiss to the top of my head.

It's little moments like these that make it hard to accept what he might have done. That make it hard to accept that in order to truly move forward with Jude, I have to hear the truth.

And hearing the truth could destroy everything that exists between my dad and I—no matter how strained it is.

Dad picks up the pile of mail from the counter near us but he doesn't look at it. From the corner of my eye I see him study me. The silence between us is filled with tension, something that doesn't typically exist around us.

"What's going on, Abbey?" He puts the mail back down where he found it, his attention entirely focused on me.

If I ask him point blank if he threatened Jude, will he tell me the truth? Do I want to hear the truth from him?

I've been hiding out in his house for seven days now and I still don't know the answer to either of those questions. I know I want the truth. I just don't know if I can trust my father to give it to me. Even after all these years, he still hates the Murphys.

Rinsing my hands, I give myself another second before I shut the water off and turn to face him. "I've been spending a lot of time with Jude lately." If it's even possible, his spine straightens even more. He opens his mouth to speak, but I don't let him. "He's been helping out at the bookstore and I've been keeping him company at the bar. It's just...it's brought up a lot of memories."

I search his face, looking for any sign of guilt or pain, but all I see is anger. "I don't know how you could let that man back into your life. Not after what he did to you."

"People change."

"Not him. Not that family," he seethes.

"What is it about Walt and Jude that you don't like? I've never understood your hatred of them." I keep my tone even, wanting to make it clear I'm not accusing him of anything. It's entirely possible there's a valid reason he doesn't like them, and I'm desperate to know.

"It's not important. All that matters is that they aren't good people and you shouldn't be involved with them." He doesn't wait for my response. Grabbing the handle of his suitcase, he storms out of the kitchen.

Two months ago I would've let him go. I would've finished cleaning up the mess I made and I would've gone home, ignoring my need to know the answers to my questions.

Now, though, I can't let it go.

"I'm not a child anymore," I say, marching after him. "I deserve to know why you think they're bad people. Walt has never done anything but care for those around him. Even when I cut him out of my life after Jude left, he let me back into his life like no time had passed at all."

This time there's pain in his eyes, but I get the sense it's not from his actions. No. I'm pretty sure it's because of how I look up to Walt. I don't have to say the words for my dad to know that Walt is like a second father to me. Walt's filled the gaps my father chose to leave in his absence, and I can only hope he's regretting that decision.

Hoping he feels some kind of guilt about missing out on my childhood makes it all that much harder to push for answers from him. But I can't keep living in denial. I don't want to lose my father from my life and I think if we have any hope of keeping a relationship alive, we have to get rid of the lies.

"It doesn't matter, Abbey." His tone is hard, one I used to hear all the time back in high school. One I haven't heard since Jude left.

"It matters to me," I whisper. "I need to know," I beg.

He hesitates for only a moment. "Abbey. Let it go."

My shoulders slump and my eyes fall closed. I give myself a moment to feel the disappointment, and then I try one more time. I open my eyes and meet his head one. "Dad, I'm telling you I need to know the truth. I need you to be honest with me. If there's a valid reason for everything that's happened, I'll hear you, but I can't go off your word alone anymore."

Nothing about his body or face changes. He stands there just as stone faced as before.

"Dad," I beg one more time, tears burning my eyes. "Why can't you say whatever it is? If you're worried about hurting me, you already are."

His eyes harden and I know there's nothing I can say or do to change his mind. "It won't matter, Abbey. It never did for your mother and it never will for you."

"Don't tell me how I feel. You can't know what I'll do or say."

"I can, because just like your mother, you love that boy more than anything else, and you will always choose him."

He doesn't wait for my response, and this time when he turns around I let him walk away.

September 1, 2023

Do you remember the day I left?
I wonder if you wish I stayed.
I don't think you do, but I still wonder.
Dad tried to talk me out of it. He tried
so hard to get me to stay, to try and work
it out.

I never told him what happened—the
truth or the lie. I wasn't brave enough—
strong enough—to tell him any of it. I was
afraid if I told him the truth, he'd convince
me it didn't matter if he lost the bar. And
I was afraid if I told him the lie, he'd
never look at me the same again.

I was afraid to see the disappointment
in his eyes.

I wonder if you ever told him what happened.

He's never said anything to me, but then again, he doesn't talk about you—he never has.

I didn't ask him not to, it's just something he assumed. Not that he was wrong. I can't handle hearing about your life.

I couldn't stand the thought of running into you around town, of seeing you fall in love with someone else, of having to watch you live a life without me by your side.

That's why I left. And it's why I'll never go back.

Fifteen years to the day since I said goodbye, and I can't get your face out of my head. I thought I'd seen heartbreak in your eyes before, but that day proved me wrong.

You were just eighteen years old, barely married two months, and your marriage was already over.

I hope you've found peace and happiness with whatever you're doing. I hope all your dreams have come true. I hope...

CHAPTER
Twenty-Three

JUDE

SHE'S NOT GOING to answer. I know it, but that doesn't stop me from knocking anyway.

"Abs, talk to me," I beg, resting my forehead against her door.

It's been seven days since that night in my apartment, and maybe I should be giving her space to come to me when she's ready, but I just don't have it in me—not after all this time away from her.

Not after how it ended.

Being with Abbey was always amazing. Even when we were bumbling teens with absolutely no idea what we were doing. Learning and growing with Abbey created a connection I've never had with anyone else. And even though it's been seventeen years since we were last together, Friday night felt like we were on a path to something truly transcendent.

Not a single part of me has thought of walking away from Abbey since I came home, but after that night—after remembering what it's like to be pressed against her, to have her pressed against me—there's nothing anyone or anything can do to take me away from her.

The only way I leave is if Abbey tells me to.

"Abbey, please open the door," I plead. "You can't avoid me forever. I won't let you." I wait a few minutes, listening for any sounds on the other side of her door but hear nothing.

I know she's here. I heard her come home for the first time all week a few minutes ago. She probably thought I was down in the bar and wouldn't know she was home, but fortunately for me, I've hired help and don't need to be there every minute it's open anymore.

I've been so absent from the bar all week, Gage, Caleb, and Declan all showed up at my door at different times wondering what was going on. I couldn't keep it from them, what happened seventeen years ago. I didn't tell them everything—Abbey deserves to be the first person to hear the full story—but I told them enough to understand why I was even more of a broody ass then normal.

"Mo ghrá," I choke out. "I'm not gonna leave until you talk to me."

I lift my head, my eyes catching on my left hand resting against the door. The word tattooed across my knuckles steals my attention and I'm instantly taken back to the day I decided to get those letters permanently inked on my skin.

It was my first tattoo and the artist tried like hell to convince me to start with something else. Hand tattoos fade the fastest and often have to be touched up. A lot of tattoo artists won't even bother with hand tattoos, but I was adamant. I needed the reminder of everything I left behind only three months before. I needed to see it on a daily basis, and the Gaelic word fit perfectly.

Four letters, a connection to the heritage my father always took great pride in, and a reminder of what I left in Ashford Falls.

ANAM.

Soul.

"Abbey." I pause, listening for anything, and this time I hear the faintest shuffle behind the door. I don't let the fact the door isn't opening stop me from finally speaking the words I've bottled up for so long. "I want to say I'd take it all back if I could, but I wonder where we'd be—who we'd be—if we hadn't spent at least some time apart. I've loved you my whole life, Abbey. That has never changed and it never will." The sound of the lock turning stops me, but when the door stays closed I continue.

"I hate that it's been so long since I've seen you and heard your voice. I hate that I don't know every tiny facet of your life over those years, and if I could take that back without losing all the growth both of us have had, I would—in a heartbeat."

It's silent on the other side of the door, but there's something in my gut telling me she's still there. She's still listening.

"Abbey. Open the door. Let's talk about it."

I don't hear anything, but the door stays closed for so long I think she might really be telling me it's done. I know she felt what I did Friday night, but maybe too much time has passed. Maybe we've grown apart more than I thought. Maybe everything we felt was just leftovers from our time before.

Maybe it was the final piece of closure Abbey needed.

I don't want to believe it, but I can't deny that it's a possibility.

Then I hear the sound of metal slowly shifting and my eyes fly to the doorknob as it turns. Abbey stands there, her hair in a messy knot on top of her head, still in the dusty, paint covered overalls she always wears while working in the bookstore, with eyes red and puffy—likely from crying. Even in the picture of mess and sadness, she's the most beautiful woman I've ever seen.

I don't let her say anything before I pull her into me, my

arms wrapping around her as I simply hold her. It's the feel of her arms winding around me and gripping the back of my shirt so tight I think she might tear it that tells me everything will be okay. We still have a lot to talk about and work through, but I know all those thoughts that just raced through my head are wrong.

Abbey's not trying to move on from us either.

I don't know how long we stand here holding each other, but I won't be the one to pull away first. I'll stand here for the rest of my life if that's what she needs. It's the sound of the door at the bottom of the stairs leading up to our apartments that has us slipping away from each other.

My eyes don't travel to the stairs as I hear the footsteps moving closer. My gaze stays trained on Abbey, which is why I see the exact moment her entire body goes still when the voice calls up the stairs.

I don't know what I expected. I guess I assumed I'd know the person showing up at our doors at ten o'clock on a Tuesday night, but the voice that sounds is not one I recognize.

"Abbey! You home? I know it's late, but I was passing through and thought I'd stop by."

It's subtle, but her eyes go wide for a moment before she wipes quickly at her cheeks, her eyes bouncing between mine and the stairs behind me. Whoever it is has her nervous.

"Hey." The voice is quieter now, and maybe a little surprised to find someone else standing here with Abbey, but that doesn't stop the man from stepping around me to place a kiss to Abbey's cheek. "I'm glad you're still up."

There are so many reasons for me to hate this man. Not only did he brush past me like I wasn't just in Abbey's space, but his lips were centimeters from my wife's lips.

"Chuck, what are you doing here?" Abbey asks, pushing him away.

"I missed you, and I figured since I haven't seen you in a while..." His words trail off as he offers her a crooked smile and steps back into her space, bringing his hand to her waist in a possessive hold.

And then it clicks. These two are together, and I'm the one in the way here.

Without waiting to see where this goes, I spin on my heels and rush down the stairs—away from the love of my life with another man.

"Jude, wait!" Abbey hollers after me, but I don't slow down. "Chuck, I need you to go."

I hear her door slam and hurried steps rushing down the stairs, but I can't stop moving. I don't know why I'm so surprised, but I am. I'm also hurt. Abbey has every right to do whatever she wants with her life, but the idea that she could be with someone else is like a pain I've never experienced before —not even when I ruined everything all those years ago.

"Jude, please!" Abbey catches up to me, grabbing my arm and tugging. "Stop, please. Talk to me," she begs.

"There's nothing to talk about." I stop walking, but don't turn around. I can't bring myself to look at her.

Those words aren't fair, especially when all I've wanted since I came home was for Abbey to listen to me. And now, when she wants the same from me, I can't give it to her.

"Clearly, there is." She steps around me, forcing my eyes to meet hers. "Jude," she whispers. "You can't seriously tell me you thought I'd never be with someone else for the rest of my life."

"Why not? I haven't been."

"What?" She stumbles back, shocked by my words. Honestly, so am I.

It's another unfair statement to make. I may have been celibate for the last seventeen years, but I never thought or wanted Abbey to be alone. I always wished and hoped she found someone else to be happy with. Abbey deserves to spend her life with someone. To have a family with someone. I just never wanted to witness it.

"There's been no one. I've only ever been with you," I whisper.

Her mouth opens and closes, her head moving back and forth so minutely it'd be easy to miss. "What do you mean?" she breathes out. "That can't be right." Her eyes fill with tears, and all the fight and anger falls away.

"I never cheated on you, Abbey. You said it yourself. I lied to you, I just didn't know how else to get you to hear me." Not when I'd been telling her for days that we needed to end things. That I wasn't good enough for her.

"If it was a lie back then, how can I believe you now?" she whispers.

Through the tears I see the hope in her eyes. She wants the truth, and I want to give it to her, but I know it's going to hurt her, and I hate that I'll be the person causing her pain yet again.

"Are you ready to hear it? All of it?"

Her breath stutters as she prepares herself. She doesn't need to know the specifics to know this is going to change her. And change, no matter what kind, is scary.

"Yeah, I want to know. I need to know."

The door behind us—the one leading up to our apartments —opens, and I don't have to turn around to know it's Chuck finally listening to what Abbey shouted at him before she came running after me.

Abbey wipes her cheeks, her eyes trained on me for another moment before she looks over my shoulder.

"Everything okay here?" Chuck asks. I feel his presence behind me, but I can't bring myself to look at him. Hearing the protective bite to his words already has me on edge. I hate the jealousy coursing through me, but I never wanted protecting Abbey to be anyone's job but mine.

"Yeah, everything's fine." Abbey glances at me quickly before looking back at Chuck. "This is Jude."

I don't need to see his face to know he understands exactly who I am to Abbey. The quick intake of breath and the lack of any other explanation is enough for me to know Abbey has shared exactly who I am.

"Got it. I guess I'll be leaving then." Chuck steps around me, his hand moving to her waist as he presses a kiss to her cheek again. "Have a good life, Abbey. You deserve it." The words are said so quietly I know I wasn't meant to hear them. The quick understanding makes it hard for me to hate him.

Without waiting for Abbey to say anything Chuck walks away, leaving Abbey and me staring at each other.

"Do you want to come up to my apartment so we can talk?" Abbey asks, her voice still choked with tears.

"Yeah," I murmur, reaching out to wipe the lone tear that slips free. I don't know if it's intentional, but she leans into my touch, her eyes closing as if savoring the feel.

It's a moment before she opens her eyes and takes my hand, leading me back into the building. We're quiet as we make our way up the stairs and into her apartment. The warmth and feeling of home the second I step through the door is just as powerful tonight as it was the first time, and it doesn't shock me in the slightest that I feel comfortable in Abbey's space.

"I want to make it clear that Chuck and I aren't in a relationship. I don't know if that makes it better or worse, but I don't want you to think that what almost happened last week—"

"Abbey, you don't have to explain it to me," I interrupt. "I know I didn't react well, but we're divorced, you have every right to live your life however you want."

"I know, but—"

"Abs," I plead. The fact that she stops and knows exactly what I mean from her name alone is evidence enough how well we still know each other.

"Okay. Then let's start at the beginning. What really happened?"

CHAPTER
Twenty-Four

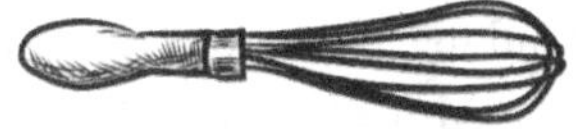

ABBEY

I LEFT my dad's knowing I needed to talk to Jude, I just thought I'd have a little more time. I should've known Jude would be listening for me to come home.

Chuck showing up was not on my bingo card. It's been two months since I've seen him and we've barely even exchanged texts over that time. I honestly thought we'd both moved on, but I guess that's proof about what they say when you assume something.

No matter what, Chuck and I were casual. I have no doubt he's slept with at least four other women over the last two months. I shouldn't—and I don't—feel bad for what happened last week. Especially since nothing will ever be casual between Jude and me.

I look at Jude, standing only a few feet in front of me, and feel like he's miles away.

"I don't know how to start." Jude shifts his weight from foot to foot, as if deciding whether he should stay where he is by the door or move further into the apartment.

"How about I tell you what I think happened, and you tell me if I'm right?" At his slow nod, I swallow and start. "I think my dad threatened you somehow, and when I refused to listen to you telling me you weren't good enough and we needed a divorce, you decided the only way I'd give in was if I hated you."

His eyes fall to my feet and he brushes an agitated hand through his hair. I don't know if I'm right, but the energy pouring off him has me nervous.

"He didn't threaten me directly," he murmurs before bringing his eyes back to mine. "He threatened to take your mom away to DC and make sure you never saw her again, and he threatened to take Murphy's away from Dad. To make his life so miserable here he'd have no choice but to leave Ashford Falls."

I freeze at his words. I knew my father hated Walt and Jude, I just didn't realize his hate went to such lengths. I never would've thought my father would use my mother against me like that. Taking her away and ensuring I never saw her again wouldn't have only hurt me, it would've destroyed her. And that's something I never expected from my father. He loved her more than life.

"Why didn't you tell me back then?" I whisper.

I feel the tears building in the back of my eyes, the pressure in my nose stinging, but I can't figure out if it's from the thought of my father being that cruel or if it's because Jude wasn't honest with me about any of it.

"Because you were already losing your mom, and I didn't want you to lose your dad too." His hands twitch as if he wants to reach for me, but he doesn't. "I didn't want to make you choose because I knew you'd choose me."

"That should have been my choice." A tear escapes and I brush it away fiercely, anger starting to wash over me.

I should have been allowed to decide what I wanted to do with my life—with our life. It wasn't his place to make this massive decision without giving me all the facts.

"I know that now," he whispers. "But I was nineteen and thought I knew best." He takes a few steps closer to me, but he shoves his hands in his pockets, forcing himself to keep them off me. "I believed your dad when he told me all I'd do was bring you down in life, that I was holding you back from every-thing you wanted."

"What did I want that I couldn't do with you by my side? You knew me better than anyone else. You knew all my wants and dreams, and they were all right here, in this town, with you."

His eyes bore into mine and I see the tears pull in the corners. "I know, and I second guessed everything," he chokes. He swallows the lump and lets his head fall forward for a moment before lifting his eyes back to mine. The tears are still there, but there's a strength in them that was missing before. "It's not an excuse. I know every decision I made back then was the wrong one. I didn't believe in us the way I should have. I didn't trust my own heart or mind when I should have."

"It's not just that you didn't trust yourself, it's that you decided what was best for us without any input from me. No matter what, it's never okay to do someone's thinking for them."

"I know." It's said so softly I almost miss it.

We stand there staring at each other, both of us lost in our own thoughts.

I wish I can say I'm not angry about it, that I understand it, but I can't. Rationally, I can recognize that at nineteen he was still a kid, learning who he was and how he fit into the world, but emotionally? My heart can't move on from that fact that he'd known me for thirteen years, he'd seen me through every stage of my life and never once did I have big dreams that would take me away from him or this town.

How could he believe anything my father spouted?

But then again, Jude was always insecure around others.

The only people Jude ever found real peace with could be counted on one hand. He was a master of blending in with the crowd, of making himself small and invisible. Though he was never truly the bad boy people whispered about, he believed he was, and that belief became so deeply rooted in him it destroyed everything.

"Is he why you've never come back?" I know the threat of losing his father is what brought him back to town, but it would've been entirely possible for him to fly under the radar while he's here. He didn't have to take care of the bar, or move into the apartment across the hall. He could've hid out at his dad's house on the outskirts of town and visited Walt at the hospital with nobody being the wiser.

"Yes and no. His threat kept me away at first, but..." His words trail off and I can see the question to share more in his eyes.

"Jude, you can't hold back from me. I don't know how we heal from this if you do."

"I know." He swallows, shaking his head. "It's not that I don't want to tell you, I just hate hurting you."

"I'm not saying this to be mean, but you can't hurt me any more than you already have. And I think, at this point, it'll hurt me more if you keep something from me."

He nods his head, his eyes moving to the shelves in the corner of my living room. I'm not sure what he's looking for, but his focus stays there for a moment before he finally looks at me again. "I came home for your mom's funeral."

"What?" I step toward him, not letting him finish. "I never saw you."

"I didn't want you to." This time when he reaches for me, he doesn't stop himself from stroking my cheek. It's a quick, light touch—one I don't want to end. "I was just starting to think I made a mistake leaving like I did. But seeing you with your dad, leaning on him..." His hand falls from my face as his words trail off, pain etched across all of his features.

"Who else was I supposed to lean on?" I whisper. It's another comment I know will hurt, even though that's the last thing I want. I may be upset learning the truth, but I still love this man in front of me, and hurting him hurts me.

"Of course, you should've been leaning on him." Jude reaches for my hand, gripping it tight. "Even if things had been different and I'd stayed, I never would've asked you to avoid him. No matter what, Grace loved both of you and was loved by both of you. You two would've needed each other that day regardless of anything else."

"Jude." My voice wobbles, tears forming in my eyes.

"I ended up back in Minnesota after the funeral," he practically blurts, continuing as if I hadn't said anything. "I needed the feeling of home, and Willie and Mae were the closest thing outside of you and my dad. They didn't know the whole story, but they knew enough." A wry laugh escapes his lips. "They almost convinced me to come back, but it'd been over two years and I didn't believe you could ever forgive me, even if I told you the truth."

"So you stayed away." I don't need to ask; I already know the answer. I've lived it for the last seventeen years.

"I might've started realizing the truth of everything, and I know you won't agree with me, but I wasn't good for you." I open my mouth to interrupt, but he doesn't let me. "I wasn't good for anyone, and I needed to figure out my own shit— forgive myself—before I could ask anyone else to stand by my side."

"But you're only here now because of your dad. If he didn't have a heart attack, you'd still be in Harborview."

The grip on my hand tightens for a moment before he speaks. "I don't know if I ever would've come back in any other circumstance."

I tear my hand from his, turning away. I'm not shocked by the answer, but I still hate it.

"Abbey," Jude says gently. I hear him move closer, his heat hitting my back as he rests his forehead against the back of my head. "I know I had a really shitty reaction earlier outside your apartment, but I always expected and wanted you to move on. I never wanted you to be alone, but I couldn't watch you move on with someone else. I couldn't stand the idea of watching you build the life we always planned without me."

"I never moved on from you," I whisper. Somehow it's easier to admit that without looking at him, but something makes me turn around. "I may have tried, but it never worked. You're a part of me, and I don't think I ever really wanted it any other way."

"When I got back and saw you sitting in that hospital room, all I could think about was how much time I'd wasted. I knew the moment I saw you that the only way I was leaving again was if you told me to."

We're already close, but I step even further into his space, only inches separate us now. "And if I told you I never wanted to go another day without seeing you?"

"I'd be outside your door every morning to make sure you'd never have to." He doesn't touch me, but I can tell he wants to.

"This doesn't magically fix everything between us." I reach for his left hand, running my index finger and thumb against his ring finger where I know that little A sits.

"I know," he murmurs, his eyes searching mine.

I let my fingers travel up his arm, trailing behind his neck to pull his head down to mine. "But I don't want to talk anymore tonight," I whisper, right before my lips meet his.

There's still a lot for us to talk about and figure out, but I've never stopped loving Jude Murphy, and clearly he never stopped loving me.

Right now, that's enough.

—

February 28, 2025

Do you know how much I love you?

I don't know how you possibly could, but I hope with everything I am, you know how much I love you.

I hate that for the last sixteen years, I've had to call you my ex-wife, but I think I might've finally learned that lesson I wrote about so long ago.

I don't know who you are anymore. My actions cost me that privilege, and while I regret them because they hurt you, I can't help but wonder if we might be better people because of them.

I have to believe you're still the strong,

amazing, beautiful soul I met almost thirty years ago. I know I hurt you, but I hope I didn't change you at your core.

I wish I could say I got to watch you grow through all the hardships I know you've faced, but I also know you came out stronger because of them.

Today might mark sixteen years since our marriage was dissolved in the eyes of the law, but in my heart, I've been married to you since the day we met when I was six. I didn't know it then, but you have always been the one for me.

I thought about coming home so many times over the last sixteen years, but the day our marriage ended was the hardest one to deny myself. I had to fly halfway around the world just to make sure I wouldn't show up at your door, begging you to forgive me.

It was the first birthday I missed since we met, and I gave you the worst possible birthday gift. Or maybe, in your eyes, it was the best possible gift I could've given you.

Part of me still thinks if I could take it all back and do it again, I would, but who would we be? Would we still have grown the same way we did over the last sixteen years?

The one thing I know for sure is how much I love you, Abbey. That has always stayed the same and never wavered.

You are the love of my life, and you always will be.

CHAPTER
Twenty-Five

JUDE

THE MOMENT her lips touch mine I finally give in to the urge to touch her. My arms wrap around her, pulling her close. I've craved the feel of her body pressed against mine since I lost it a week ago.

I've craved the feel of her since I left seventeen years ago, but I didn't realize how much until I had her back in my arms.

Abbey already said it, things aren't perfect between us. We aren't picking up where we left off seventeen years ago, but we are moving forward—and I wouldn't trade that for anything. Not even the time we've lost.

"Mo ghrá," I groan against her lips.

Part of me thinks I should be embarrassed by how quickly my body reacts to Abbey's nearness, but I'm not, especially when she presses her body closer to mine. She's just as needy for me as I am for her.

I let my hands trail from her back down over her ass to her thighs where I get enough leverage to lift her. Abbey doesn't hesitate to wrap her legs around me, pressing her core against my aching cock.

"Jude," she moans as she grinds her hips against me.

"I don't want to rush this," I breathe against her cheek. "I want to take my time. I want to cherish you."

She pulls her face away from mine, just enough to look me in the eyes. "Cherish me later."

My lips crash back onto hers, that desperation from last week is back as if it never left, and maybe it didn't. Maybe it's been just under the surface since she rushed out of my apartment.

I'm still going to cherish her—there's no way I can't—but I'll give her a taste of what she wants.

I carry her to the bedroom, never letting my lips leave hers. Not until I feel the foot of her bed press against the front of my legs.

With her legs wrapped tight around me, I bend, bracing one hand on the bed and the other on her back as I lower her. She releases her legs from around me, but grips my shirt so tight I think she might rip it, and the heat in her eyes as she looks at me does something to my soul.

"I don't know how I survived without you all these years," I whisper in the quiet of her room.

I know I got this sight last week, but it wasn't enough. I love the look of her sprawled across her bed, peering up at me with lust in her eyes.

"Let's not worry about that right now." Her hand cups my cheek as her eyes bounce between mine. "I know we still have a lot to figure out, but we have time, and that's all that matters now."

I let my eyes wander her face, studying every inch, trying to find some part of her that doesn't believe what she's saying, but I can't. She's in this for the long haul and a weight is lifted from my shoulders at that realization.

My head falls to her chest in disbelief. I can't believe I'm this lucky to get a second chance with her.

"Babe," she whispers as her fingers thread through my hair

at the nape of my neck, and when I lift my eyes to meet hers again, I know she sees the tears I'm trying desperately to hold at bay.

"I'm going to do everything in my power to make it up to you."

I don't let her respond before my lips are back on hers in a bruising kiss. I'm going to focus on this moment like Abbey asked, and worry about the rest later, but there's no way I don't at least start proving how much I've missed her now.

Abbey's hands slip down my back, pulling at my shirt. "I need to feel you," she moans.

I give her what she wants, pulling away enough to pull my shirt off, but then my lips are back on her skin, this time trailing a path down her neck and to the swell of her breast peeking out from the top of her tank top.

"Don't tease." She squirms beneath me, wanting more than the feather light touches I'm giving her.

"Hmm," I hum, my hands lightly trailing across the bare skin above her shorts where her shirt has risen. "I'm not teasing, I'm savoring."

"Savor later," she pleads, and I can't help but chuckle.

"Patience, love." I lift my head, meeting her eye for eye as I slide a hand down her thigh, caressing the exposed skin before sliding up, pulling the hem of her loose shorts with me. "You know I'll take care of you."

"Jude," she groans, her hips jerking when my fingers slide under her shorts and graze over the wet spot growing on her panties.

I keep my eyes on Abbey's face as I pull her panties to the side, letting my knuckle brush against her soaked clit. Her eyes flutter closed as her back arches and her hips roll, her body searching for more friction. I don't make her wait. My fingers find her clit and give her the pressure she wants.

"I need more," she breathes out, her eyes landing on mine.

"I need you inside me." She reaches between us, fumbling with the button of my jeans.

"Not yet." I shift my hips out of her reach, but give her a touch of what she's looking for as I slide two fingers into her dripping pussy. "God, you're soaked."

"Yes," she moans, her hips grinding down on my hand as I swipe my thumb across her clit.

God, how I've missed this. Being this close to her, knowing her better than I know myself, bringing her this kind of pleasure. I don't care that she's been with other people, not when I can make her feel like this. Not when I know I make her feel seen and cared for.

"Jude." She bites her lip, her eyes trained on mine and I know she's about to come.

"That's right, fuck yourself on my hand." I want to kiss her, to leave a mark on her skin, but I don't want to stop watching her as she gives into her desires, her hips moving in rhythm with my touch.

"I'm close. Don't stop," she pleads.

"Do it, love. Let go."

Her eyes fall closed as her body goes tight, her walls clenching around my fingers and I finally cave, bringing my lips back to her neck as she rides out the waves of her orgasm. I should give her another minute or two, but I need her just as much as she needed me only moments ago. I need to feel her skin against mine.

"Mo ghrá," I whisper against her neck as I slide my hand up her sides, pushing her top up and sucking a nipple into my mouth the moment it's exposed to the air around us.

"How—how in the world..." She doesn't finish her thought before another moan leaves her lips. "Jude, please." Her thighs hug my waist and her hips shift, pressing her core against me as her hand reaches for my jeans once again. And this time I let her have her way.

I groan as I rise to my knees, looking down at her. She's the picture of desire. Her shorts and panties still pulled to the side, exposing her beautiful pussy, her tank pushed up above her breasts, and her hair a mess as it falls from the messy knot that used to be on top of her head.

"What a gorgeous picture you make." I ghost my fingers up her exposed legs, feeling the goose bumps pop along her skin. "I'll never get tired of seeing you like this," I murmur in the quiet of the room, reaching the band of her shorts and tugging them down her legs with her panties.

Abbey doesn't let me take my time, and I don't fight her. If I'm not inside her soon, I'm going to embarrass myself—I'm about to explode. She pulls her legs back and pushes to sit so she can remove her own top, before her hands are back at the button on my jeans.

"Jude, if you aren't inside me in the next minute, I'm going to take matters into my own hands." As if to prove her point, she slips her hand in the top of my boxers and slides her silky fingers across my steel cock, toying with the bead of liquid at the tip.

"Abbey," I hiss, my hips jerking at her touch. I put one hand to her chest and gently push her back, forcing her to lie down. "If you keep touching me, this is going to be over way too soon."

"I don't really care, as long as you're inside me when it does." She reaches for me, her arms sliding around my neck before she pulls my lips to hers.

I get so lost in the feel of her lips on mine and her bare chest pressed against mine, I don't notice her hands aren't around my neck anymore until I feel her push my pants and boxers down just enough that my cock pops free.

"Abbey," I moan.

"Jude," she returns, brushing the head of my cock against her clit.

I drop my head to her shoulder, basking in the feel of being this close to her—of feeling her everywhere around me. I force myself away from her, only long enough to shed my pants and boxers.

As I crawl over Abbey on the bed, I let my hands travel up the outside of her legs, over her hips, and up her sides, ghosting my fingers over her pebbled nipples before trailing down her arms, taking her wrists in both of mine and moving them over her head.

"I don't think I can trust you to keep these to yourself." I thread my fingers through hers and grind my hips into her, my cock sliding over her soaked center, causing both of us to moan and shiver.

"I promise to behave if you stop teasing me."

"How many times do I have to tell you it's not teasing?" I cross her wrists over each other and grip them in one hand, letting my other trail down the side of her body in a feather light touch. "Okay, maybe I'm teasing a little bit," I breathe in her ear, nibbling at her earlobe.

"Jude," she whines. "Please."

"Okay." I line myself up at her entrance. "I'll stop teasing." My lips land on hers and I press forward, entering her in one hard thrust, giving her exactly what she wants. My breathing stops at the feel of her wrapped around me. How have I survived without her? Without this?

I study every facet of her face as I pull back slowly, wanting to drag out every second of this bliss between us. Part of me wants to drive into her, give it to her hard like she's begging for, but I need the slow connection more than anything else right now. And I know that no matter what she says, she likes it slow too.

"Yesss," she moans against my lips, dragging the word out. Her wrists strain against my hold and her body arches against me, her hips meeting mine as I sink into her.

I thought the feeling of our bodies pressed together was like coming home, but it's this feeling here—the feeling of our bodies joining together and becoming one that feels like coming home. It's the feeling of knowing nothing else—and no one else—has ever felt like this before.

"You feel so good. Like nothing else I've ever experienced before." I tell her, my eyes boring into hers as I pull back and slowly thrust back in. It's entirely possible she'll have bruises on her hip from the grip I have.

"Let me touch you," she begs. "I need to touch you."

I release my hold on her wrists and her hands immediately move to my back, her nails digging in as I move my hand from her hip and press my thumb to her clit. I keep my rhythm slow, trying to draw the pleasure out as long as I can, but Abbey has other plans.

She pushes at me and I give her what she wants, rolling us so she straddles my waist, her hands pressed against my pecs.

"Thank you." Her eyes are trained on mine as she rolls her hips against me. My thumb lands back on her clit, needing her to come. The feel of her around me, the sight of her pierced nipples and her lust filled eyes—even going slow I'm going to come faster than I want.

"Come for me, mo ghrá."

She shakes her head but moves faster, and at the feel of her thigh twitching, I know she's close.

"Yes, let it go."

"Jude," she moans, her head falling back as her hips move faster over me.

I surge forward, wrapping my arms around her and press our bodies together. Our lips meet and our tongues dance. The connection between us is more than it's ever been before.

And just like that, both of us go over the edge, my balls drawing tight as I release everything I am into Abbey.

CHAPTER
Twenty-Six

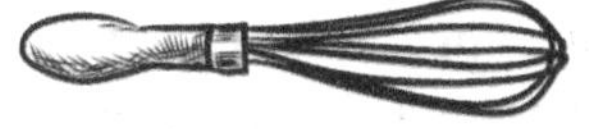

ABBEY

I CLING to Jude like he's my life raft, keeping me afloat as I drift at sea.

My arms are wrapped around his shoulders, my legs around his waist, and I can't stop myself from rolling my hips against him one more time, feeling his cock jerk inside me.

"Abbey," he moans, his lips pressed against mine.

"I can't move," I whisper, pulling away slightly. "I don't want to move." I dig my nails into the skin at his back and I can't tell if it's voluntary or not.

I'm desperate for him.

The contrast of his rough palms running down my back and his smooth chest pressed to mine makes me shiver. I don't care that we're sweaty, I want to stay exactly as we are right now.

Jude grips my hips and shifts just enough for his half-hard cock to slip free, but the feel of something wet sliding down my thigh makes me freeze. I know the second Jude realizes the same thing when his back goes taut.

We're both quiet. There used to be a time I could tell

exactly what Jude was thinking, but in this moment I can't. And I don't think I hate anything more.

"Abbey," he whispers. "I'm sorry. I didn't think. I was to—"

"No, it's not just on you," I interrupt, my eyes staying focused on his. "I'm—I'm on birth control, but I haven't been tested since I last…" I don't need to finish the sentence; Jude knows exactly how that thought would end. "I've never had sex without a condom," I rush to say. I hate it's even something I need to say.

I see his Adam's apple bob as one of his hands at my hip flexes, and I hate the pain I'm causing him right now.

"I haven't been tested recently, but I've also never been with anyone else, so I assume I'm clean." There's no malice in his words, but I still feel a tug in my chest.

The quiet returns, and I have something else to hate now… I hate how we went from riding this high of being together again to this low of hurting each other.

"Jude, I'm sor—" I try to move out of his hold, but his grip around me tightens.

"No. Don't apologize." He cups my cheek in one hand, smoothing his thumb over my lips, stopping my words. "You have nothing to apologize for."

"Jude—"

"No, Abbey." Like always when his hands frame my face, I melt into his touch. "If we let ourselves, we'll spend the rest of our lives apologizing to each other for everything that's happened over the last seventeen years. If we're really going to move on, we have to forgive each other." He pauses, his eyes tracing over my face. "And ourselves."

My eyes fall closed as a tear slips from the corner of my right eye, but he wipes it away with his thumb almost as soon as it appears.

Jude's right.

That doesn't mean we stop talking about everything that's

happened over the last decade and a half, but if we're truly moving forward together, then it does mean we can't hold our pasts against each other. And I desperately want to move forward with Jude. I can't go back to him not being part of my life, not when I've gotten used to him being here again.

I bury my face in the crook of his neck, breathing in his musky scent. "Okay," I murmur against him. "No more apologizing."

He holds me close and shifts his head, pressing a kiss where my shoulder and neck meet. "No matter what, we're going to be okay."

Choking back the tears, I simply nod my head, wanting him to know I hear and agree with him, because I do. We've both grown a lot over the last seventeen years. We're older and wiser. We won't make the same mistakes we made before.

I hate that we spent so much time away from each other, but I can't help thinking that Jude is right. We're better people for having spent time away from each other. We appreciate what's between us even more because of the time apart.

THEY SAY HINDSIGHT IS TWENTY-TWENTY, and I agree, because this sight right here? The one of Jude sleeping peacefully in front of me? I took that sight for granted, and I hope I never do again.

I'd like to think that most people don't go into their marriage expecting it to end, so maybe everyone takes it for granted—waking up next to the person they love—but even after only having it for a little over two months, I got used to waking up to Jude by my side.

It took far longer for me to get used to him not being there than him being there, and I fear after only one night...I'm already desperate to make sure it happens again and again.

I let my gaze travel his face, and even with the fine lines starting to make an appearance at the corners of his eyes and across his forehead, I still think he's a beautiful man.

If I'm being honest, I've spent a decent amount of time over the last seven weeks watching Jude. Something about him calls to me, and I can't stop my eyes from finding him whenever he's near. A lot of things have changed, but one thing that hasn't changed is how he holds himself in a crowd. He may have that confidence he lacked when he was a teenager, but he still holds himself back from everyone around him.

There's a rigidness to his posture and a cloud over his eyes, never really letting you see the real man behind all of it. But when he's sleeping? All of that slips away. There's a peace around him that I can't find when he's around other people.

Thirty-five years in this world, and Jude is still the man I compare everyone else to. He's still the one I want more than anyone else.

The sheet's fallen to his hips, exposing his back to me, and just like I was last night when I saw it for the first time, I'm surprised by the amount of open space he has. I want so desperately to trace a finger over the blank canvas, but I'm not quite ready for him to wake up. I need a bit more time to think without his presence surrounding me.

I have to physically remove myself from the temptation before I let my desire take over. I slip from the bed as quietly as I can, grabbing the first thing I can cover up with—Jude's T-shirt—before slipping out the door of my bedroom.

A responsible adult would've had a conversation about safe sex *before* the sex actually happened, but a woman desperately in love with the man before her? No one can claim she's smart in that situation.

The logical part of my brain can't quite grasp how we didn't have that conversation, especially when we'd just established I haven't been celibate for the last seventeen years—unlike Jude.

I don't even know how I feel about the fact that Jude hasn't been with someone else. I may have realized the likelihood of Jude cheating on me back then was slim, and I may have hoped our story wasn't over, but I never thought Jude would choose to be alone for the rest of his life. No matter what happened between us, I never wanted Jude to be alone.

The idea that Jude regretted how everything happened between us, knew he never planned on returning home, and still chose never to sleep with someone else makes me a little nervous. I know I love him. I know I never stopped loving him —even when I thought he betrayed me in one of the worst ways. But I don't know if I ever thought it was possible to love someone so much you'd never move on from them, even if you thought they'd never be part of your life again.

That's a whole level of dedication that never crossed my mind, and it's a lot of pressure to live up to.

I move into the kitchen and begin the process of brewing a pot of coffee. I know I'm a coffee snob, and on any other morning I'd take the time to grind some beans for the freshest taste, but grinding beans means making noise that I don't know if Jude will sleep through. Seventeen years ago I knew he'd sleep through a bulldozer hitting the side of the building, but now? Maybe his sleeping habits have changed—I know mine have.

While the coffee brews, I pull the fridge open looking to see what I can make with the ingredients I have. I don't have much, considering I've been out of the apartment for almost a week. But making something from practically nothing in the kitchen is one of my favorite things to do. The idea that you can take a whole bunch of random things to make something beautiful and enjoyable does something good for my soul.

Being in the kitchen has always been my greatest outlet.

It's the place I think the most clearly, and right now I really need to figure out what in the world I'm thinking. I pull out the ingredients for some omelets and let my mind wander as I move on autopilot.

Can I forgive Jude for everything that happened in our past?

I know I agreed with him last night about truly moving forward with our lives, but in the bright light of day...*can I?*

Part of me gets it. In the eyes of the law we were adults, but the reality is something else entirely. We were eighteen and nineteen years old. Maybe we thought we were adults—and acted like it—but we weren't. It's not hard to see how someone threatening the people Jude loves most in the world would scare him and make him do whatever they wanted.

I can even understand why he wouldn't tell me about any of it for fear of repercussions.

There'd been so many changes in such a small amount of time. I graduated high school, we got married and moved in together, and shortly after that we found out that my mom had been diagnosed with ALS.

Dad knew exactly what he was doing when he threatened Jude.

Looking back on who we were at the time, I understand it. But I can't help wondering how it all could've been different if he'd simply told someone. Not telling me, I can accept—I wasn't in the right headspace after learning about Mom's diagnosis and I know I wouldn't have reacted well—but not talking to his dad? That's more of a struggle for me.

Anyone who knows Walt, even the smallest amount, knows he would've given up Murphy's in a heartbeat if it meant his son was happy. But I also know Walt wouldn't have given up without a fight.

We've all lost so much time and nothing we do can ever get

that back. Of course, who would we all be if Jude never left? What kind of life would we have?

There's no guarantee Jude and I would've stayed together the last seventeen years. We could've ended up divorced no matter what. And say we divorced ten years ago, five years ago, would there have ever been a chance we'd find our way back to each other?

We may have lost seventeen years together, but there's a chance we have the rest of our lives to make up for it.

We are who we are because of our time apart. And even if I've been lonely more often than not in the last seventeen years, the last seven months have been pretty amazing. The friendships I've made and the steps I've taken to make my dream of owning a bookstore a reality are things I might've missed out on if even one moment in my past changed.

What good did playing *what if* ever accomplish?

"Something smells good in here." Jude's sleep filled voice hits my ear at the same time his arms wrap around my waist, making me jump in surprise. "Sorry. I didn't mean to startle you," he murmurs against my neck where his lips rest.

The comfort that washes over me is instant, and I can't deny how right it feels—being in his arms, having him in my space, waking up next to him.

"Not your fault," I whisper, resting my hand over his where it sits on my stomach. "I tend to get lost when I'm in the kitchen, nothing else exists around me."

"Now, that I remember." Even if I didn't feel the smile against my skin, I hear it clear as day in his voice, and a bit more of that fear disappears.

Neither one of us are shying away from our past, and that feels like a good foundation for our future.

CHAPTER
Twenty-Seven

JUDE

"WHAT ARE YOU UP TO TODAY?" I lean back in my seat next to Abbey at the table, my eyes focused on her.

I haven't been able to take my eyes off her since I walked out of her room this morning. There was a moment of pure panic when I woke up and she wasn't in the bed next to me. I thought I imagined everything that happened last night—the intimacy we shared, the trust I thought we'd been rebuilding—but then the smell of something amazing wafted through the door, and I knew it wasn't a dream.

I slipped from the bed and pulled on my boxers before opening her bedroom door. The sight of her in the kitchen made me pause. She was in profile, her hair thrown up in a knot on top of her head and her bare legs peeked out from the hem of my black T-shirt where it fell to her mid-thigh.

There was something about Abbey in my clothes that made me feral for her, and I hoped that feeling was something I never got used to.

Abbey's always been a fan of cooking and baking, so seeing her in the kitchen at any point during the day wasn't out of the norm when we were together, but it was a sight I thought I'd never see again.

I leaned against the doorjamb, simply watching her as she moved about the space. There was a grace to her movements, almost like a choreographed dance designed to draw the audience in, and I didn't want to disrupt her, but the need I had to touch her was something I couldn't ignore.

The way she immediately melted into me when my arms wrapped around her had that last remaining bit of panic disappear entirely. I know we still had more to work through, but I truly believed we could do it.

"I need to stop by the store. I haven't been all week, and I know George will be there today. And I need to go to the grocery store. I was barely able to pull this together with everything I had in the fridge." She chuckles as she places her napkin on the table next to her plate and brings her eyes to mine. "I was thinking about going to visit your dad too. I haven't been to see him in a while."

I contemplate keeping the next words to myself, not wanting to come off as needy, but I quickly decide that I don't care if she thinks I'm needy. When it comes to Abbey, I'm absolutely desperate to spend time with her. "Mind if I tag along?"

Her eyes fall to the table but the smile that splits her lips is still visible, and I can't help but smile in return. "You want to come along on my errands day?" She lifts her eyes back to mine and leans her elbow on the table, bringing herself closer to me.

"Abbey, I want to spend all my time with you," I tell her honestly.

I don't want to smother her, but I've gone way too long without her in my life, and now that there's a chance we might be able to find our way back to each other? I don't want to miss a single opportunity to be with her.

"Okay," she says softly.

Her eyes bounce around my face, studying me for a few moments before she lifts her hand to cup my cheek, her thumb stroking back and forth across my beard before she leans in to press a kiss to my lips.

I know it's supposed to be a quick peck before we start our day, but the moment her lips touch mine I need her. Wrapping an arm around her waist I lift her into my lap, her legs straddling mine. She releases a gasp of shock at the sudden move and I take full advantage, slipping my tongue between her lips.

The moan she releases has me shifting my hips, my hardening cock pressing into her core, desperate to feel her again.

My reaction to her closeness is instant. There's nothing but tenderness in her look and touch, and yet my body is ready for so much more with her. Not just my body, my mind and heart too.

"Jude." She breathes against my lips, her arms snaking around my shoulders and holding me tight against her.

Thank God I'm not alone in this.

"What is it, love?" I ghost my lips across her cheek, searching for the spot below her ear that I know makes her melt.

"I need you," she gasps as I suck on her neck, her body sinking into mine.

"You have me. You always have," I whisper against her.

Her hand slips from my shoulders and reaches between us, pushing my boxers down to release my aching cock. Our eyes meet as she takes me in hand and rubs my leaking tip against her already soaked pussy.

"Where are your panties?" I hiss at the feel of her bare against me.

"Wherever you left them last night." Her head rolls back as her hips continue to grind against me.

I force her eyes back to mine and lift my hips to meet hers.

"You're telling me you've been prancing around here all morning without any panties on? Been sitting next to me all morning without any panties on?"

"Yesss," she moans, drawing out the word. She releases me from her grip, bringing herself closer to me with my cock sandwiched between us. Every shift of her hips has her clit sliding along the length of me.

"Abbey," I plead. I want nothing more than for her to sink onto me, but I know it's not smart, especially after last night. I've made so many bad decisions when it comes to Abbey, and I don't want her to regret anything that happens between us moving forward.

This is the last chance we have, and I'll do everything in my power to make sure it lasts.

I can't lose Abbey.

I won't survive it—not again.

"Do you have a condom?" Her voice is breathy and I know she's close.

I shake my head. "Something we'll have to pick up on your errands," I say, palming her ass in my hands.

Her head falls against my shoulder and I know she's disappointed, but that won't stop me from making her feel good, and it doesn't stop her hips from moving against me.

"That's it, love. Use me to make yourself come," I grit from between my teeth. I'm so close to losing it, but I refuse to go before she does.

"Jude," she pants, her head buried in my shoulder and her grip around me tightening.

She lifts her head and meets my eyes for only a second before her head falls back. Her movements become more frantic, and I know the moment she flies over the edge when her entire body goes taut. I'm not far behind. I wrap my arms around her and pull her close for a demanding kiss, my cock pulsing between us, making a mess against my stomach and my shirt.

The kiss turns leisurely, but neither of us release each other, needing the closeness we both feel.

"Condoms are a definite must on our errands today." Abbey pulls away, a smile tugging at her lips. "At least until I can get in to see a doctor." She shifts against me, and I grunt as my still half-hard cock twitches.

"Mo ghrá," I warn.

She laughs, pressing one more quick kiss to my lips before she lifts herself from my lap and saunters away toward her bedroom. She pauses halfway there and glances over her shoulder. "You gonna stay there or join me in the shower?" Abbey doesn't wait for my response before she's pulling my shirt over her head and tossing it away as she continues to her room.

I'm not even upset when I find myself following her like a lost little puppy.

The truth is, I am lost without her.

"HEY, WALT," Abbey whispers as she leans down to press a kiss to his cheek. She brushes a lock of hair from his forehead before looking at the nurse on the other side of his bed. "How's he doing today?"

"He's doing good." Sarah, one of Dad's nurses smiles at Abbey before her eyes shift to me in the doorway, shock filling her features. I know it's not a surprise that I'm here to visit Dad—I'm here almost every day. It's shock that Abbey and I arrived together.

Things between Abbey and I may be improving since I returned to Ashford Falls, but this is the one space I haven't invaded with Abbey—I never wanted her to feel like she couldn't visit Dad—and anyone who saw us interact the few times our visits overlapped could feel the tension between us.

Sarah visibly shakes herself from her shock and looks back down at my dad. "It's going to feel so strange when he transfers. Do you have a date for that yet?"

"Not yet, but it should be soon. Dr. Winters said after eight weeks if there's no change, he'd be better served in a long-term facility."

Sarah's gaze shifts back to me and offers a small smile. "Speaking of, Dr. Winters rounds just started. She should be in soon to give you an update."

"Thanks, Sarah." Abbey smiles as she takes a seat in one of the vacant chairs next to my father's bed.

"Of course. Someone will be at the desk if you need anything."

I step further into the room, giving Sarah space to step past me. She smiles once more before sliding the door closed behind her.

"You gonna stand over there the whole time, or are you gonna come sit down?" Abbey glances over her shoulder, a teasing glint in her eye. She's been in a good mood all morning, and I can't help but smile knowing I'm partly the cause.

After our steamy shower—for more than one reason—I rushed over to my apartment to change and grab my computer before meeting Abbey back in the hallway. Maybe one day I won't be stunned every time she walks into a room, but today isn't that day. With her hair still damp from our shower hanging over one shoulder and her focus entirely on making sure she had everything she needed in her purse, I couldn't take my eyes off of her.

She stepped out of her apartment in what's probably one of the simplest summer dresses I've seen. It's long with short, flowy sleeves, a neckline that dips just enough to tease at her cleavage, and a slit that goes all the way up her leg but was only noticeable as she stepped toward me. Even though I'd been with her four times in the last twelve hours, I couldn't stop myself from pulling her into me. And the fact she moved into me the second my hand touched her hip made me the happiest man around.

"I have to run my errands. If you're going to continue to distract me I'm going to take back my permission for you to join me," she whispered against my lips, a smile forming with the words.

"I'll be good, I promise." I pressed one more kiss to her lips before taking her hand in mine and leading her down the stairs.

While she stepped into the bookstore to check on things with George, I went into the bar to make sure everything was closed up properly. I'd been surprised to find Jane behind the bar, but it was evidence I made the right decision in hiring her to manage the bar in my absence. Hopefully Dad will agree once he's recovered and working behind the bar again.

"You're in early."

"Not really." Her brows pinched when she glanced at me but quickly focused back on the open drawer in front of her. *"You gave me the night off and I know you weren't here last night, so I wanted to make sure we were in good shape before we open in a bit."*

I glanced down at my watch and saw she wasn't wrong—just after ten thirty. *"Well, clearly I've left the bar in good hands."* I chuckled, realizing I'd been coming in to do the same thing.

Jane didn't acknowledge me before she closed the drawer and moved on to her next task. It didn't bother me; her straightforwardness is one of the reasons I hired her. Without waiting for a response I knew wouldn't be coming, I tapped the bar twice before turning to leave the way I came. *"Call me if you need me,"* I called over my shoulder and returned to Abbey.

I stood near the door to the bookstore and watched Abbey

move around the space talking with George about the remaining items on her list. They'd made a lot of progress in the two weeks they've been working at the bookstore and were estimating they'd be done in another two weeks max.

It was officially time for Abbey to start planning for her grand re-opening and I knew how excited she was the second she turned her beaming smile to me when she heard the news.

"Babe." Abbey's voice brings me back to the present, and I don't waste another second standing on the other side of the room.

"Yeah, love. I'm with you." I cup her cheek and lean down to press a kiss to her forehead, lingering there before I finally take my seat next to her.

There's nowhere else I'd rather be.

CHAPTER
Twenty-Eight

JUDE

I SHOULDN'T BE SURPRISED that the words are suddenly flowing for me. My writing has always been connected to my mood, and I've never been able to write when my mind was more focused on Abbey than anything else going on in my life.

Everything I wrote around our birthdays or wedding anniversary was always trashed when I finally came out of my emotions enough to truly pay attention to what I was writing.

There was only one time I kept what I wrote on Abbey's birthday—and according to her, it was the worst thing I've ever written. Not that she knows they're my words yet.

Four days surrounded by all that's Abbey Selbey and I haven't figured out how to tell her my biggest secret. I've told her so much about our time apart, but for some reason I can't bring myself to tell her about that.

She knows I lived a truly nomadic life, never staying anywhere long enough to make a true connection. I told her all about the Hawthornes—the family from Stonebridge Hollow that gave me my first job when I left Ashford Falls—and how they're some of the few people I stay in contact with. She knows all about Willie and Mae and how they're the ones who truly saved me after that first year on the road. She knows about the most memorable places I stayed and why I wouldn't let myself fall in love with any of them.

She even knows about the journals I've kept and how it was writing in them that made me come to terms with where my life took me. She knows everything there is to know about the last seventeen years, except that.

And yet...even with the weight of needing to tell her the truth, I can't stop the words from pouring from my fingertips.

There might be guilt for holding this last secret so close, but the joy of going to sleep next to her every night and waking up next to her every morning far surpasses any other negative emotion.

I'm not the only one who's shared about their life over the last decade and a half.

I've hated almost everything Abbey's told me—the fact that she closed herself off so completely from everyone around her breaks my heart. Knowing I'm the one who caused it tore me in two. But seeing who she's become and how strong she is makes me so damn proud.

I've been in love with Abbey since I was six years old, and there wasn't a moment in time where I thought that love disappeared. But getting this second chance with her? I want to shout it from the rooftops how in love with her I still am.

I'm so focused on the screen in front of me, I don't hear anything going on around me. I know Jane and Cole, the newest bartender I hired, are behind the bar serving the few patrons that came in for lunch today, but I haven't been paying the slightest bit of attention to them.

I hear Cole shout to someone but I don't let my eyes wander from the screen. It's not until hands cover my eyes that I'm forced to pull away from my computer.

"Guess who?" Abbey whispers, trying to disguise her voice with a terrible Irish accent, but her scent gives her away. Lemon and lavender surround me, and I immediately melt into her.

"Sorry to disappoint, love, but I'll always know it's you." Her hands fall from my face but slip around my neck as I spin in my stool, pulling her between my spread thighs. "How's your morning been?"

"Good. George and the team are ahead of schedule. They're confident they'll be done by next week." The smile that breaks out on her face is so contagious, I can't help but smile in return.

My grip on her hips tightens slightly as I press a quick kiss to her lips. "That's amazing, mo ghrá."

The shiver that runs down her spine makes me chuckle. I love that she can't help her physical reaction to my nickname for her. It's nothing different than what I call her in English, but something about the Gaelic term does something to her and I hope that never changes.

She presses herself further into me, her lips landing on mine in a demanding kiss. It's Cole's whistle that tears us apart.

"All right, you two, that's enough of that. Some of us have yet to find our person." Cole smiles at us, making it clear he's only joking as he steps up to us from behind the bar. "Can I get you anything, Abbey?"

"No, I just came from The Diner with Emily."

"Do they have a new menu or something? Maybe that's where everyone is?"

Cole's only lived in town for a few weeks now and is still learning all the ins and outs of small town living, but the fact that even he's noticed the change in customers around here makes me a little nervous.

I've been trying to be optimistic about the lack of people

coming through the doors, but it's getting harder and harder to ignore.

The people of Ashford Falls have changed a lot since I've been gone. People who never would have stepped foot in these walls before I left are now regulars, but it's also true that they've stopped coming around recently. And the only thing that's changed around here is me.

Abbey's brows pinch as she glances around, noticing how empty it is for the first time. "Well, it is lunchtime on a Wednesday afternoon and school just started back up two weeks ago." Her eyes come back to mine and I see the worry starting to pour out of them.

"Good point." I reach over and squeeze the back of her thigh. "This could be totally normal for Murphy's at this time of year."

"Maybe," Cole murmurs. "You sure I can't get you anything?"

"No, I'm good. Thanks, Cole." She offers him a smile as he walks away and steps from between my legs, slipping onto the stool next to me. "What are you up to?" Abbey asks, gesturing to my computer.

My next move isn't subtle or cute in the slightest. I slam my laptop shut and offer her the goofiest smile—not intentionally. "Nothing." I'm the least nonchalant I've ever been, and Abbey is far too smart not to call me on it.

"Yeah, okay." She reaches for my computer and I push my hand down on top of it, holding it in place.

The second her eyes meet mine the guilt settles in. It's hurt that fills her eyes and after everything we've been through, I can't blame her. My eyes fall to the floor between us as I lift my hand in surrender.

She slides the laptop in front of her and because I'm a chicken, I spin in my seat to face the bar. I don't watch her reaction head on, but I can see her out of the corner of my eye. I shouldn't be surprised at how quickly she figured it out.

The little gasp she releases a few minutes later confirms she's learned my last secret before the words leave her mouth. "You're AJ Doherty?"

I turn to face her slowly, not entirely sure how she feels about this news.

"Yeah." I release the simple word on a breath, having no idea what else I should say.

"Why didn't you say anything? We've talked about his books..." Her words trail off as she looks at the computer screen once more. "Your books," she whispers.

"The first time I saw you reading *The Silent Promise* was a few days after I got back to town. Talking about that book was the way I got you to talk to me, and I didn't want to lose that."

Her eyes come back to mine and I hate that I see tears welling in the corners. I reach for her but she doesn't let me. She slides from her seat and rushes away.

"Abbey, wait!" I call after her, grabbing my laptop and following her path out the back door and up to our apartments.

Her door is open when I make it up the stairs, and relief courses through me at seeing that. She may be upset, but she wants to talk about it.

"Mo ghrá." I'm not fighting fair using that name, but I'm okay with that. I'll use anything I can to make her listen to me.

I place my computer on the island in her kitchen and walk up to her where she stands facing her bookshelves. Just like the bookstore downstairs used to be—and how I'm sure it'll look again—they're filled to the brim. And right in front of her, at eye level, is the shelf filled with my books.

"Jude." She sighs, spinning on her heel to look at me. Her eyes are still wet, but now I see anger building in their depths. "I understand not telling me at first, but how many chances have you had since then?"

"I know." My eyes fall to the floor for only a moment before I face her again. "I know I should have told you. If not when you were tearing my book apart, then definitely at some point over the last few days."

"Oh god." Her eyes fall shut and she lifts a hand to cover them, as if she needs the extra layer of protection. Like if she's unable to see me, I won't be able to see her. "I can't believe you let me say all those things."

"No, Abs." I grasp her wrist gently, pulling her hand away from her face. "That's why I didn't say anything that day. I always want the truth from you. I never want you to filter your thoughts with me—about anything."

She studies me for a moment, the tears making another appearance. "Exactly."

"Abbey—"

"No, Jude," she interrupts. She pulls her hand from mine, crossing her arms over her chest, but she doesn't step away from me. "That's the point. You've shared so much with me over the last four days, except you've been filtering yourself. It's not like you're some unknown author. You're literally one of the best in your genre."

"I know."

"It might be dramatic, but if you've kept this from me, what's to say there isn't something else you're keeping from me? Or what's to say something doesn't happen in the future that you decide to keep from me?"

"It's not dramatic," I whisper, lifting my eyes to the shelf over her shoulder.

She's right. It's not the biggest thing I've kept from her, but that doesn't really matter when you take our past into consideration. The entire reason I needed this second chance was because I kept something massive from her. If I want this to work, I can't keep anything from her, big or small.

"I'll tell you everything you want to know about this part of my life"—I gesture to the books behind her—"but I think there's something else I need to tell you first."

Abbey's entire body deflates as her arms fall to her sides. "What?" The word is pure dejection, and I hate that her mind has probably gone to the worst possible scenario.

I don't beat around the bush; I tell her the truth—hoping she'll forgive me for keeping yet another secret from her. "Your dad's been in to see me at Murphy's three times since I've been home. Each time he's warned me to stay away from you."

"What?" She gasps in disbelief.

"I'm not saying me being AJ Doherty isn't important—it absolutely is—but you're right that I need to be better about not keeping things to myself. If I want this to work, and you know I do, then I have to do better."

"Jude," she chokes out, the tears back with a vengeance.

Without holding anything back, I pull Abbey over to the couch and tell her everything.

I tell her about the first time he came into the bar after he saw me at the bookstore with her. I tell her about the second time shortly after Ava and Declan's birthday party, after he heard Marybelle talking about how sweet it was that I'd been helping out at the bookstore. And I tell her about the last time he showed up, the same night she came to my apartment after her ladies' night at Emily's.

I fill her in on my belief that it's him causing the decrease in customers at Murphy's—I don't have any proof, but it fits with his initial threat to me seventeen years ago. And finally, I tell her about my concerns with him being an investor in the bookstore.

After the threats he's made—especially the ones that I know would hurt Abbey the most—I don't trust he won't do something to destroy her dreams.

"I'm sorry I didn't tell you the truth sooner, Abbey." I squeeze the hand I've been holding in mine since we sat down, trying to make her meet my eyes. "It shouldn't have taken you pointing out how important it is for me to tell you what's been going on. Especially when this is the reason for everything that happened before."

"Is this all of it?" she asks quietly, her eyes still focused on our hands in my lap.

"Yeah, love. That's all of it."

She doesn't move or say anything at first, just sits there cross-legged on the couch facing me, but without warning she falls forward, burying her head in my chest and wrapping her arms around my shoulders.

"I swear I'll never keep anything from you again. The only secrets I'll keep are the good ones, like surprising you with your favorite meal," I whisper, trying desperately to lighten the mood.

It works partially. I feel the muffled laugh against my neck more than I hear it, but the thing that makes me relax is when she climbs into my lap, making herself more comfortable with her legs wrapped around me where I sit on the couch.

"That sounds like a good plan." She clings to me like a monkey and I love every second of it.

I don't move or say anything else, not wanting to ruin this moment between us. I know I still need to fill her in on the author front, but the fact that she's not demanding I leave after revealing everything with her dad feels far more important.

"Are we okay?" I tighten my arms around her, a little scared of what she'll say.

"Yeah, we're okay." She pulls back just enough to meet my eyes, and even though it's clear she's been crying, I'm still struck dumb by how beautiful she is.

"I don't know how I've gotten lucky enough to have another chance with you, but I swear I've learned from my past—even if this doesn't look like it." I tuck a piece of hair behind her ear, cupping her cheek in my hand. "No more secrets, I promise."

Her lips land on mine, and I know we're going to be okay—we're going to be more than okay.

CHAPTER
Twenty-nine

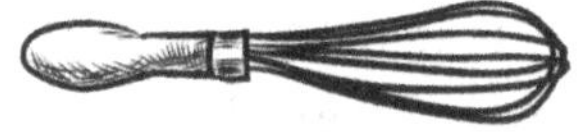

ABBEY

"I'M SORRY. It's been how long?" Ava asks in disbelief. "Why the hell haven't you told me sooner?"

"Yeah, that's the most important part of this?" Quinn rolls her eyes in exasperation.

"You two are like children," Emily murmurs, her eyes focusing on me. "We're gonna need you to go back to two weeks ago and tell us what happened, because last we all talked you weren't sure what really happened when you were a teenager."

My eyes wander to Jude where he stands with the guys by the grill. It's nice to see the small smile on his face as Declan, Gage, and Caleb laugh at something Max must've said. Unsurprisingly, his eyes meet mine a few seconds later.

Ever since he came clean about everything that happened with his author career and my dad, we've been so connected to each other. I felt connected to him the second he walked back into my life a little over two months ago, but this link between us is different. There's a peace now that wasn't there before.

I still find myself staring at him whenever he's around, like

I'm afraid he'll disappear if we're away from each other for too long. But that thought evaporates quicker and quicker every time it shows its ugly head.

"I didn't go home after I left your place that night." I bring my focus back to the ladies in front of me and tell them the truth. "Well, I mean, I did. But instead of going into my apartment I went to Jude's."

"And he told you what happened?" Ava raises a hand to cover her mouth at the look Quinn and Emily throw her way. Not that it stops her from talking through her fingers. "Sorry. I'll hold my questions until the end."

"No, he didn't tell me what happened, but only because I wouldn't let him." I fidget with the bottle in my hand, not loving the light I'm about to paint myself in. "Honestly, I threw myself at him, begging him for sex, and then I ran out just as things were getting good because I realized it was a mistake."

"Oh-kayyy..." Quinn drags the word out, emphasizing each syllable, but there's no judgment in her eyes.

When I look at Ava and Emily, they're both staring back the same way, simply waiting for me to continue. I don't know what else I'm expecting. If there's one thing I've learned about these women, it's that we've all used sex in one way or another. Whether it was to prove we still had power and control in those moments, or because we just needed to feel something, we've all tried to make sex the answer to our problems.

Taking a breath, I give them the rest. "I missed helping out at the bookstore because I ran away to my dad's in an effort to avoid Jude. There was no way he wasn't going to try talking to me when I work and live next door to him. Of course, my dad came home from his business trip and made it very clear his feelings about Jude have not changed." I pause, taking a gulp of air and then my drink, letting my mind settle before I continue.

"I asked him point blank why he hates Jude and he refused

to tell me. All he said was that I'm just like my mother and no matter what I'd always choose Jude over him."

"Wow. Did your mom ever choose Walt over your dad?" Ava asks quietly.

"I have no idea." I throw my hands up in the air, more than exasperated with the entire situation. "I can't think of any time my mother didn't drop everything to be there for my father when he asked, but then again, I know I don't know everything about their relationship. Is it possible?" I shrug. "Of course, it's possible."

"What happened after you talked to your dad?" Emily asks in the silence that follows.

"I went home." My eyes move back to Jude and I feel my shoulders relax. I didn't even realize I'd been holding so much tension in them until I felt them physically deflate, just from laying eyes on the man across the yard.

"You went home and..." Ava probes when I don't continue.

"And Jude showed up at my door. He refused to walk away until I agreed to talk to him."

"So you opened the door, and he confessed his love for you and told you it was all a lie!" Ava rushes to say, interrupting me yet again.

I chuckle softly, shaking my head at her antics, and the glint in her eye tells me that was exactly what she was aiming for.

"I opened the door, and just as we started talking Chuck showed up."

There's no need to explain who Chuck is, Ava met him once when he showed up at the bookstore one night while we were closing, and she didn't pass up the opportunity to know more at our very next ladies' night. Chuck has been the topic of conversation a few times...none of them loved the idea of me and Chuck, not that I can blame them.

It was clear from the start nothing serious was going to

happen, and considering the three of them have found their happily ever after, they want the same for me.

"That couldn't have been good." Quinn grimaces.

"I mean...it could have been worse. Him showing up made Jude reveal more than I think he'd been planning on."

"Oh? Like what?" Ava bounces in her spot slightly.

"Like the fact he's never slept with anyone else...ever."

"What?" all three of them shout.

The silence that washes over the yard is a little comical. Everything goes still as the guys turn to look at us, concern evident in all their expressions.

"You all okay?" Declan asks from his spot behind the grill.

"Yeah, we're good," Quinn yells back, waving him off like he's the one who disrupted the story. "I'm sorry, but I think you're going to have to explain that one."

Before I say anything else, I feel the weight of Jude's stare on me and let my eyes meet his, silently telling him I'm fine. With a slight nod of his head, his attention turns back to the guys in front of him and mine comes back to the ladies in front of me.

"I mean, there's not much else to it than that. Jude's never been with anyone else."

"Hold up." Ava shakes her head, her brows pinched. "There's so much more to say. I mean, the whole reason you broke up was that he had an affair. At least, that's what he claimed."

"The affair was a lie." I lift a hand when I see Ava's mouth open. "Look, I said it that night, I didn't trust the affair was real. He'd been telling me for weeks before that we should get a divorce, I just refused to listen to him. I thought it was nerves about being married so young. I thought it was something we'd be able to move past."

"I don't blame you. The way you two were with each other

was enviable." Quinn reaches out and squeezes my hand before releasing it.

"Honestly, if I didn't have Caleb I'd be envious watching you two together now."

"Ditto. Well, I mean, if I didn't have Gage." Ava raises her drink in an imaginary toast, making all of us smile. "So, the affair wasn't real. Not that I thought it was. That man has looked at you like you're his entire world since the moment he showed up in Ashford Falls. Anyone with eyes could see that."

"What really happened?" Quinn whispers.

"My father." It shouldn't surprise me the lack of shock on their faces. My father's been showing his true colors more and more lately. "He told Jude if he didn't leave me, and Ashford Falls, he'd take my mother to DC and make sure I never saw her again, and that he'd destroy Murphy's and make it so difficult for Walt to be here, he'd need to leave to find peace. He threatened to destroy the people Jude cared about most."

"And instead of talking to you about it, he decided what was best for everyone involved and left?" Emily asks in bewilderment.

"Hindsight is twenty-twenty," Ava whispers, her eyes shifting to Gage for a few seconds before they return to me. But when they do, there are tears building in them. "You can't take what you know now and apply to a situation from the past. At nineteen, Jude probably thought Edward could do some horrible things if he wanted to."

It's my turn to reach out and offer comfort. Ava was the queen of beating herself up for decisions she made that she thought she should have known better. It wasn't until Gage came into her life that she started to believe what she just told me.

"You're right." I offer her a small smile. "I'm still angry with him about it, but I understand it. We were kids and he thought he was doing what was best. My mom had just been diagnosed with ALS and I was going to lose her no matter what, he wanted me to have as much time with her as I could."

"He still could have given you the option," Emily mumbles.

"But that's just it, he knew me—he still knows me—better than anyone else. If he'd told me back then, I would've chosen him. I would've been devastated not having those last two years with my mom, but I would've chosen him because she would've been so mad at me if I'd made any other decision."

Quinn doesn't say anything, but she grabs my hand and holds on tight, a tear slipping down her cheek. It's the worst club to be in—the one where you've lost a parent—but sometimes having someone to lean on who truly understands the pain makes it just a little easier to bear.

Quinn's gaze shifts away for a minute before she pulls herself back together. "So, he didn't cheat, he's been faithful to you this whole time, and you've forgiven him."

"We're still working through some of the trust issues—it's not something that can be fixed with the flip of a switch—but we're both more than willing to work on them. So, yeah, I've forgiven him."

Ava releases a massive sigh, her entire body deflating. "Oh, thank goodness. When you first told us about the alleged affair, I hated him on principle, but he just kept worming his way back." A soft chuckle escapes my lips. "Seriously, that man is obsessed with you and you deserve to have someone obsessed with you. You're fucking amazing." She springs forward, pulling me in for a quick hug before she practically skips away.

"I feel sorry for anyone who doesn't have an Ava in their life," Emily murmurs quietly at my side as Ava joins the guys by the grill.

"She's definitely a force of nature." Quinn laughs.

"Honestly, I feel lucky to have all of you in my life," I tell them.

It's crazy to think how much my life has changed over the last year. I never thought I'd have friends like them—I wasn't open to that possibility—but here they are, and I wouldn't change that for anything.

CHAPTER
Thirty

ABBEY

"I'M NOT SAYING I'm not grateful that you're doing this, but are you allowed to do this? You're a general surgeon," I ask as Emily shuts the door to the exam room.

"Sure, any doctor can pull a swab and run some tests. Now, if you needed medical care to treat a specific ailment, I would absolutely send you to the right specialist. But I'm literally just grabbing some spit and sending it to a lab." Emily laughs as she gestures to the chair for me to sit and pulls her own stool over, taking a seat in front of me. "You didn't really say why you needed to see a doctor when you asked for a recommendation on a new gynecologist. Everything all right?"

"Oh, yeah. My last gynecologist moved recently and I haven't gotten a new one. And, you know, safe sex is the best sex." It's an uncomfortable laugh that breaks through as I cover my face with my hands. "I can't believe I just said that."

Honestly, I'm so glad Emily is doing this for me. I called three doctors trying to schedule an annual visit and was told they couldn't fit me in for another month before I finally cracked and called Emily to see if she could recommend anyone.

It's been two weeks since Jude and I had sex without a condom, and while I'm not worried about pregnancy or disease —I'm on birth control and have never been with someone without a condom—it's always better to be sure.

Jude has been so understanding, but—even though it doesn't make sense—I have all this guilt around the need for this appointment. I had every right to move on from Jude. Our marriage was over. He left town. And yet...knowing that *Jude* never moved on gets my stomach in a twist.

The sooner I get these results, the sooner I can stop letting this affect me, because it's just me. Jude has been nothing but understanding and supportive. Minus his reaction to finding out I'd been with someone else—which was a really shitty way to find out—he hasn't said anything about my sexual history. And I think that might be feeding the guilt.

Emily's laugh pulls me back to the present, and I have to remind myself what she asked. "Jude and I were a little too into the moment to pay attention to using a condom the first time, and while he's obviously good to go, I haven't been tested since my last time with Chuck."

"Gotcha." Emily doesn't even bat an eye as she stands from her seat and starts pulling out supplies. "I think we'll go with a blood test instead of a cheek swab. No reason other than it's quicker and will give you peace of mind sooner." She rushes to say when she sees my look of concern.

"Oh. How quickly will the results be ready?"

"For most tests it'll be a couple days, but some will take about a week."

I nod absentmindedly as she wheels the tray over with everything she'll need to draw my blood. All of a sudden nerves hit me and I don't know why. I have no reason to believe anything bad will come back in these results. I feel confident in thinking Chuck wasn't only sleeping with me, and while we always used condoms I know they can fail.

Emily doesn't push me to talk more. She goes through the motions and draws a couple vials of blood before placing a Band-Aid on my arm and asking me if I want to join her for lunch. I know she's doing it because she can clearly see my thoughts spiraling, but I appreciate the distraction all the same.

And I let my lunch with Emily become a distraction. It's been a while since I've had the chance to spend one on one time with her, and I'm glad for the opportunity. Emily has a calming presence that's hard to ignore. Somehow her calmness always seeps into me and I walk away feeling more at peace than when we first started hanging out.

"I'VE BEEN CALLING you every day for over a week," I bite into the phone, letting my anger pour out more than I want. I take a breath before I continue. If I let my anger get in the way, I'll never have the conversation I both need and want to have with my father. "I know our last conversation wasn't great, but you've never blatantly ignored me." I soften my tone, truly trying to understand.

"I've been busy. Things at work have been hectic." There's a rushing sound in the background, like he's outside and the wind is whipping past, and I know it means he's calling me on his way somewhere else.

This call is something he quickly penciled in between things he's deemed more important. It's not new to me, but that doesn't make it any less disappointing.

"Dad." I sigh. I'm exasperated, and I have no doubt he hears it. The sound of rushing air stops and I'm not sure if he's stepped into a building or if he's simply stopped moving. No matter, we're both silent, and I can't stop the next words that come out of my mouth. "Has there ever been a time where you wanted me as a daughter?"

I'm not sure where the words come from, but once they're out, I realize I've never felt truly wanted by him. Besides my mother, it's like family as a whole was an obligation, or some item to check on a list of things to prove one's success.

I know he loves me, but you can love someone and not appreciate them. You can love someone and not want them.

"Abbey, what kind of question is that? You're my daughter," he huffs.

"That's not actually an answer," I whisper. I feel my nose burning, but I refuse to let the tears free. I have so much to love about my life, so many people in my corner, I won't let my father bring me down—not today.

"Abbey, I don't have time for this." He sighs and I can imagine him pinching the bridge of his nose in annoyance. "What is it you wanted to discuss?" And suddenly he's all business again. "Is it something about the bookstore? I told you I wouldn't transfer the money until I saw the itemized list from your contractor."

I look around the space George and his team just vacated. The renovations are done and the store is officially mine, and not once has my dad stopped in to see how everything has progressed. It's yet another thing that shouldn't surprise me.

"No, it's nothing about the bookstore."

The bell above the door rings—the first thing I put back in place after George left—and I spin to find Jude standing there, his eyes taking in everything around him.

I wanted to have this conversation with my dad in person, and I definitely planned for it to be without Jude around, but the second his eyes land on mine and that smile he only ever has for me makes an appearance, I know that second idea was a mistake. Having Jude by my side will only ever be a benefit to me.

"I wanted to talk to you about what happened when you threatened Jude, the first time."

With my eyes focused only on Jude, I see the moment his smile falls and his body goes taut. I didn't tell him I was planning on having this conversation with my dad, but he should've known I wasn't going to let it go. Especially when he's continued to threaten Jude.

Jude doesn't let the tension coursing through his body stop him. He moves into my space, gripping my free hand in his, proving that he's here with me for whatever I need.

"Abbey." Dad's tone is so sharp, it almost makes me flinch, but with Jude's strength I push forward.

"It's time you stopped hiding behind whatever perceived wrong you believe to be true. Just tell me what happened."

"There's nothing to tell." His words are so low, I almost miss them. It takes a moment for him to continue. "I thought I was keeping you safe. I still believe I'm keeping you safe. The Murphys will only bring you pain, but if you need to learn that for yourself—again—then so be it."

"Dad—"

"I told you work's been busy," he interrupts. "I don't have time to discuss this more." His words are clipped, and I'm shocked when he continues with an almost proper goodbye. "I'll be back in Ashford Falls in time for your opening. Talk soon." And with that, the line goes dead.

It takes me a couple seconds to finally pull the phone away from my ear, but Jude is instantly moving further into my space, ensuring all my focus is on him. "What do you need?"

Trying like hell not to let the tears slip free, I let my head fall against Jude's chest and my arms wrap around his waist. Jude doesn't hesitate to wrap his arms around me, pulling me in tighter to his body. When his lips land on the top of my head, I can't stop the tears from leaking out.

This comfort right here, it's everything I've always wanted

—knowing there's someone I can lean on to help support me through the tough times. I know I'm capable of doing it on my own, for the most part I have ever since my mother died, but just because I can doesn't mean I have to.

"Love," Jude whispers against me. "What can I do?"

"Nothing. This is more than enough." And it is. Being in his arms is exactly what I want right now.

Jude lets me soak in the comfort of his arms for a few minutes before he asks the question I knew would eventually come. "Can you tell me what he said?"

"Nothing new." I release my grip around his waist and pull back to look him in the eye. "Honestly, at this point, I don't really care what he has to say. I don't think there's anything he can say to make me forgive him. Even if there's a valid reason for him to hate Walt, you never did anything to deserve his behavior."

"Abbey, I don't want—"

"No," I interrupt, slipping out of his arms. "A child does not deserve to be treated like the perceived sins of the father are their fault. That belief is complete bullcrap." I have to stop myself from stomping my foot like a child throwing a temper tantrum. "I'm done letting his beliefs and actions impact my life. It sucks that I have such a shitty father, but I've got Walt and you, and the rest of the group. I have far too many people in my corner to let him affect me anymore."

Pity never crosses his features, but that doesn't stop him from stepping forward and taking my hand in one of his. "Love," he whispers, cupping my cheek in his other hand. "You set whatever boundaries you need to set, but don't act like this doesn't hurt—not with me. He can be the biggest asshole, but he's still your father, and he still supported you through some of your hardest moments. It's okay to be disappointed in him and hurt by his actions."

My eyes fall shut as I suck in a breath of air. His words hit more than I want them to. Jude's right—no matter what bad he's done, there are good moments with my dad, and those are the moments I wish for over and over again. I thought, when he accepted my business proposal, that we'd have a chance to build on the relationship we had, but that's clearly not the case.

What I need to accept is holding onto those moments—building expectations off of childhood memories—is setting myself up for disappointment. While I can feel whatever negative emotions I have right now, I can't let myself sit in them. If I want a real chance at living a full and happy life, I have to let it go.

"I know I can feel whatever I'm feeling, but I don't want to feed the negative emotions. I want to move on and chase those dreams." I place my hand over his on my cheek and sink into the touch. "I want to keep moving forward with you."

"Okay, mo ghrá," he whispers, pressing a kiss to my forehead. "Where do we start?"

CHAPTER
Thirty-One

JUDE

THE CALL CONTINUES to ring as I tuck the phone between my ear and shoulder, stuffing my keys and wallet into my pockets.

"Jude Murphy. What have I told you about letting so much time go between phone calls? It's bad enough I don't get to see you very often," Mae chides as soon as she answers the phone.

"You know the phone works both ways, Mae. You could always call me." I can't help the chuckle that falls from my lips. Mae might be giving me a hard time, but I know she's only teasing me. It's been too long since I talked to her and Willie.

I called them a few days after I got settled in Ashford Falls, letting them know what was going on, but have only shot them a text here or there over the last two and half months. They're far too important to me to have let this much time pass between phone calls. The support they've given me since I first met them means the world, and just because I'm getting my life back doesn't mean I don't still need them, because I do —probably now more than ever.

"How's your dad doing?" I hear the screech of their screen

door through the phone, and I know she's stepping out the front door, probably on her way to the garage where Willie likely is.

"No change. They move him to the nursing home next week."

"No change is better than bad news."

"I know. I just wish he'd wake up already."

"Is that our boy finally calling us?" Willie's booming voice sounds in the background, and I'm grateful for the smile that pulls at my lips. I've missed them. Hearing their voices always has a way of calming my spirit.

"He had the nerve to tell me it's my fault we haven't talked!" Mae hollers back to him.

"Hey now! That's not true." I laugh as I close the apartment door and head down the stairs to meet Abbey at the bookstore.

There's a rustling on the other end of the phone for a second before I hear Willie more clearly. "It's been a while, kid."

"I know. I'm sorry I haven't called more." I pause as I step outside, taking a second to enjoy the fresh air and soak in the fondness of that nickname, before I make my way around the building.

"Oh, you know we're only giving you a hard time. We just miss you." There's no censure in his voice, but it doesn't stop the pang of guilt in my chest.

"It's been too long since I've been out to visit you two." *Way too long.*

"Does that mean we're getting a visit here soon?" Mae's excitement at the simple possibility of me coming to visit makes me smile.

I laugh, unable to stop myself. "I think that's definitely a possibility."

Pausing in front of the bookstore, my eyes catch on a hole

in the paper covering the front windows. The paper's been up since Abbey started renovations, wanting to keep everything a secret from the town, and I know that hole is an accident. That doesn't stop me from stepping up to it and taking full advantage.

"How are things going there, kid? Everything all right?" Will's voice sounds in my ear, but I don't take my eyes off the sight in front of me.

George and his team cleared out of the bookstore and handed the keys over yesterday, and Abbey jumped in with both feet to get the place ready for her grand re-opening in just over a week. After giving herself a few minutes to come to terms with the stagnant conversation with her dad, she started figuring out exactly how she was going to get everything ready. Without even an hour passing, the entire gang showed up and boxes of books started coming in through the back door.

I don't know why, but it blew my mind to see everyone piling in through the front door asking about how they could help. Declan and Quinn showed up with pizza and beer, Ava and Gage came with a speaker and playlist ready to keep us motivated, and Emily—with Fiona strapped to her chest—Caleb, and Max arrived with snacks to keep us energized.

With everyone working together we were able to bring in all the boxes of books, the new furniture Abbey bought, and all the supplies she got for the café. There's still a lot for her to do, but having everything in one space means she'll have a much easier job doing it.

But now, instead of unpacking the boxes like I thought I'd find when I walked through the doors, she dances around the space, the most radiant smile on her face, and I fall in love with her all over again.

"Yeah." I smile, my eyes never leaving Abbey through the window. "All things considered, everything is pretty great."

"Well, there's definitely a story to tell there," Mae calls, and I can imagine her clearly, leaning forward with her chin propped in her hand, eagerly waiting for me to say more.

"Abbey and I are back together."

"Oh," Mae gasps, and when she speaks next, her voice is choked. "That's wonderful, Jude."

I have to look away from Abbey and swallow the lump in my throat before I'm able to speak. Even with them not knowing the full story, I know they understand how big of a statement that is. After Grace died, and I went back to Minnesota needing the comfort I couldn't find anywhere else, I couldn't help but think I'd ruined everything. I was so adamant I'd never find true happiness again, that Abbey had been my one true love. I didn't need to tell Mae or Willie that for them to know I'd practically given up all hope. They didn't necessarily push me to reconsider going home, but they definitely pushed me to think about what I wanted out of life. They pushed me to find new passions and things to bring joy.

"You're gonna bring her on your next visit?" Willie asks.

"Yeah." I chuckle. "Abbey's already said she wants to meet you both before the end of the year. She said she wants to meet the people that kept me in check all these years."

"I like her already." Willie laughs.

"Yeah, I have no doubt you'll love her," I answer absent-mindedly, my gaze moving back to Abbey through the window.

I hear Willie and Mae talking, but I lose all focus on the conversation. I'm a lucky bastard to have this woman back in my life. How I managed to make up for the biggest mistake of my life, I'll never know. But I'll also never take her or this life we're building for granted.

When I left before, I thought I was doing the right thing. I thought I was making life easier for Abbey by not forcing her to choose between her family and me, but I never should have done her thinking for her.

From this moment forward, everything I do will be with Abbey at the forefront of my mind, and she'll be part of every decision I make. I know she's forgiven me and won't hold onto this as some tool to use in a future fight, but she deserves to truly understand exactly what I've been doing since I left Ashford Falls.

"Hey, can you do me a favor?" I ask, interrupting whatever Willie and Mae were talking about. My eyes stay glued to the woman through the bookstore.

The woman I can't stop thinking about.

The woman I've been obsessed with my entire life.

"Of course. When have I ever denied you anything?" Mae's voice is soft, and I hear the smile as clear as day through the phone. I love her for many reasons, but her ability to jump to a new topic without question is one of them.

"Can you send me that box of journals packed away in the closet in the guest room?" The other end of the call goes completely silent. It's so quiet, I have to pull the phone away from my ear to make sure the call wasn't dropped. "Mae? Willie? You still there?"

"Yeah. I'm just a little surprised. I thought they'd live in that closet for the rest of our lives."

"I know," I whisper. I let my eyes leave the image before me and turn to walk up to the door, pausing outside to finish this conversation first. "I think Abbey should have the chance to read them. If she wants."

"That's a pretty big move." Willie's words are hushed, and I don't blame them. I've kept those journals so close to the chest, only ever talking about my story ideas with select people. But opening them up in their entirety to read? It's big.

"If anyone deserves to read them, it's Abbey."

"We'll get 'em packed up and shipped out today."

"You don't need to rush. In the next few days is fine."

"Oh no," Mae insists. "I don't want you to have any time to change your mind. I'm hanging up and getting them now."

"Wait—"

"Nope. We love you and we'll talk to you in a few days," Mae shouts.

"Take care of yourself and your woman, kid," Willie offers right before the line goes dead.

I shake my head and laugh at their antics before shoving my phone in my pocket and finally walking through the door to the bookstore. Abbey's smile when she turns to look at me grows even wider, and I'm lost to her all over again.

———

"WHERE'D AJ DOHERTY COME FROM?" Abbey pauses in her movements, her focus on the box of books she's opened in front of her.

I don't need to look to see what books she's staring at. That question wouldn't have popped into her brain without prompting, not with her attention so focused on getting the bookstore ready.

It's been ten days since Abbey found out I'm AJ Doherty—one of her all-time favorite authors—but she hasn't asked as many questions as I assumed she would. I haven't pushed, wanting her to set the pace on learning everything about our time apart. If I had it my way, I would've dumped it all at her feet if that's what she wanted. But I didn't want her to become overwhelmed with so much information—we have seventeen years to catch up on and hopefully we have a lifetime to do it.

"I'm sure you could guess the initials A and J," I tease, moving to stand across from her, three boxes stacked between us.

"Abbey and Jude," she whispers, her eyes moving up to mine.

"Yeah." I nod. "And Doherty—"

"Was your mom's maiden name," Abbey interrupts, her gaze falling back to the book in her hand.

"When my agent asked me what name I wanted to publish under, I knew immediately I wanted to use a pen name, but I still wanted the name to represent me in some way."

"It's a good pen name." The words are said so quietly I don't think she even realizes she said them.

Knowing Abbey, there are more questions forming in her mind, but I can see she's working through something in the way her fingers smooth over the cover of the book, tracing my name almost tenderly.

"Why'd you pick a pen name? Why not use your real name?" Her focus stays on the book when she asks, but I don't mind.

I'm not surprised by the question, but I wasn't looking forward to it either. "The honest answer is that I didn't think I deserved it." Abbey lifts her head and opens her mouth to say something, but I don't let her. I need to get this out. "When I signed my first deal with my publisher...it was more money than I knew what to do with—it was more money than I thought I'd ever see in my lifetime." It's my turn to trace the title on the cover of the book between us.

I still don't understand why they'd been willing to offer so much to a nobody like me. I had absolutely no training or formal education and was truly flying by the seat of my pants. But they took a chance on me and somehow it all paid off.

"I thought it was insane they wanted to pay me so much money to write a few books for them, and I thought putting a different name on it would let me dissociate from the entire thing." I lift my eyes to Abbey's—she deserves the next words to be said to her face, not to an inanimate object. "After everything I'd put you and my dad through, I didn't think it was fair to have so much security."

"Jude—"

"I know it doesn't make sense, and you probably never would've agreed with me, even when you hated me—"

"I never hated you." Abbey leans against the top of the box between us, bringing her face closer to mine, a small smile forming on her lips. "That was part of the problem," she teases.

I wonder if I should hate that she can joke about the pain of our past, but the truth is that I love it. For me, it's proof that we really are moving forward. That we can build a life together. One so much stronger than the one we had before.

"Well, you never hating me isn't a problem for me," I croon, mirroring her position against the top of the box.

"No, I guess it isn't." Her eyes dip down to my lips inches from hers and the second she swipes her tongue across her bottom lip, I can't help myself—I don't want to stop myself. I know she still has a bunch of questions simmering in that head of hers, but they'll have to wait for later.

My lips land on hers in a demanding kiss, and when she responds in kind, I don't even stop to contemplate that the door to the bookstore is unlocked and anyone could walk in. I crave her with everything I am.

Pulling her around the boxes between us, I devour her, lifting her into my arms and pressing her into the shelves against the wall. Everything about her reaction pushes me forward—the moan that slips from her lips, the way her hips grind against my hardening length, the grip she has on my shoulders.

Nothing could pull me away from her. Not now. Not ever.

CHAPTER
Thirty-Two

ABBEY

A SOUND from the front of the store draws me out of the kitchen where I've been testing out different recipes for the opening next week. I know there's still a lot for me to organize and set up, but most of the books have been unpacked and I couldn't wait to play in my brand new commercial-grade kitchen. It's quite literally my dream come true.

As I step out into the store, I immediately hear someone knocking at the door, and the longer it goes, the louder it becomes.

I haven't removed the paper from the front windows and door yet, wanting to keep everything about this place a secret until the very last moment, and being here alone makes me quite nervous to open the door. I'm well aware I live in a small town where I know almost everyone, but I'm still a woman living in a world that constantly teaches us to be cautious, and opening that door goes against every instinct I have.

I contemplate calling Jude, who I know is in the bar helping Jane with the morning delivery, but as I'm turning to go back to the kitchen for my phone, the person on the other side of the door calls for me.

"Abbey, I know you're in there. Jude told me when I knocked at your apartment."

The sound of Emily's muffled voice instantly calms me, and I rush to unlock and open the door. "Hey, what are you doing here? I thought you worked today."

"I do, but I've got about an hour before my shift starts. I figured I could stop by and help for a bit." Her gaze drifts around the space, and while the act on its own isn't alarming since so much has changed since she's been here, the tension pouring off her is.

"You thought you'd stop by to help for...what? Fifteen minutes?" My brows pinch and my concern grows when she refuses to meet my eye.

Last I saw her was Friday night when everyone showed up to help move everything into the store, and as far as I know, everything was great. We all had such a good time, laughing and goofing off. It felt good to be with everyone, it felt like I had my family with me. The only person missing was Walt.

"Oh god! Did something happen to Walt?" I turn to run for the kitchen, wondering why Jude wouldn't come get me if something happened.

"No!" Emily shouts. "Walt's fine!"

Her eyes finally meet mine when I turn to look at her, but the way she bites her lip doesn't help me feel better. "What is it? You're freaking me out." My arms band around my waist, holding myself tight against whatever Emily's about to say.

"I got your lab results back." My entire body tightens, preparing for something unimaginable, but her next words are out before I can say anything. "You're pregnant."

"No," I refuse immediately. "I'm on birth control. I can't be pregnant."

I don't know if I ever seriously thought about having a baby. In an obscure way I've always known it was something I wanted to do, but the older I've gotten the less likely I thought it was. No matter what, this wasn't the way I imagined it happening.

"I can't be pregnant," I repeat. "There's no way."

"You never missed a pill?" Emily steps closer to me, her tone soft. There's no judgment, just support. When I don't answer, she pushes gently. "There's been a lot going on in your life—problems with your dad, the bookstore, learning the truth about Jude. It'd be understandable if you missed a day or two."

"No, I haven't missed a pill," I answer emphatically. "I was late taking a few, but I never missed one entirely."

"Well, unfortunately, no form of birth control is completely effective. It's rare, but even people who take the pill exactly like they're supposed to can still end up pregnant." She reaches for me, grasping my hand tight in hers. "You're a special one, Abbey Selbey."

I can't be pregnant. Jude and I are only just starting to get our shit together. We're just starting to get used to each other again.

So much about the last two weeks has felt easy and carefree, but there's still so much to work through. I know we're both consciously trying to move forward. Neither of us wants to forget the past, but we also can't keep it in our back pocket, ready to throw it at the other person in a moment of anger. That's not what a relationship should be. If I want a real future with him, I have to let go of the past.

My eyes dart to Emily's and I feel the panic rising. My heart feels like it's beating out of its chest. "I can't be pregnant," I whisper.

"Do you not want kids?"

"No, I do." I shake my head, trying to clear my head, but I can't and every random thought comes pouring out. "Jude absolutely deserves to be a dad. He'd be an amazing dad. I mean, look at his own father. But we're just starting again. I know it seems like we're picking up where we left off, but it's work. I forgive him for what happened, but I still struggle with trusting him."

"Babe, no one would blame you for feeling a little uncertain. You lived almost half your life thinking the man cheated on you. It'll take time to fully recover from that."

Tears fill my eyes, and I have no way to put into words what I'm thinking or feeling. On one hand, I'm so incredibly nervous. Not just for what it means for mine and Jude's relationship, but also for how he'll react to the news. On the other hand, I couldn't be happier.

I'm thirty-five years old. I know they don't call it a geriatric pregnancy anymore, but that doesn't negate the risks. I'd come to accept children wouldn't be in my future. To be pregnant now, and by the man I've never stopped loving...that seems too good to be true.

"Abbey, I know it's not what you would've planned for yourself, and maybe this looks nothing like you imagined, but it's okay to be happy about it." Her smile is soft and reassuring. "Two things can be true at once. You can be both scared and thrilled about this news."

I nod, unable to form words with the lump in my throat, but I know Emily understands. She wraps her arms around me in a tight embrace, not letting me go until I loosen my arms from around her.

"You'll keep this to yourself, right?" I pull away and wipe at my cheeks, my eyes meeting hers.

"Of course. Until you make the announcement, I know absolutely nothing."

"Thank you," I whisper, a small smile playing across my lips. "I promise I won't make you wait long. I just need to figure out how to tell Jude."

"Don't stress about me keeping this quiet. That's the absolute last thing you need to worry about. Technically, you're my patient. Telling anyone else would break HIPAA, and I'd never do that."

I pull Emily into a hug once more before we say our good-byes and she leaves for her shift at the hospital, leaving me to contemplate what my next move is going to be.

How the hell do I tell Jude?

"MO GHRÁ," Jude's voice reaches me in the small office in the kitchen, and I take a deep breath before meeting him in the store.

I've thought about nothing else except the news Emily dropped on me this morning, and no matter how much I want this, I just don't think Jude and I are ready for it.

Maybe that's not fair.

I'm not ready for how this could change us.

After hours spent googling anything and everything I could think to ask, I've learned I know absolutely nothing about being pregnant, giving birth, or taking care of a baby. I mean, I know exactly what day we conceived this baby, and yet, I'm somehow five weeks pregnant already. How is that even possible when it was only two weeks ago Jude and I had sex for the first time in seventeen years?

If Emily had decided to do that cheek swab instead of the blood test, I wouldn't even know. Even if I thought pregnancy was a possibility, and I bought a home pregnancy test, it's entirely possible that test would be negative right now. And don't even get me started on everything that happens to a woman's body when she's pregnant.

I know having a child is something I want, but I figured I'd have time to prepare for everything. Getting pregnant was going to be a planned thing where I'd have all this time to figure out everything that entails. I know I still have nine months to figure out the taking care of a baby and what happens during birth, but the pregnancy side? I'm all out of time.

"Hey, love. I know it's Ashford Falls, but if you want to keep this place a secret until opening day, you should probably lock the door, especially when you're in the back." Jude smiles, placing a hand on my hip and a kiss to my temple as he steps past me, toward the still swinging door. "Something smells amazing! You working on recipes instead of unpacking today?" he teases, tossing a wink over his shoulder.

I force a laugh, trying desperately to keep my racing thoughts to myself and follow after him. "Yeah. But technically, I had to unpack and organize most of the kitchen before I could start baking. So it's not like I've only been baking."

"I'm not complaining. I've missed a lot of things over the last seventeen years, and your sweets are definitely high on the list." His attention is drawn to the mess in the kitchen.

While the boxes are dismantled and piled in the corner, ready to be taken out to the dumpster, ingredients and bowls litter the counter tops. And I know he's wondering how I have so little to show for supposedly spending the entire day in the kitchen, when the only finished treat is the lemon bars Ava told me had to be on the menu for opening day.

"Why does that sound dirty?" I tease, trying to distract him from looking too close to what I've done today.

This man loves me and knows me better than anyone, even with so much time apart. The second he realizes how little I've actually accomplished today is the moment I have to make a decision—tell him about the pregnancy or lie to him.

Is it really a lie if I'm going to tell him eventually?

Waiting to tell him is just postponing the inevitable. Why am I waiting?

But then I think about all those tabs open on my computer —all the unknowns of what having a baby means for us. Would having a baby change anything about our future? I mean, I know having a baby changes practically everything, but the fundamentals of what we both want—will the news of this baby change that?

My eyes track Jude as he prowls toward me, a playful smile tugging at his lips. I'm so freaking nervous about this news dropped in my lap this morning, but when Jude looks at me like that—with so much love and desire—I can't help but focus on only that.

Even with all the pain and heartache in our past, having Jude back in my life brings me so much joy. I'm not ready to dampen that.

I'll tell him about the baby. Just not right now.

CHAPTER
Thirty-Three

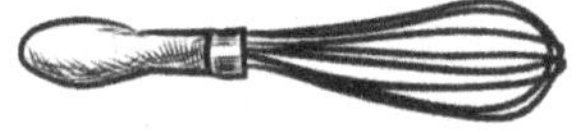

ABBEY

"HEY, Dad. I know our last call didn't go very well, but I need to talk to you about the bookstore." I pinch the phone between my ear and shoulder while juggling my coffee and keys in one hand and pressing the button to the elevator with the other. "George called and said he hasn't received the final payment yet. I sent you the itemized list like you requested last week. What's going on?" I hang up without saying goodbye and glare at my phone.

I'm well aware he's upset with me—I'm pretty upset with him myself—but that doesn't excuse refusing to pay George. He can be mad at me all he wants, but this is business. I've never known my father to shirk his responsibilities.

The second the doors to the elevator slide open I step into the empty space and press the button for the third floor. My body instantly slumps against the back wall when the doors close. It's been barely seventy-two hours since Emily told me about the pregnancy and I'm already exhausted from hiding the truth from Jude. It takes work trying to act like nothing's wrong.

The truth is, I'm pretty confident Jude knows something is

bothering me, but for some reason, he's not pushing me on it. Part of me thinks he's not pushing me because he's still concerned I haven't forgiven him about the past. Like maybe he's afraid to push me because he thinks I'll decide trying this again won't be worth it. And if that's the case, how in the world will we ever survive?

Or maybe he trusts that I'll come to him when I'm ready. When we were younger I always ran to Jude when I needed comfort, but I didn't always tell him what happened right away. I've always been a person who needs to work through things on my own before I can get other people's opinions. But that never stopped Jude from asking what was bothering me— even if he knew I might not answer him right away.

Of course, if I stopped trying to do Jude's thinking for him...

The elevator doors slide open on the third floor, revealing an empty hallway, the sign across the way reminding me to turn left for the ICU. I've been here so many times I don't need the reminder. I could probably make it to Walt's room with my eyes closed.

When I woke up this morning, aside from the growing guilt for not telling Jude the news about the baby, I felt this pressing need to be with Walt. I needed the comfort only a father's embrace could provide. I knew I wouldn't get that warm hug I was desperate for, but I knew being in his presence would bring me peace.

I press the button to be let into the ICU and wave when the nurse inside the glass door catches my eye and smiles.

"Oh! I'm glad you stopped by once more before they move him. I made you a little something." Sarah springs up from her seat and rummages through a bag beside her. "I know how much you like to read and I saw these book sleeves online and I couldn't get the idea out of my head to make you one."

"Sarah, you didn't have to do that." I gasp.

Walt always has the same nurses rotating through his room and watching over him. You get to know the nurses just as they get to know you, and somehow it feels like you've grown a new little family in these walls. It's both strange and wholly appreciated. There's this comfort in knowing someone who cares for your loved one is keeping them safe.

"Oh, I know, but I can't keep making quilts. I'm running out of people to give them to and I don't have any more room for them in my house." She laughs. "Ah-ha! Got it." She pulls a beautiful pastel purple and yellow fabric from her bag and presents it to me with a flourish.

"The idea is that you slip your book into this little pouch to keep it safe inside your purse. You can put any book that fits, but for the most part it keeps your corners safe. Or, if you have an e-reader without a case, it keeps your screen from getting scratched." Sarah's enthusiasm is contagious, and I can't help the smile from breaking free as I take the gift from her.

I don't own any book sleeves myself, but I know what they are. Holding this in my hand, I can't stop an idea from forming. "Was this hard to make?" I ask, fingering the squishy pocket.

"Oh, not at all. It was actually quite easy. I had to stop myself from making more." She laughs again.

"I know you have a full-time job you love, but if you like making these and want to make a little extra cash, I'd love to sell these at the store." I meet Sarah's eyes, a broad smile tipping at my lips.

"Are you serious?" The disbelief in her tone makes me laugh.

"Of course, I'm serious. I'm mad I didn't think about stocking something like this, and to have them hand made by someone local? That's the cherry on top of a perfect sundae."

"Oh, I'd love to do that. I love sewing and quilting, but I'm not lying about running out of people to give things to."

"Perfect. Come by whenever you have time and we can

work out all the details. I want to make sure it's worth your while."

Sarah nods but isn't able to say anything else before she's called away. I wave her off, letting her know we'll catch up again before I leave. I have no doubt she'll be in to check on Walt at some point during my visit.

I know there's plenty I could be working on at the store, but I want to be here right now. Jude was surprised when I told him I wanted to come visit his dad this morning, but he didn't question it or ask to join me—more proof he knows something is going on with me.

The beeping from the machines in Walt's room have become so normal there's a comfort in hearing them the moment I cross the threshold. The rhythmic sound is a constant reminder that his heart is still beating, that he's still with us.

I slide the door closed behind me, closing out the sounds of the rest of the unit before stepping forward and pressing a kiss to Walt's forehead.

"Come on, Walt," I whisper. "It's time to wake up. We need you." I pause where I am, inches from his face, as if he'll open his eyes on command even though I've made this same request numerous times over the last two months and nothing has happened.

"Oh, Walt. I don't know what I'm doing." I fall back into the empty seat next to his bed, dropping the bag I brought with me onto the floor at my feet. My gaze stays focused on his, looking for the smallest sign he can hear me.

It surprises me how little has truly changed about Walt in the last two months. It just goes to show how bad he was looking before the heart attack. I remember thinking how sick he looked back in January when I stepped into Murphy's for the first time over a decade and a half. I'd been concerned then and that concern only grew from that point on. Ava, Gage, and

I tried to convince him to take some time away from the bar, or at the very least hire some full-time staff to help carry the load, but he refused.

Gage and Ava assumed it was his inability to give up the smallest amount of control, but I knew it had more to do with Jude than anything else. Walt is a family man through and through—he lived for his family—and when Jude left to never return home, it broke something in Walt. Staying busy and keeping all of his focus on the bar made it easier to cope with Jude's absence.

Walt never said that was why, but I know that's exactly what I did after Jude left. I focused all of my time and energy into my mother—spending time with her, taking her to doctor's appointments, keeping her company as her body started to deteriorate. If I didn't have time to think about Jude, I couldn't hurt because of Jude.

Of course, that coping mechanism only lasts for so long.

"All right." I lean forward in my seat, placing my elbows on the edge of his bed. "I'm going to tell you this because maybe you can hear me and it'll bring you back to us. And because I need to tell someone but I'm not ready to tell your son."

I pause, waiting—hoping—just that little bit is enough to entice him back to this side of life, but nothing changes. His eyes don't flutter open, his breathing doesn't pick up, and the beeping of his monitor is as steady as ever.

"Walt," I whisper, leaning closer. My gaze shifts to the finger of his left hand and I don't try to stop myself from tracing the Dara Knot tattooed on his ring finger. I don't remember exactly what it means, but I know it represents love in some way.

"I'm pregnant." It's the first time I've said those words and somehow it makes it all more real.

There's a baby growing inside of me. A human life that's

made up of me and Jude. A little person that will bring so much joy to everyone around us. And all of a sudden all that fear and anxious energy washes away.

Tears well in my eyes and I can't stop the watery laugh from breaking free. None of this is happening the way I wanted it to, but when does life ever go according to plan?

"Walt, can you believe that?" I stop tracing his tattoo and grip his hand in mine, my eyes focusing on his face before I continue. "Jude and I are having a baby. You're going to be a grandfather." I choke on a sob. There's both joy in the news I'm sharing and fear that Walt won't come back to us to be a part of this new life, but I don't let that stop me. "You have to wake up so you can meet this little person. They're going to need a fun, loving grandparent to spoil them."

And unlike all the movies and TV shows, there's nothing dramatic about what happens next. The machines don't start blaring. Doctors and nurses don't come barreling through the door. It's a simple squeeze of my hand and a fluttering of his eye before a small groan breaks through the beeping, and then the tears flow freely.

"ABBEY." Jude's panicked voice reaches me before I realize he's standing in front of me in the waiting room of the ICU. "What happened?"

"He's awake," I breathe out, the tears that started in Walt's room thirty minutes ago still pouring down my cheeks.

"What?"

All I can do is smile and nod, emotion clogging my voice.

As soon as I realized what happened I was sprinting out of his door, calling for Sarah. In retrospect, I feel horrible for the panic I caused her, but I was too overcome with every emotion to form any words. She rushed into Walt's room and came back out almost immediately, paging for Dr. Winters. She told me I needed to go to the waiting room and someone would be out to update me as soon as they could.

I wanted to fight her, to be with Walt, but I followed orders. Sarah was the one who came out five minutes later with my bag and told me Dr. Winters wanted to run a few tests before I could go back in. My phone call to Jude after that was a jumbled mess of incoherent words, but he understood the important ones.

"He's awake?" Jude whispers, his eyes shifting to the door behind me, the door he knows Dr. Winters will come through.

"Yeah. He's awake."

I don't even care when his arms band around me in an almost painful embrace. I know I'm holding onto him just as tightly. We may not have voiced the thoughts out loud, but I know we were both terrified this day would never happen.

I'm so glad we were wrong.

CHAPTER
Thirty-Four

JUDE

"MO LEANBH." Dad sighs in exasperation. "It's all right to leave. I'm not going anywhere."

"Two months, Dad. That's how long you were in a coma."

"I know, clearly I've missed a lot." His eyes shoot to my left where Abbey's curled up in the seat next to me, her knees tucked up to her chest and her head resting on top of them.

I don't know how she does it, sleeping like that, but she refused to go home without me, and I haven't been able to pull myself away since Dr. Winters let us back into his room.

Aside from natural muscle atrophy due to lack of use, all of his tests came back normal. Dr. Winters, for having a typically cold demeanor, couldn't stop the smile from forming on her lips when she gave us the news.

He'll have to stay in the ICU for observation for another twenty-four hours, but then he'll be transferred across the floor for inpatient physical therapy. They aren't positive how long he'll need to be inpatient, but it's looking like he'll be here at least another month.

I don't really care how long he's here. All I care about is the fact that he's awake and able to hold a cohesive conversation with me. I never would've forgiven myself if he didn't wake up from this.

"It's still pretty new," I tell him quietly, not wanting to disrupt Abbey's sleep.

"Hmm," he hums, a twinkle lighting his eyes. "You two have been in love with each other since you were six years old and you never stopped loving each other."

"Dad—"

"No, mo leanbh," he interrupts, reaching for me. I don't fight him and place my hand in his, my grip instantly tight against his. "I never doubted you two would find your way back to each other. I just wish I'd known it would be me landing in the hospital to get you back here. I would've done this ages ago."

"That's not even a little funny." His normally contagious laugh doesn't pull me in. I don't care that everything's okay now, the last two months were terrifying.

"Oh, son. One day you'll be able to laugh about it, but I understand why that day isn't today."

It's been over twelve hours since Abbey called me in hysterical tears, unable to get any words out other than I needed to get to the hospital. And even with all that panic coursing through my body, I kept my emotions in check. My biggest display was when Abbey said those two words I'd been begging to hear for months, "He's awake." The relief and joy that coursed through almost got me, but I kept it together.

When Dr. Winters came out and told us the good news, I kept it together.

When I walked into my father's room and saw him sitting up in bed, alert with a smile on his face, I kept it together.

But now, seeing him radiating that spirit I'd come to expect from him, I lose it.

I bury my face in the blanket draped over his legs and breathe deep, trying to keep the tears at bay just a little longer.

But the second I feel his hand on the back of my head, offering that comfort I haven't felt in far too long, they break. My shoulders shake and my body trembles with the force of my tears. I don't know how I'm able to stay silent with the force of the emotion moving through me, but somehow I manage it.

"I know, mo leanbh. I know," he whispers in the silence.

I don't lift my head from where it rests until I'm positive the tears have dried up, but when I do, my dad's eyes are just as wet as mine.

"I love you, Dad. And I'm so sorry I let anything keep me away. I swear, no matter what happens with Abbey, I'll never stay away again."

"Oh, Jude. You don't have anything to be sorry for. I love you with everything that I am. I understand why you stayed away, and I never needed an apology for it." He swallows, his Adam's apple bobbing in his throat. "I'm sorry I held on so tightly to that bar. If I'd been willing to step away from it, I could have gone to you. I should have done that more."

"No, Dad. You don't have to apologize. I know how important Murphy's is to you."

"It's not more important than you."

I chuckle softly, the sound a little watery from the tears. "We're just as bad as Abbey and I were." His brows pinch and I don't let him voice the question before I answer. "We'll keep apologizing to each other for the rest of our lives if we let ourselves."

"You're right." He laughs. "How about we both agree to forgive and forget. All that matters now is what we do moving forward."

"Yeah, that sounds good."

"ABBEY," I whisper in her ear late the next morning, her back pressed against my front.

I want to let her sleep, but considering she missed a whole day of working in the store yesterday, I don't think she'll forgive me if I let her sleep the day away.

After one of the most emotional conversations of my life last night, I woke Abbey up and got her out to her car before she fell asleep again. When we made it back to the apartment I didn't even try to wake her up. I slipped her out of her seat as gently as I could and carried her up the stairs and into bed. Even with stumbling to unlock the door and slipping her out of her clothes and into one of my shirts, she didn't move a muscle. It was an emotionally exhausting day and I didn't blame her in the slightest.

But it's a new day and I want a chance to talk to her before she gets distracted by the bookstore. Things have been strange between us all week and while I've tried to give her time to come to me with whatever's bothering her, I can't take it anymore. If she's changed her mind about being together, I need to know now.

"Abbey," I whisper, pressing a kiss to her neck. "It's time to get up."

"Hmm," she hums, her body pressing further into mine. "I wanna keep sleeping," she whispers groggily.

"It's almost ten o'clock, love. We need to get down to the store so you can finish setting up for the grand re-opening in just a couple days."

"You're right," she groans, stretching. Her body arches against mine before she turns in the bed to face me. "Good morning," she whispers, a small smile playing at her lips.

"Good morning," I whisper back, my arms wrapping around her and pulling her close.

"Your dad woke up yesterday."

"Yeah." I chuckle. "He did."

"I'm so happy," she whispers, almost like she's afraid if she admits it something bad might happen.

"Me too."

We're silent, the both of us studying the other. I'm the one who breaks the silence, unable to stop myself from asking the question I can't stop thinking about. "Want to tell me why you went to visit him yesterday?"

Her body goes taut as she tries to pull away. "Am I not allowed to visit him now?"

"Abbey, you know that's not what I'm asking. I'm just surprised you went to see him this close to the opening of the store, and things have been off between us all week." I smooth a piece of hair from her face, gently forcing her eyes to meet mine. "I want to know what's bothering you."

"It's nothing." She pushes at my chest, and this time I let her pull away.

I sit up in bed and watch her pad across the room, saying my next words to her back. "Abbey, if you've changed your mind about us, just tell me." She freezes, but doesn't turn around. "I don't want you to be unhappy."

She spins to face me and the tears in her eyes have me on edge. I want to go to her, but I force myself to stay where I am. I won't push her more than I have. I need her to want to tell me what's going on.

"I haven't changed my mind." Her voice is quiet as she fidgets with the hem of my shirt, flashing her pale yellow panties.

"All right," I say gently, shifting to the edge of the bed and planting my feet on the floor. I have to hold onto the edge of the mattress to stop myself from going to her. She might not want to break-up, but something is still bothering her. "What's going on, love?"

"I'm pregnant," she whispers, so quietly I'm not sure I heard her correctly.

"What?"

She releases my shirt and squares her shoulders, her voice much stronger the second time around. "I'm pregnant."

The second her words penetrate my brain, I'm off the bed and she's in my arms. I never thought I'd be happier than the moment Abbey let me back into her life completely, but this beats it, hands down. She's the love of my life and creating a family with her sounds like the perfect thing.

I slide my hands up her side and cup her cheeks, making sure she sees how serious I am when I speak my next words. "Nothing could make me happier than starting a family with you."

"You're sure?" she whispers, tears filling her eyes.

"I couldn't be more sure."

"Oh, thank God." Abbey springs to her toes and wraps her arms around my neck, molding her body to mine. "I didn't know how you'd feel. I know we have so much history, but this is still new."

"Mo ghrá, you've always been in my heart. A lifetime could pass us by and I'd still want everything with you."

I feel her tears hit my neck, but I know they're tears of joy. We may not have talked about it first, and this might not be the way we planned it, but it's still a dream come true.

CHAPTER
Thirty-Five

JUDE

"YOU'RE GONNA MAKE ME LATE," Abbey moans out, the sound echoing off the shower walls around us. Her body arches and she presses her ass into my aching cock.

"We have time." My hands on her hips separate, one moving up her body to toy with a pebbled nipple while the other slips between her legs, finding her already soaked clit.

Three days since she told me about the baby growing inside her, and we can't keep our hands off each other. She may have been nervous to tell me about the baby, but I've spent every moment I'm with her making it clear how happy and excited I am to be taking this next step.

Nothing about this baby changes any of my wants when it comes to Abbey. I was desperate to keep her in my life before we found out, and I'm just as desperate to keep her in my life now.

"Babe," she gasps as I slide my finger down to her entrance and back up. "I don't have time for your teasing." She turns her head to catch my eye as she reaches between us, her grip on my cock tight, teasing me like I'm teasing her. "Fuck me, or I'll take care of it myself."

I groan at her words, but do as she says—I want her just as much as she wants me. "Hands on the wall, love."

Her hands land on the wall and she bends at the waist, arching her back and presenting her ass to me in the most delectable way. I can't stop myself from smoothing my hands over her cheeks first. "There it is."

I line myself up at her entrance and bury myself to the hilt in one thrust. I don't give her time to adjust, I keep one hand on her hip, holding her in place and slip my other around to play with her clit. If she wants this hard and fast, that's exactly what she'll get.

"Yesss," she hisses as my fingers circle her clit, her ass grinding against me when I have yet to move.

"Stop trying to control it, love. You know I'll take care of you." I nip at her neck, careful not to leave a mark—not today anyway.

I start to rock my hips, my pace picking up speed as her body starts to go taut, her orgasm building more and more. "That's it. Let go, mo ghrá."

"Jude," she moans, pushing off the wall, forcing my cock to slip free, but it's clear what she wants when she spins around to face me. "I need to see you."

I don't wait for more from her before my hands are on the backs of her thighs and I'm lifting her, pressing her back into the wall for more leverage. I easily slide back in, finding the rhythm she needs.

With her eyes on mine and our bodies wound around each other, we both find our release quickly, everything about the moment exactly what we need.

Those three little words almost slip past my lips, but I don't want to say it quite yet. I don't want the first time I say those words after seventeen years to be right after sex. I never want her to think I didn't mean it when I say those words again.

"EVERYTHING LOOKS AMAZING," Ava gushes as she bounces up to Gage and me an hour before closing. "Abbey did amazing!"

"She knocked it out of the park." I smile at her before searching for the woman of the day. Everything's been perfect since she opened the doors at noon this afternoon.

Just before the clock struck twelve, I pressed a kiss to her lips, wished her luck, and the two of us tore the paper off the windows and door. The crowd Abbey saw outside brought tears to her eyes. I wasn't surprised in the slightest at either sight. This town loves Abbey and was always going to come out in droves to support her. And Abbey, while strong, isn't afraid to let those beautiful emotions shine.

She had every right to be emotional about today. This was a dream come true and a long time coming. The pride I had coursing through me was unlike any I'd felt before.

The only thing that was dragging her down was the lack of acknowledgement from her dad. She hasn't talked to him since that conversation I walked in on. I know she's reached out a few times, but he hasn't returned any of her calls. She was both panicked about the fact George had yet to be paid—though he wasn't pressing her about it—and hurt that he was treating her like this.

Honestly, even I was surprised he was ignoring her. He may be an asshole, and I might hate him, but when it comes to his family, he's normally a decent guy. When he said he'd show up for her, he always did. The fact that he hadn't shown up today was pissing me off more than normal.

"This place is going to be so freaking popular." I don't even try to fight the laugh that breaks free at the way she pulls at Gage's arm. He doesn't even care when her bouncing makes him spill his drink. The love he has for her pours off him in waves, and if I didn't have the same feeling for the woman striding toward me right now, I might be a little jealous of him.

"Hey." She leans up to press a kiss to my cheek, her eyes shining bright with happiness.

"How you feeling?" I ask, wrapping an arm around her waist and pulling her front to my side. I'm so proud of her, but I also miss her. Even if I've spent the whole day in the same room as her, she's been moving nonstop talking to people and being a proper business owner.

"I'm great. Everything has been perfect." She beams.

"I was just thinking the same thing, mo ghrá." The smile that breaks out across her lips is one I know is meant for only me. It speaks of love and comfort, and the dreams of our future. Of the secrets and hopes we share.

"You two are so cute," Ava practically shouts, breaking the moment, but nothing could ruin the happiness coursing through me, not when Abbey keeps looking at me like that.

"I told you to stay away from my daughter," a voice seethes quietly behind me.

I understand why Abbey removed the bell from above the door today—with people coming in and out all day it would've been ringing nonstop—but in this moment I'm wishing I had the heads up.

Abbey's entire body goes stiff against mine, but I notice she doesn't try to pull away. If anything, she presses in closer.

"That's the first thing you have to say on a day like today?" I answer just as quietly, turning slowly to face him.

Edward seethes before us, and I'm afraid he might hit his breaking point and snap.

I'd prefer not to do this today, but I won't cause a scene out here on Abbey's opening day. "Let's go to the kitchen."

Releasing my hold on Abbey's waist, I take her hand in mine and lead the way. I don't look to see if Edward is following us, I have no doubt he will.

"Dad, I've been trying to get a hold of you all week," Abbey says as soon as the door swings closed behind Edward.

"I've been busy."

"That's all you have to say? George hasn't received the final payment. What's taking so long?" Abbey crosses her arms, her posture straight as she faces her father head on.

"I've decided to withdraw my investment. I'm not sure I can trust you to run a business seeing how you run your personal life." His tone is flat, his gaze never moving from mine.

"What?" Abbey's arms fall, and I hear her voice waiver, but only for a moment. "You can't do that. We have a contract."

"There's always a way out of a contract. I thought I taught you better." Now his eyes shift to Abbey, and I swear it's disgust I see in the curve of his lips. "The morality clause would suffice in this situation."

Abbey takes a step away from him, her back hitting my front. I lift a hand to her hip and squeeze, making sure she knows I'm here. I want so desperately to come to her aid, but I know she needs to do this on her own.

"How?" she whispers.

"Take your pick. Cohabitating with a man you're not married to. Public indecency."

"Excuse me?" Abbey shouts. "Public indecency?"

"Are you telling me you two haven't been together in this bookstore?"

"There's no way you can know that," she coughs out.

"Your reaction is proof enough."

The words are barely out of his mouth before the door swings open, Ava, Quinn, and Emily stepping through the door.

"All right. That's enough," I snap, stepping in front of Abbey. "You can hate me and threaten me all you want, but you will not talk to my wife like that." The gasps that sound around the room aren't only from the three women who just walked in. "I don't want to make Abbey choose between us."

"Jude," Abbey interrupts, placing a calming hand to my back. I take a deep breath, stepping back to Abbey's side to let her talk. This is her fight, and I'll support her however I can. "He won't have to ask me to choose. If you can't respect me, I don't want you in my life."

I can't tell if the words hit Edward the way they should, nothing about his expression changes. "Is that how you really feel?" he asks, his tone flat.

"Yes." Abbey's voice is strong, not an ounce of hesitation in her response. "But let me make something very clear." She steps forward, her tone softening with her next words. "You've hurt me more than anyone else ever has and I think more than anyone else ever will, but even knowing that, I still want you in my life. You're my dad." Her voice cracks and it takes her a second to continue. "I love you, and I know you love me, so please, figure your shit out so we can have a relationship."

Edward doesn't move, but his eyes bounce between Abbey's, and maybe it's wishful thinking, but I swear I see pain and guilt in them.

"And one more thing, something I need you to really hear." She glances at me over her shoulder for only a moment. We haven't talked about telling anyone, but I know the words that are about to come out of her mouth before she even starts. "I'm pregnant." This time there are only two little gasps to accompany that announcement. "If you don't want to figure this out for me, then do it for your future grandchild. Because I can promise, you won't be a part of my child's life if you continue down this path."

Edward may not verbally respond to the news, and if I hadn't been paying attention I would've missed the slight widening of his eyes. But as quickly as it happened his expression clears.

"Sir." I step up to Abbey's side, taking her hand in mine. "I don't know if you heard, but my father woke up from his coma last week." His eyes shifting to mine is the only indication he's listening to me. "I finally asked him if he knew why you hated our family so much, and the story he told was honestly heartbreaking."

It wasn't the first thing I talked to him about on my visits with him, but it was probably one of the most important things we talked about. And the second he finished telling me that story, I wished I'd asked him sooner.

Grace and my dad were the very best of friends. They shared everything, just like Abbey and I did. But where their relationship differed from ours? They never loved each other the way Abbey and I do. People like to say men and women can't be friends, but that was truly all Grace and Dad were.

When Grace went away to college she fell madly in love with Edward. Dad said Grace called it a once in a lifetime love, the kind that made it impossible to ever fall in love again. Over time, as Edward watched Grace's relationship with my father, jealousy morphed and grew into obsession and possession. Dad tried to convince Grace to leave, but she loved him too much, and then she found out she was pregnant with Abbey.

Grace was so happy about getting pregnant, and she saw how happy Edward was at the idea of having a daughter that she believed everything would get better. But of course, that didn't happen.

Grace never said it, but she didn't have to. After my mother died, my father leaned heavily on Grace for support, and when Edward witnessed that support, his jealousy grew. Edward loved Grace so much and feared losing her to another man that he internalized everything so much he couldn't let anyone else into his heart—especially his daughter for fear he'd lose her too.

And after all the threats Edward threw my way, I can't help but agree.

I don't think it would've mattered what man tried to be a part of Abbey's life, Edward was always going to find a way to come between them. But being the son of the man he thought would steal his wife definitely didn't help.

"I don't know what I can do or say to make you believe me" —Abbey's hand smooths down my back, giving me the strength to continue—"but I swear to you, if you want it, you will always be a part of our life."

Edward's eyes shift to Abbey and for a split second I see the love shine through, but it's gone in the blink of an eye and then he's spinning on his heel, marching out of the room.

CHAPTER
Thirty-Six

ABBEY

"WHAT AM I GONNA DO?" I ask no one in particular.

I can't believe he pulled out of the contract.

I can't believe he just walked out the door without saying anything.

I can't believe some of the things he said to me.

"How am I supposed to pay George?" I gasp, turning to look at Jude.

"Don't worry about that for a second." Jude takes my hand in his, keeping my attention on him. "I've got it covered."

"I can't ask you to do that."

Jude has more than enough money to cover this, but that's asking too much—especially with everything else going on. I know we just had a big conversation about what our future holds—the two of us together, raising our baby—but that doesn't mean all of my problems become his. Or at least it shouldn't.

"You didn't. I offered."

"Jude—"

"Wait," Ave interrupts. "Sorry, but why isn't your dad

paying George like the contract says?" She steps forward, her hand landing on my shoulder and squeezing.

"He said he was pulling out of the contract. Something about a morality clause."

She shakes her head, a look of confusion crossing her face. "That's not how that works."

The door swings open, Declan, Gage, and Caleb stepping into the kitchen with the rest of us.

"Number one, I don't remember seeing a morality clause in the contract—I never would have let you sign that. Number two, what in the world is he saying you did to break this imaginary morality clause?"

"It doesn't matter," Jude interrupts. "What's mine is yours. I have more than enough to take care of this."

"Jude—"

"I don't want any more hidden vows," he shouts, and I step back as if the words are a physical blow.

"You're it for me. You always have been." His voice quiets as he takes a step toward me, erasing the space I created, and ignoring the audience surrounding us. "You always will be." He reaches out, cupping my cheeks and wiping at the tears I don't realize are tracking down my face. "And I want the world to know it."

I hiccup, trying to keep even more tears from falling from my eyes. He's shown me over and over again since he's come home how important I am to him, but it's not until this moment it finally clicks.

All the coffees, the talks, the little moments, the big ones. His reaction to the news about the baby, his love and excitement for the future. Every single thing this man has done since he walked back into my life has been in an effort to prove to me I've always been in his heart.

"I love you, Abbey. So much it physically hurts sometimes." His voice cracks, and I see him swallow before he continues. "These last seventeen years have been hell for me, and I hate that they've been even worse for you."

His eyes bounce between mine, searching for something before he continues. "I know I've said it before, I wish I could say I'd take it all back, but we don't know where we'd be if we did, and I wouldn't trade anything to be where we are now." He steps closer, erasing the last inch of space between us. "You're it for me," he repeats. "And I'll stop at nothing to prove that to you."

"Jude—" I start, but I have no idea what I want to say. Words can't express what I'm feeling in this moment.

He's right. No matter how terrible these last seventeen years have been, they've led us here—back together and with a baby growing inside me.

I don't know where we'd be if we never split up, but I know we wouldn't have made this baby, and even if I haven't met him or her yet, I already love them more than I thought possible.

This man was my whole world. Everything I did revolved around him, and him around me. That's not healthy for a relationship. We both needed to find out who we were as individuals—our likes and dislikes, our wants and needs.

I hated not having him in my life, but I also like who I've become over this last decade and a half. I'm stronger because of our time apart, and so is he.

Jude's thumbs stroke my cheeks, bringing me back to this moment. "You don't have to say anything. I just don't want you to doubt my feelings for you. Not anymore."

"I love you too." I bring my hands up to his wrists, gripping them tight, not wanting him to move. "You're right. We wouldn't be where we are today—who we are today—without you leaving when you did, and I wouldn't want to be anyone other than I am now." I take a breath, and with it, all the pressure in my chest releases. It's easier to breathe now, easier than it's been my entire life.

"It doesn't take away all the pain we've both been through, but it somehow makes it easier knowing I have you now. And nothing anyone does or says is going to change that." I move to my toes, bringing my lips within an inch of his. "I love you too," I whisper, finally touching his lips with mine and kissing him like he's the last man I'll ever kiss again—because he is.

"Wow," Ava says, right before she grunts. "What was that for?" she whisper-shouts.

"Ruining the moment," Quinn responds in kind.

"Now you are too," Emily growls.

"All three of you are." Caleb laughs, but then I hear the sound of the door swinging back and forth and know he's ushered them out the door.

"I'm gonna marry you," Jude whispers against my lips.

"Hmm," I hum. "I like the sound of that." My body melts into his.

Jude pulls back, just enough to look me in the eyes, his hands still cupping my cheeks. "Yeah?"

"Definitely." I sigh.

"Big wedding?"

"No, small. Just our family."

He quirks a brow. "We've got a pretty big family."

"We have the perfect family."

He pulls me back in for another kiss, this one just as slow and methodical as the last one. There's no rush, not anymore. We both know the other is in this for the long haul. I was pretty confident in that before today, but now there's not a single ounce of doubt.

"Next month," he demands, his lips never leaving mine.

"That's not enough time to plan," I whine, pulling away slightly.

"Plan what? It's a small wedding." He grins.

"November," I counter. "As long as Walt's out of the hospital," I rush to add before he can say anything.

I want more time to plan something a little more formal than our first wedding. I loved our courthouse wedding, but this time we get to share the day with everyone we hold close to our hearts and I want to make that special.

"All right. As long as Dad is out of the hospital, November it is." The relaxed smile that slips across his lips makes my heart leap.

There's still a lot for us to figure out. Where we're going to live, for one, because neither of our one bedroom apartments is meant for raising a child.

And I'll need to talk to my dad. Even with the horrible things he said today, I don't want to lose him. I still have hope we can fix our relationship. It'll never be what I want it to be. It'll never be the kind of relationship Jude has with Walt, or Gage has with his parents, but it could still be something. Maybe it's wishful thinking but I have to believe he walked away the way he did tonight because of the audience we had.

But for now, I'm going to focus on the man in front of me.

The man I love loves me too.

The man I love wants to marry me and be my husband again.

The man I love, the father of my child, couldn't be more excited at the idea of having a baby with me.

There might be some obstacles in our future, but I have a lot to be grateful for.

CHAPTER
Thirty-Seven

JUDE

MY EYES BLINK open and it takes me a few seconds to take in the numbers on the clock on Abbey's nightstand, three in the morning. It takes me even longer to recognize that Abbey isn't here.

It's too early for her to be up, even with her hours prepping for the café, this is too early for her. I question if she ever came to bed last night, but the rumpled sheets answer that question—she was here, but for how long?

I slip from the bed and step into my boxers before moving to the door. The second I pull the door open I see her. She's curled up in her reading nook surrounded by the box of journals I gave her last night.

I'd been a day away from asking Willie and Mae if they shipped the journals when they surprised me last night by walking through the door of Murphy's. We'd talked a few times since I asked them to mail the journals, but they never gave away that they were planning to come for a visit.

Things had picked back up at Murphy's since the bookstore opening and I'd been busy helping Jane behind the bar while Cole and Abbey helped on the floor—somewhere I honestly hadn't expected to need extra help. I found myself wondering many times over how the hell my dad managed to run this place on his own and not have a heart attack sooner.

It took Willie and Mae calling my name for me to look up and find them standing across from me. Once it actually registered that I wasn't imagining them, I rushed out from behind the bar and pulled the two of them into a hug. I knew I missed them, hearing their voices always brought a wave of sadness over me, but seeing them in person? It really brought home just how much I missed them. Exactly like it'd been with Abbey in my dad's hospital room, and just like it'd been when I finally got to talk to my dad again face-to-face.

They say distance makes the heart grow fonder, and while I believe that, distance also makes it easy to compartmentalize and forget the importance of being with the people you love.

Bringing myself back to the present, I carefully make my way to Abbey, not wanting to startle her. "Mo ghrá," I whisper, crouching in front of her. "These journals aren't going anywhere. You don't have to read them all in one night." When she lifts her eyes to me, tears well in the corners. "Baby," I plead, unable to see her cry.

I move to my knees, taking the space on the floor in front of her as I gently pull the journal from her hands and glance at the date, trying to figure out what journal she's on—2015, the year I published my first book.

There were a lot of emotions coursing through me that year, the biggest one being guilt. The guilt ate at me so much I avoided everyone I cared about—I literally flew to another country half-way around the world to make sure no one could be with me. And I know the journal entries this year were some of my worst. I explored every negative emotion in the book and I beat myself up over and over for all the mistakes I'd made that led me to being alone—something I thought I more than deserved.

A sentence from the middle of the page she has open catches my eye and part of me regrets giving her these journals, but this isn't who I am anymore, and it's not how I feel either.

Looking back, I can see that night for what it really was—the start of the end for us.

Placing the journal on the floor next to me, I take her hands in mine, holding them tight in her lap. "Mo ghrá. You know most of this is the farthest thing from how I feel now. I'm the happiest I've ever been, and that's all because of you."

"I know," she whispers, the simple words choked on a sob. She shakes her head before pulling her hands from mine, and there's a moment of panic that maybe I shouldn't have given her these journals, but she collapses into my chest and her entire body wracks with the force of her tears.

"Abbey," I croak. Lifting her from the seat, I switch places with her, cradling her in my lap. I don't try to talk to her, not right now, I hold her and sooth her as best I can while she calms down.

This woman's heart is so big, feeling this pain for a man who doesn't exist but in the pages of these journals, and it's one of the things I love most about her—her empathy.

I know we went through some hard times before we made our way back to each other, but I'm so happy with where we ended up. Giving her these journals was simply meant to help her learn about our time apart. It was my way of proving just how much I love and trust her. It was my hope that giving her these journals would help rebuild her trust in me.

I never wanted to cause her more pain.

"I just hate all the time we wasted," she whispers once her tears have dried up.

"I know, love, but we can't live in the past." I press a kiss to the top of her head and tighten my arms around her. "We have the start of a beautiful life right here at our fingertips, and I want to keep building on that."

She lifts her head to meet my eyes—they're red and puffy, but she's still my breathtaking Abbey. Her mouth opens and closes, but no words come out. I smooth a hand over her cheek, wiping at the tears that still wet her face, and give her whatever time she needs to organize her thoughts.

"We can accept that we wouldn't change our past because it would change our future, and still be upset about everything we missed out on—two things can be true at the same time."

"You're right," I admit.

She presses a light kiss to my lips before she nestles her head against my chest, and I know she's listening to my heart beat in time with hers. I should probably pick her up and carry her back to bed, but I don't move from where we are.

Abbey's soft voice breaks the silence what feels like hours later, but is really only minutes. "Thank you for sharing these with me. For sharing all of you with me."

"Mo ghrá," I whisper. "You've always had all of me, and you always will." I shift, pulling her face from my chest to meet her eyes. "But maybe you should take your time reading these," I suggest. "It's going to be years before I start being nicer to myself, and I can't stand to see you cry—not over these." I gesture to the piles of journals around us.

"That might be a good idea," she concedes, her eyes taking in the mess she's made before her gaze comes back to me. "Are you still writing in a journal?"

"Yeah, I don't really have a specific routine, but since I got home I've been journaling in the morning. I fit it in wherever I have time." I shrug.

"Will you let me read your current one?" A sly smile forms on her lips, and I don't even try to stop my laugh in response.

"Love, you can read absolutely everything I write whenever you want."

"Including your next manuscript." Her eyes sparkle and I melt into them.

I'd give her anything she asked for right now.

"Anything and everything, Abbey Selbey."

Her smile beams before she presses a quick kiss to my lips, springing out of my lap and practically leaping to the kitchen island where I left my laptop.

"Mo ghrá." I laugh, standing from the chair and taking the space behind her. "How about you start on that later. We're meeting Willie and Mae for breakfast in four hours and you've barely gotten any sleep."

"I'm not tired," she says distractedly as she opens my computer.

"I can help with that," I murmur against her neck, nipping at the skin below her ear.

"Hmm," she hums, leaning her body into me. "You're right, this will be here later."

I don't give her a chance to change her mind before she's in my arms, my lips on hers in a heated kiss.

"I love you, Jude Murphy," she murmurs against me as I lay her on the bed. "More and more with every passing day."

"I love you too, Abbey Selbey. With everything that I am and everything I can be."

———

November 8, 2025

Do you know how happy you make me?

Seriously, Abbey. I know I've told you plenty over the last four months, but I don't know how I survived without you.

I don't know how I got lucky enough to get a second chance with you, but I'm taking it and I'm never letting you go.

We got married today.

It may be our second wedding, but in my heart I've always been married to you. You are the love of my life, and today I got to share that with everyone I hold dearest.

I thought you were beautiful at our first wedding (and you were), but today? Mo ghrá, I've never seen you shine so bright. Your joy was the greatest gift you could have given me (well, at least for another six months).

I know we said our vows under the oak tree in Dad's backyard, with all of our loved ones surrounding us, and while I meant them with everything I am, they weren't the ones I would've written.

So, my love, my greatest treasure, and my everything, before the clock strikes twelve and our wedding day is officially over, I want to make these vows to you.

I vow to keep you safe and warm in the shelter of my arms, always.

I vow to help you and support you with all that I am.

I vow to cherish you for everything you are, and everything you have yet to become.

I vow to keep choosing you and this life we're building together.

I vow to grow with you and never apart from you.

I vow to love you every day as if it were my last.

I could go on and on, but you're looking at me like it's time to be done writing in this journal and I don't want to disappoint you on our second first day as husband and wife.

I love you, Abbey Murphy, with all that I am and so much more.

I love you, Abbey Murphy, with all that I am and so much more.

Epilogue

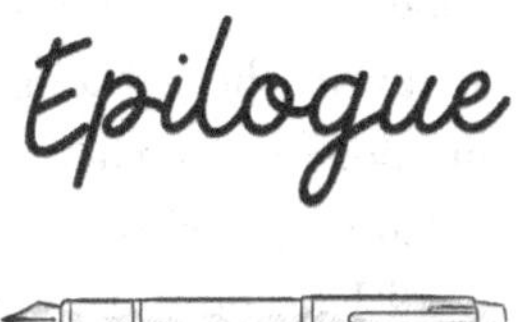

JUDE

"MO GHRÁ, YOU ALMOST READY?"

"Yeah, I need to grab my shoes and I'm good to go. Where's Ronan?" Abbey calls over her shoulder

"With my dad in the living room." I lean against the doorway, watching her put her hair up in the mirror.

Her eyes meet mine through the reflection, and the heat that sparks lights me up.

Almost four years married and we still can't get enough of each other. I knew this woman was the love of my life long before I married her the first time, but it's the little moments like these that help prove me right.

"We don't have time for that. We need to leave in the next ten minutes if we want to be on time."

I may not have known Scott well, but he was an important person in our friends' lives—Quinn and Caleb's dad, Ava and Declan's surrogate father, Abbey and Gage's friend. Being invited to help celebrate the man on one of the hardest days of their lives was a privilege neither my wife nor I took for granted.

"You could do it in ten minutes." She spins to look at me head on, her hands moving to grip the edge of the counter behind her.

"I could, but that doesn't give me time to savor you the way I'd want to." I prowl toward her, placing my hands on the counter beside hers, but not touching her.

"You can savor me later," she whispers.

"Or, I can wait until later and really make it worth your while," I murmur right in her ear, my breath tickling her skin.

"Jude," she groans, trying to press her body into mine, but before she can touch me, I step back, a teasing smile on my lips.

"My dad is taking Ronan tonight. We'll have the whole house to ourselves, and I really want to hear you scream."

"That's just mean," she whimpers, and I can see her thighs clenching, trying to relieve some of the pressure building in her core.

"But you know it'll be worth it." I spin on my heel and walk out of our bedroom, only stopping when I make it to the living room.

Three years later, I still don't take for granted the image before me as I cross the threshold.

There on the floor with his grandson is my father, looking healthier than ever.

I hate that it took almost losing him for me to truly recognize what I had, but I thank my lucky stars I got more time with him.

I wish every day Abbey had the same kind of relationship with her dad, but I'm thankful they have something. It might not be what she always imagined it would be, but it's better than it's ever been, and that's a pretty good place to be.

After her grand opening, she let Edward cool off for a few days before she went to see him, just the two of them.

She told me there was a lot of yelling and a lot of tears, but they came to an agreement, one that meant he was a part of our lives, but only as a father and grandfather, not as a business partner or investor.

Even after that conversation, things between them were still strained. It wasn't until three or four months later that things between Edward and Abbey really got better.

Edward showed up at the bar one day—very differently than any of his previous visits—and apologized for everything. I thought it was fake at first, but when I truly looked at him, I saw the sorrow in his eyes.

It was the look in my father's eyes over Edward's shoulder that made me realize he stepped in to help.

It didn't surprise me to learn he went to Edward to talk about their past. Once Dad woke up from his coma, I couldn't avoid telling him the truth forever.

I'd been right about his reaction, though—he'd been mad and disappointed I never went to him in the first place. But he loved me, and was happy I was home and working things out with Abbey.

Abbey hated taking the money from me for the bookstore, but the way I saw it, there was no one else I'd spend the money with or on. Her dreams were my dreams, and this was an easy one for me to help make a reality.

Besides, having Abbey in my life had those creative juices flowing, and my books were selling better than ever before. I still don't make public appearances, and my identity's still a secret from the world at large, but the people who matter most to me know the truth, and that's more than enough.

Arms slip around my waist as a body I know well presses into my side. Abbey's soft voice sounding in my ear pulls me back to the moment in front of me. "What are you doing?"

"Feeling very thankful for the life I have." I wrap my arm around her, pulling her front even closer into my side.

"We've built a pretty amazing one." Her eyes drift to our son, laughing at the silly face my father makes.

"It's perfect. Better than I ever imagined."

NOT
Done Yet?

Neither was I.

Scan the QR code below to get your copy of an exclusive bonus scene.

If you'd like to stay up to date on all things Erin Graves, including new releases, bonus content, behind the scenes, give-aways, and more, be sure to sign up for my newsletter.

ENJOYED
Hidden Vows?

Or even if you didn't, please consider leaving a review on Amazon, Goodreads, Storygraph, and/or anywhere you review books.

Reviews are one of the easiest ways to help indie authors. Even a simple sentence and star rating can go a long way.

WANT TO READ ABOUT

Read Quinn and Declan's story in *Shuttered Hearts*!

A brother's best friend, return to hometown, strangers to friends to lovers romance.

Read Ava and Gage's story in *Unexpected Love*!

A new in town, one night stand to more, hurt/comfort romance.

Check out Reid and the mystery redhead's story in *Nine Holidays Falling*!

A sister's ex-boyfriend, loathe to love, forbidden romance.

Acknowledgments

Abbey and Jude's story came to me about halfway through writing Shuttered Hearts, and the second I wrote 'the end' on Quinn and Declan's story, Abbey and Jude started screaming like there was no tomorrow. But alas, I had to write Ava and Gage's story first.

I'm honestly so happy I finally got to tell Abbey and Jude's story. As with the rest of the Love in Ashford Falls series, Abbey and Jude did not stick to the script I had for them. Their story went its own way, and I think it turned out perfectly.

This series might be over, but we aren't completely done with Ashford Falls yet. We'll see it at least one more time before we travel somewhere new.

I'm sad to be leaving these characters, but I can't wait to introduce you to a whole new cast...mostly.

Before you go, I've got to thank the people who truly made this book possible.

From my alpha readers: Kelly, Paige, Emily, Gina, and Michelle. I know I took you all over the place, and I truly cannot thank you enough for your support.

To my beta readers: Sarah, Annelise, Katie, and Mary. You all were truly amazing jumping in on such short notice. Your feedback had me smiling and so freaking giddy to continue making Abbey and Jude's story better. From the bottom of my heart, thank you.

And my editor, Caroline. I think you might be the real MVP for this one. Maybe one day I'll learn the proper use for commas, but until then, you are truly wonderful.

My sibling. As always, the way you bring my characters to life is one of my favorite things. I don't know where I would be without you.

You. Yes, you right now, reading these words. None of this would be possible if you didn't pick up this book and read these words. So, thank you. I hope you'll stick around on the next journey.

And finally, my wonderful husband. I know you hate when I mention you don't read my books (and here I am doing it again), but it truly doesn't bother me. You support me in every way that truly matters, and that's what's most important to me. Thank you for always pushing me to achieve my goals.

CONTENT
Warning

Please note that these trigger warnings are considered MAJOR spoilers for the plot of the story. That being said, please take care of yourself first and foremost.

- Death of a parent (both MC's mothers, off-page)
- Allusions to cheating
- Accidental pregnancy
- Mention of the death of a side character's parent due to cancer

ALSO BY
Erin Graves

The Love in Ashford Falls Series

Shuttered Hearts

Unexpected Love

Hidden Vows

Forever in Stonebridge Hollow Series

Three Months Yesterday

Standalone Novellas

Nine Holidays Falling

Holiday Haven

ABOUT THE
Author

Erin Graves writes small town contemporary romance novels with a lot of heart and a touch of spice. She's a wife, cat mom, author, and sometimes crocheter. She was born and raised in Maryland and now lives in Pennsylvania with her husband and two cats. She started writing in high school but stopped when she thought she could never be a published author. Fifteen years later, her first novel was published.

STAY

You can find Erin Graves in all the usual bookish places...

Website:
eringravesauthor.com

Instagram:
instagram.com/author.eringraves

Goodreads:
goodreads.com/eringravesauthor

BookBub:
bookbub.com/authors/erin-graves

Amazon:
amazon.com/author/eringraves

Pinterest:
pinterest.com/authoreringraves